Cal struggled to his feet . . .

Lush green trees and grass reached all the way to the far end of Daedalus.

"How did I ever get myself into this?" he said.

"You're going to have to be a lot more specific than that, Captain."

He turned quickly, looking for the speaker, before he realized that the voice had come from his wrist computer.

"Who are you?" he asked.

"This is Vincent. You feeling okay?"

"Vincent, my wristcomp. What's my name?"

"Cal Donley." The computer fell silent, as though surprised. Then it produced a long, low whistle.

"Yeah, I know," said Cal. "It seems I'm missing a few memories."

Ace Science Fiction Books by John E. Stith

SCAPESCOPE
MEMORY BLANK

MEMORY BLANK

JOHN E. STITH

ACE SCIENCE FICTION BOOKS
NEW YORK

This book is an Ace Science
Fiction original edition, and has
never been previously published.

MEMORY BLANK

An Ace Science Fiction Book / published by arrangement with
the author

PRINTING HISTORY
Ace Science Fiction edition / January 1986

ISBN: 0-441-52417-6

Ace Science Fiction Books are published by
The Berkley Publishing Group,
200 Madison Avenue, New York, New York 10016.
PRINTED IN THE UNITED STATES OF AMERICA

For my mother and father,
Virginia Franklin Kenway Stith
and George Allen Stith.
And for my brother,
Richard Warren Stith.

Contents

Prologue

EVEN before the man entered the room, he had known there were two bodies on the floor. A monitoring camera had told him that much. What he didn't know was that one of the bodies was not dead.

He stepped over the man nearer the exit and turned off the alarm that had summoned him. Once finished, he stooped to examine the first intruder. The man's chest was crushed. Even if that hadn't been enough to kill him instantly, the gaping wound on his forehead would have sufficed. The massive amount of blood on the man's body had resulted from the sudden large breaks in the skin, not from a single wound that had kept bleeding as the intruder slowly died. Death had not lingered here.

The man was glad the victim had not suffered. The world was too full of pain already.

He crouched over the second body, and only then did he realize this man was still alive. The injured man's breath was shallow, uneven. His pulse was weak.

Complications. The crouching man rolled the prone form onto its back and then looked appraisingly at it. This one was no stranger.

Applying a firm but gentle pressure at the base of the jaw could make the immediate situation far simpler. It would make everything simpler. The man liked things to be simple.

Instead, he rose and shook his head. There had to be another way. Maybe not so simple, but almost as sure.

1

———— Chapter one ————
Hillside

HE tasted dust.

Awareness returned in a series of minute steps as fragments of information came into focus. He sprawled facedown. For no reason he could think of, beneath him lay dirt and rocks.

He tried to prop himself up on his elbows and open his eyes, but the shooting pains from his lower back forced him to clench his eyes shut.

Sweat broke out on his forehead. Fighting the growing fear, he resigned himself to a more gradual investigation. With one eye open, he could make out dark shapes that looked like outlines of bushes. Blades of grass brushed his cheek, and he smelled the musty odor of earth. A constant breeze cooled his face.

He lifted his head, more gently this time. His jaws tightened as the pain lanced back, but it didn't seem so bad this time.

He rolled carefully onto his back. In the process he found another sore spot above his knee. His breath came heavily.

He was alone, outside somewhere in the dark, and hurt. He couldn't remember what had happened the night before, and, as he strained to recall, an overwhelming feeling of fear hit him.

With effort he found he could summon disjointed impressions of a college campus, but they seemed distant. The harder he tried to retrieve images, the more his head hurt. It felt as if a tattoo artist were busy engraving a mural on the inside of his skull.

His eyes felt gritty. Momentarily he was unable to focus. He must hurry. Something within him made him feel the need for haste. But why?

Stars shone off to one side. They grew brighter as his eyes adjusted to the scene, and he decided that he must be in a wilderness area. The stars couldn't possibly be that bright anywhere near Atlanta or any other city. Atlanta. He hadn't remembered Atlanta until now. Was he somewhere in the Blue Ridge Mountains?

It was as though his memory lay before him, a cavernous darkened warehouse. Far into the smoky distance, unseen hands switched on one dim light, and he felt a link to Atlanta. Now that he had at least a fragment of past knowledge, the panic lessened.

What had happened last night? His memory was foggy, as though from disuse. He looked at one of the brightest stars as he tried to force his memory to disgorge more facts. But they wouldn't come. He shifted his leg to avoid a rock that ground into his hip. And then he realized something else was wrong.

The stars lay along a straight path, perhaps forty-five degrees wide. It was as though he were in the middle of Peachtree Street, seeing the stars between the parallel rows of building tops.

He moved his head so he could better see what bordered the stars. Now in his field of view lay *another* strip of sky. His stomach knotted. His memory loss couldn't possibly have been for merely a day or even a few days. He knew where he must be, and he knew the points of light he saw were not stars. He was a long, long way from his college days and the Chattahoochee River Valley.

He swung his gaze back in the opposite direction for confirmation. Two corridors of "stars" radiated from a vanishing point many kilometers ahead of him and stopped overhead. Between the strips of "stars" lay a straight band of much fainter "stars."

Daedalus. He had to be on Daedalus, the orbital colony.

His head throbbed. During college his foremost goal had been to go to Daedalus. Now he was here, and he remembered nothing of the preparations, the training, the journey. It was all blank. His memory had to be missing at least several months. Maybe more. Excitement somehow managed to displace a portion of the fear.

Before him stretched the axis of the enormous cylinder that

housed Daedalus. Far into the distance the three huge strips of land, divided by three equally large strips of windows, met at the other end of the thirty-kilometer-long cylinder, like a spinning, elongated melon cut lengthwise into six slices. Along the land strips, lights of homes and public places formed the "stars" he had seen. Gigantic mirrors outside each window, now closed for the "night," merely reflected more distant images of these same "stars."

His stomach lurched as he thought about being on the *inside* of a world, rather than on the outside. The darkness helped. The jolt would probably have been more pronounced if he had revived during the day, when the outside mirrors reflected the sun's light onto the interior land strips.

He sat up slowly and examined his surroundings.

He was partway up the hill formed by the end of a land strip as it gradually curved up to the cylinder end. Below him, perhaps only a few hundred meters, lay the assorted lights that had to indicate the outskirts of a town along the foothills. Trees and shrubs and grass surrounded him. Behind him the ground rose into the darkness to the end of the cylinder's axis, where it joined the five other melon slices.

Clearing away some of his confusion, he realized that he could at least learn the date. With his watch held close to his face, he realized it was not his old watch, but he was more interested in its dimly glowing screen.

05:51 12 APRIL 2156

Impossible. That would mean he must have lost more than . . . As he tried to determine the span, he realized that he couldn't pick an exact date that it had started. The best he could do was narrow it down to maybe 2143 or 2144.

Twelve years.

He didn't for an instant wonder if someone could be playing a horrible practical joke by setting the time ahead several years. There was far too much else left to explain. His body, even making allowances for being hurt, somehow no longer felt quite as resilient as it had in his late teens and early twenties. His breath was too forced. Maybe he could have quickly lost the muscle tone he had developed by running, but it didn't seem likely.

And setting the time ahead wouldn't explain all the bewildering changes. Patches were torn out of his memory, leaving only fragments behind. For those incompletely removed portions, there were ragged edges he could get his fingers under, to pick at, to feel the boundaries so he could deduce the missing portions, like Atlanta—he could start there. But what about those sections ripped whole? If no clues waited for him to follow the trail, if in fact the start of the trail were gone, what then?

Surprised that he had not thought about it before, he realized that he could not recall his name. What other basic information was he missing? Fear came back stronger.

As he probed for links that might reveal his name, the area around him began to lighten. Far up the hill behind him a patch of brilliant sunshine lit a mass of light and dark greens of pine trees and grass, marking the start of sunrise on Daedalus. The light split into two overhead spokes and spread down the hill he was on. The sun's image entered the overhead mirror, and he could feel the slight warmth. Squinting, he watched day come to the colony.

Slowly at first, but now gaining speed, the light moved along the length of the cylinder and finally reached the far end, where again the three land strips joined at a point.

For a moment he thought he might escape the vertigo, but then it hit even worse than unexpectedly going to zero gravity, forcing him to lie down again. His eyes closed, he felt the firm ground beneath his outstretched arms. After a long moment he tried again, only to reexperience the feeling of being suspended upside down, a half-dozen kilometers in the air.

He saw in his brief examination that small villages marked the locations of clusters he had originally mistaken for stars. The sun appeared to be directly centered in the overhead window, brighter than he had ever seen it. The other two windows were dark. From here he couldn't see the latticework that he knew supported the millions of small panes, which at this distance appeared to be one enormous, solid window.

In stages he could keep his eyes open for lengthening intervals, finding that it helped not to look at the two other land strips. As he watched, his peripheral vision picked up the Earth moving briskly down out of view of one window. About a minute later it traveled up past the window on the other side. Then he saw a distant shiny cylinder following the Earth. That would be Icarus, the agricultural and industrial counterpart to Daedalus.

Minutes later he could sit up again. Down the hill lay a city with brown and green buildings set irregularly into the slope. But for now he was more curious about himself.

Bringing his left knee up convinced him the knee was unbroken. He wore brown running shoes. His tan trousers were soiled by several large stains. His queasiness returned.

The stains were black, but with a tinge of dark red. He reached gingerly forward, ready to roll up a pants leg, and then he saw his hands.

They were splattered with what surely must be dried blood.

Only his palms were fairly clean, as though he had rubbed them against a flat surface until the blood was gone. It must be his own blood, but from what injury? He rolled up his pants leg, but his knee showed no particular concentration of stains.

On the cuffs of his long shirt-sleeves, prominent against the pale blue of the material, there was more blood. Again he felt the urge to hurry, without knowing why.

On impulse he checked his pants pockets. There were three reddish capsules with no designations. They could have been anything. With the capsules lay a short rod, flattened like a key on one end so it could be held conveniently. At least he knew what it was. The rod was a bank stick. He wouldn't be able to make any financial transactions without it. Stamped into the flat part were three tiny letters: CTD. His initials? They must be, but they meant nothing to him now.

A brief scolding bird cry came from a nearby pine tree.

There was no name on the back of his wrist computer. The silver and gold case had a few specks of blood on it, but it had suffered no permanent damage. He pressed the ON button as he put the watch back on, but nothing happened.

He struggled to his feet. Lush green fruit trees, shrubs, and grass reached all the way to the far end of Daedalus, broken only by a modest number of towns, isolated dwellings, and a few large lakes.

"How did I ever get myself into this?" he said.

"You're going to have to be a lot more specific than that, Captain."

He turned quickly, looking for the speaker, before he realized that the voice had come from his wrist computer.

"Who are you?" he asked.

"This is Vincent. You feeling okay?"

"Vincent, my wristcomp." So the new one had voice.

"You'd better sit down. You don't sound too great."

"You called me Captain." He thought back to "CTD."

"Figure of speech. Say, you really are having trouble today, aren't you?"

"My name. What's my name?"

"Cal Donley." The computer fell silent, as though surprised.

Cal. Did he remember being teased long ago with the nickname "*Cal*culating"? He knew he had a gift for manipulating numbers. Or more recently had someone called him "*Callous*"? His memories seemed to be reordered, to have linkages in some of the normal directions obliterated. He couldn't easily summon memories solely by thinking of chronologically close occurrences, but maybe he could pull fragments together if he tried seldom-used sequences. An overpowering sense of loss tore at him.

"Anything else, boss?" Vincent's voice sounded male, of indeterminate age.

"I'm trying to figure out where to start. This is Daedalus, right?"

"Right-o. But why all the questions?"

"It seems I'm missing some memories."

"I always thought the memory was the *second* to go. Care to quantify 'some'?"

"I don't know precisely. Ten or twelve years anyway."

To Cal's surprise, Vincent produced a long, low whistle.

"Yeah, I know," Cal said. "It's taking a little getting used to."

"So you want a little refresher course? Something like that?"

"The essentials. I'll worry later about the rest."

"Okay, partner. Start with me or Daedalus?"

"You. I need to work my way up."

"Me. Right. Halette Forty-Two series. I answer to 'Vincent' or 'Vin.' 'Good-bye, Vin' puts me to sleep. 'Hello, Vin' wakes me up. Or you can use my switches. I'm linked to your home computer, so I can share data with it. I'm your portable com line, calculator, timer, data base, and Computer Friday."

"Do you keep track of my activities?"

"No. When I'm awake, I mostly pay attention to things you say to me. And I pay less attention if you go for quite a while without talking to me. A lot of what I hear gets flushed after it's been in short-term memory for long enough. When I'm asleep, the only thing I can hear is 'Hello, Vin.' "

"And only with *my* voice?"

"Right, guv. You turned me on with my switch a few minutes ago, but you didn't say anything. So I decided to keep quiet."

A flash of reflected sunlight from the village down the hill caught Cal's eye. Other people must be waking up. "What about Daedalus? Orient me."

"The city down there is Machu Picchu. There are six large cities—one at each end of all three continents. There are nine villages, three in each. Current total population is a million two hundred thousand, give or take."

"What am I doing up here on the hill? Is there transportation near here?"

"Nope. You must have walked up here from town."

"Any reason not to go back there, then?"

"Help yourself."

Cal took a few steps. The pain this time was manageable, so he started to pick his way carefully down the hill.

After only a few minutes the hillside began to feel natural. Whether it was due to fringes of his memory returning, or to a superb job of interior decorating, he couldn't tell.

"Am I getting even more tired?" he asked a few minutes later. "Or has the gravity increased that much?"

"From where we were to here, the gravity has increased by one point two-two-six percent, so most of the change must be in your imagination."

"Maybe I'm just suggestible." Thinking about his mental condition triggered curiosity about his physical appearance. "Vincent, can you act as a mirror?"

"By displaying one of my video inputs? Sure."

"Do it, will you?"

It took a moment of getting used to, because the side-to-side maneuvering was opposite that of a real mirror, but Vincent's screen showed a strangely familiar face. Cal touched his cheek with his hand and saw the relayed image do the same with no mirror reversal. The face that stared back at him had a few unfamiliar wrinkles and stress lines. Had those years been happy, or depressing and disillusioning? He wondered if they had been as frustrating as the last half hour.

Into Cal's mind floated the ancient question "What are you going to be when you grow up?" He was quite obviously grown up, but what was he? What had be become? In school he had been studying computers, particularly organic machines. Had his interest survived? He wouldn't find out by waiting here, so he resumed his downward journey. Perseverance gets you more than halfway to your goal. He wondered how many times he had said that. And had he yet learned the difference between perseverance and stubbornness?

"Vincent, what's my job here?"

"Your title is Computer Systems Integration Manager."

A stream angled across his path perhaps fifty meters ahead. As he tried to follow its path upward with his eyes, he stumbled. Totally out of control, he tumbled at least two complete revolutions before slamming into an aspen.

This time the pain in his lower back was excruciating. He didn't quite black out, but wished he had. His whole body tightened up in agony. He lay there, trying to regain his energy, until he felt clammy as the sweat evaporated. He was aware of a sore spot on the back of his head. Had it been there earlier? There was no way to tell.

"You okay, Vincent?" he asked at last. His throat burned, making it difficult to talk.

"Naturally. But what about you? I can call a doctor."

Cal considered the possibility, thinking also of the blood on his hands and the way the conversation might turn. "No," he said finally. "I think I'm okay."

"You're in charge." Vincent said it the way someone else might say, "Go right ahead and kill yourself. See if I care."

"Can you do things on your own? I mean without directions from me?" Cal wondered what would have happened if he had broken his neck just now.

"In a way. I can't initiate activities that I don't know you approve of. But you can give me general directions, or tell me to do something like wake you in eight hours, or call a doctor if you're unconscious for more than ten minutes."

"Do I have any outstanding requests like that?"

"You've asked me to warn you if I see anyone sneaking up on you."

"I did?" Cal asked apprehensively. "Did I explain why?"

"Negative."

Cal sat, looking for a moment at the two overhead continents. His vertigo was still present. Toward the far end of Daedalus's cylinder, the cumulative refractions over thirty kilometers gave the distant land a faint blue tinge, but it wasn't the same as a blue sky on Earth.

He painfully pushed himself off the ground and stood until he felt steady enough to continue.

"So I can talk to anyone I want through you?" Cal asked.

"You've got it."

"I don't even know who I might want to talk to yet, besides a doctor."

"You might want to call your wife."

Cal stopped, clearing his throat before he dared to speak. His pulse pounded. "My wife?"

"Sure. She tried to call you last night. Maybe she wants to talk. Or don't you remember her?"

So he was married. Surprise and worry filtered up from the depths. He couldn't even remember dating anyone more than maybe a dozen times. He had always been too busy. Had he met her here? He wondered what would have made her special.

"What would I say to her?" he asked unthinkingly.

"That's not my specialty."

Fear and curiosity momentarily drove away all unrelated thoughts. Cal wanted to call her right then, but he didn't. Somehow it was too much like asking a stranger for help. First he had to learn more about himself. Was his marriage one of love, convenience, expediency? He couldn't imagine the latter two, but then he probably hadn't imagined waking up on Daedalus and missing a decade of memories.

"How would I call someone?" he asked.

"Tell me the name and whether you want video or voice only."

"And you'll let me know if anyone calls?"

"Unless you tell me you don't want to be disturbed."

Cal rubbed the back of his neck. "What's her name?"

"Your wife's?"

"Yes."

"Nikki."

Nikki. No image. For some reason he thought of a young

woman he had dated a few times during his freshman year. The memory seemed to be one of the most recent he could summon, but her face had faded into oblivion. Now all he could recall was her embarrassment when he had found out that, despite her request for help with physics assignments, she'd had a superb high school record and obviously had as much need for his assistance as their professor did. Had he been so insecure that she needed to overdo her modesty?

He wondered if Nikki was worried. Or uncaring. Was she a friendly roommate, a loving partner, or a bitter, angry person? Again he felt the urge to call, but refrained.

Ahead lay the stream he had seen from farther up the hill. The water's course curved so it ran parallel to the path.

"The water is pumped up here?" Cal asked.

"Correct. The lakes below feed it. It keeps them from stagnating, and people seem to like the stream."

The water was totally clear. Beneath the surface the stream bed looked like it was lined with real stones and pebbles. Cal was suddenly aware of how thirsty he was, and awkwardly knelt beside the flowing stream. The water was cool but not chilly.

He couldn't bend over far enough to drink without pain in his back forcing him to halt, so he stretched out flat on the ground. The water tasted excellent.

"Are you waterproof, Vincent?"

"Down to a hundred meters of water at Earth-normal gravity."

As he drank it occurred to him that the water might have a second use. Maybe this would be a good place to wash off the blood and see how much damage his body had sustained. No point walking into Machu Picchu looking the way he did. Twenty meters farther down, the stream ran through the concealment of a couple of large pine trees, so Cal moved on.

The water felt colder when he immersed both arms, so he concentrated on the blood adhering to his hands. The reddish-black flakes came off stubbornly in the cool water. Cal hurried. He took off his trousers and shirt and doused them. The blood clung to the thin material.

He wrung out the trousers and shirt. The bloodstains were almost as bad as before, so on impulse he crumbled a handful of dirt and sprinkled it on the pants. The dirt reduced the blood's contrast with the tan fabric. Better to look a little dirty than bloody. He was putting his clothes back on when he realized what else was wrong.

Now that he had washed off his hands and arms, he realized that he had no wounds.

There were numerous minor bruises, but no major breaks in the skin. So whose blood was it?

"Vincent?"

"Here."

"Do you know anything about the blood on my hands?"

"Not much. Last night at twenty-three fifteen you turned me on and asked me to erase all my records of your recent activities. Your sleeve was rolled down over me, so I couldn't see, but it sounded like you were dragging something heavy along the floor. Like a body."

"Did I say why, or say anything else?" Cal's head began to ache again.

"You didn't explain. But you did keep repeating a phrase. You kept saying, 'What have I done to you?'"

———— Chapter two ————
Hotel

" 'WHAT have I done to you?' I said that?" Cal asked, dazed.

"Several times," Vincent said. "And I didn't think you were practicing voice lessons."

Cal's gaze focused on the pine tree in front of him, as though by looking at a relatively normal object, he could block out all the abnormalities. Or *was* it abnormal for him to be dragging bloody bodies around at midnight? Maybe that was why he felt the need to hurry. He shivered.

"What did I do then, Vincent?" he asked at last.

"I don't know. You turned me off. But even if you had left me on, I wouldn't have saved much information unless you were talking to me."

Cal walked down the hill toward Machu Picchu. The pain was tolerable, and he felt slightly better physically. The light breeze persisted. What he had said to Vincent made it seem that he had hurt someone badly, perhaps deliberately, and then felt remorse. He forced the thoughts of a bloody body from his mind. There had to be more to the story. He couldn't have killed anyone.

"Too much is happening," he said. "I've known my name for less than thirty minutes. And I don't even know where I live. I do live here, don't I?"

"For sure. You can even see it from here."

Cal took another glance at the two overhead continents before the vertigo resumed. "I suppose that's humor. Right, Vincent?"

"Very good. Maybe you are recovering. Look down at the

13

land that runs from Machu Picchu all the way to the other end. There are three villages. One in the center, two nearer to the ends. You live in the center village, Greenwich, just beyond the lake. Want a closer look?''

''What do you have in mind?''

''I can operate as a telescope just as easily as a mirror. Hold me at a convenient position and watch.''

Cal stopped walking and did so. A color image of the center village came up on the screen and began to zoom.

''Say when,'' Vincent said.

The picture kept growing, far beyond what Cal thought was possible. Surprised, he said, ''Enough.''

In the screen were fewer than a dozen earth-sheltered houses, many with large windows, sprawled in the midst of an area almost as lush with pine trees, grass, and low shrubs as his current location. Massive windows consumed almost all the exposed area in several of the houses. Grass grew on the roofs of some of the houses, and a few had rock facing.

''That's remarkable. How is it that this image is so steady?'' he asked.

''The view I'm receiving is approximately ten times the area I'm showing you. As long as you don't move so much that I lose the primary view, I can dynamically pick the right portion so you see a steady display. If you move too much, I just repeat frames until you swing back.''

What Cal found even more surprising than the view was the touch of pride in Vincent's voice. As he watched the screen, a young blond girl, perhaps ten years old, pedaled her bicycle into view. She leaned hard and followed a sharp bend in the path, disappearing momentarily behind a large evergreen. Following behind her, running hard, was a small terrier. Apparently there were no roads, just meandering trails.

''Thanks very much,'' Cal said after just a moment longer. He had experienced a puzzling, disquieting sensation as he watched the girl and could no longer look. Did he possess an extremely powerful aversion to voyeurism? Maybe it had something to do with Carla. He realized that he had not thought about his sister until now. Had he and Carla had another fight—maybe one more serious than all their petty squabbles as kids when both of them had wanted to be the leader? No. That didn't seem right. He and Carla had become good friends once they were out on their own, competing with classmates rather than each other. At least he remembered more than he had before. He wished the triggers to more information would speed up.

"Care to see anything else?" Vincent asked.

"That's fine for now. What about transient lodging in Machu Picchu?" he asked, picking his steps carefully, convinced that he couldn't make it home, and nervous about what he would find there. Would there be a policeman waiting for him?

"Plenty there, Kemo Sabe."

"Vincent, where *do* you get your choice of words?"

"From your list. You gave me a list of a hundred books to read as part of my initialization. Most of them were novels, but I especially liked *Five Centuries of Slang and Idiomatic Expressions*."

"Do I always understand you?"

"Mostly. If it's critical, I try to confine myself to easily understood phrases. With a lot of the slang, the *sound* it makes tells you more than the word itself. But if you insist, I could limit my speech to current usage and slang no older than a year." Vincent's voice implied reluctance even to suggest such a limitation was possible.

"No," he said. "Use whatever you like for now. If I have too much trouble, we can worry about it later."

"Thanks, pal."

"Don't mention it. Wait a minute—do you take expressions like that literally?"

"Only when it's to my benefit."

Cal grinned despite his exhaustion. Ahead, a solitary hiker climbed the path Cal was on. As the figure came closer, Cal could see that it was a woman. He experienced conflicting feelings, telling himself simultaneously that she was attractive and that she was too old for him. But he looked again and realized she was probably in her thirties, so part of his subconscious message was clearly wrong.

"You're up early," she said, once the distance had narrowed. Her voice was unstrained, as though she were used to a brisk morning jaunt. The fringes of her blond hair were bright in the sunshine.

Cal said nothing at first, unsure whether he was supposed to know her. "It gave me a chance to see the sunrise," he said neutrally.

"I should do that sometime—are you okay? You look like you had a bad fall." The woman stopped.

"I'm fine. Really." Cal decided he didn't know her.

"I don't believe you, you know." She stood there smiling, waiting. Her shirt and shorts, made of thin material like that of Cal's clothes, were snug and flattering. A small pack hung from a narrow belt at her waist.

Cal stared at her eyes. She seemed genuinely interested in helping, but he couldn't accept it. Not without knowing more about what was going on. He smiled wryly at the paradox. "I'll be all right. I took a spill, but everything's under control now. Thanks for the concern."

"Wounded your pride too?" she asked. But without waiting for a reply she added, "Okay. I'm going on up. Last chance."

"I really do appreciate your offer. But I can get down fine. Thanks."

"Okay." She gave him a broad grin, as if to say she wasn't offended, and left.

"One question," Cal called before she got too far away.

"Okay."

"Do you come up here every morning?"

"Every one. Why?"

"Just curious."

She grinned again and turned away. Cal watched her until she passed behind a cluster of aspens. The sway of her hips awakened feelings that had been dormant earlier in the day, and he wondered again about his relationship with his wife.

He turned back toward the outskirts of Machu Picchu. The urge to hurry was stronger now, still unaccompanied by any idea of why.

He soon found himself on what had to be the grassy roof of one of the uppermost buildings at the edge of the city. Below him, the rest of Machu Picchu was an enormous, irregular, green-carpeted staircase. There came a distant sound like a door slamming shut, but otherwise the city lay quiet.

The buildings were mostly long, narrow structures set horizontally into the side of the hill, such that each roof was covered by grass and shrubs. Each, in turn, provided a terrace and a pleasant view to the next building up the slope. Occasional breaks between buildings on the same level formed passageways for people to travel up and down the hill. Bicycle racks were plentiful, but there were hardly any people out on the streets.

"Where are the nearest transient accommodations?" Cal asked.

"Here's a map. We're always the blinking green box. I'll show the hotel you want in red."

Cal glanced briefly at the map on Vincent's screen. "I'm too tired even to do that. How about if you just give me directions?"

"Okay, Igor. Face left. Now walk this way."

"Vincent, why did I buy a smart-ass?"

"Smart-ass? You said you wanted me this way because you worked with computers all day. You were bored with most of them," Vincent said. "Smart-ass?"

Cal followed Vincent's directions. Only one of the shops he passed, evidently a bar, showed signs of activity. Fortunately, the hotel was not far from where he had come into town.

"Here we are, killer," Vincent announced a few minutes later.

"Ah, Vincent, could you take that word off your list for the time being?"

"Cert."

The hotel fit into the general format of the buildings Cal had already passed, except it was longer than most of the stores, and a few rock benches sat on the grass in front. Like many of the stores, the hotel's facing looked like smooth granite. Bordering the lip of grassy roof that he stood on was a short rock wall.

From there Cal could see a few more people out on the streets below. Their eyes were shadowed, too distant to see clearly. Was there a policeman looking for him somewhere, wanting to ask him about a dead body or someone badly injured? Cal didn't know what privacy limits were the norm, but he gathered that if the police were searching for him, Vincent would not tell them where he was.

With a determined stride a short woman wearing a striped T-shirt and long pants gave him a wide berth as she passed and averted her eyes. Did he look that bad? The woman had also worn a wristcomp, but hers was dark brown rather than the alternating gold and silver of Vincent's case. Cal hurried inside.

On a panel in the hotel lobby there were rows and rows of

numbers, each with a light and a touch switch. Cal was surprised that only a scattered few lights were lit.

"The lights indicate occupancy?" he asked.

"Yes. Put your bank stick in the aperture and press your thumb on the white square."

Cal did so, and a deep voice sounded from the panel. "Welcome to the Machu Picchu Hilton. Rooms are available by the hour, day, or week, in accordance with this schedule." A panel lit up with a brief table of rates. "If you would like to stay, please press the switch next to the room number you prefer." A map took over the display space.

Cal pressed the nearest vacancy.

"Thank you very much. Your privacy code is on the screen. Simply type it when you wish access to your room." Displayed were very tiny letters: A K G T.

"Vincent, can you remember these for me? I'm not sure I even trust myself that far." He held Vincent close to the screen. Cal assumed that each of the small, circular indentations on the band were video pickups.

"Got it."

"Have a pleasant stay," the deep voice said. "A light above your door will blink for five minutes."

Cal could see the light from where he stood and started moving toward it.

"You forgot your bank stick," the deep voice reminded him.

"Right. Thanks."

Cal was halfway to his room, moving through a deserted lobby, when he heard sounds from across the room. The throbbing beat had to be coming from the hotel bar. But it was early morning.

Momentarily more curious than tired, Cal walked toward the sound. Maybe the night shift had their entertainment hours shifted also.

He looked into the dim interior of the room that contained the activity. The music was so loud, he almost didn't hear someone call, "Come on in, honey."

The bar was packed. There were more people in there than he had seen on his walk. He left. He had taken only a few steps toward his room before a slightly drunk, feminine voice called out more loudly, "Whatsa matter, darlin'? Don'cha feel sociable?"

Cal turned to face a tall, dark-haired woman with a hemispherical glass in her hand. Her drink almost spilled as she leaned against the wall, misjudging the distance. She moved closer and put her hand on the back of Cal's neck.

"Maybe later," he said, acutely uncomfortable, pushing her hand away.

"Anytime." She seemed undisturbed.

Confused, he walked to his room. "Nice place you got here," he said under his breath. He passed a vending machine and was surprised to see that it offered carrots and celery.

"But you wouldn't want to live here?" Vincent asked.

"I don't know yet."

Under the flashing light he tapped in his code, and the door slid silently open. A button on the inside wall caused it to close again. Cal didn't even examine the room. He moved directly to the bed and lay down. "Vincent, would you wake me in two hours? If I don't get just a little rest, my head is going to explode."

"Roger wilco."

The pain in his back flared as he changed positions, but after a minute or two, Cal felt distinctly better. It occurred to him that he rarely went right to sleep lately, but, even as he wondered where that thought had come from, sleep overtook him.

"Come on," a voice said. "Wake up." There was a pause, and the voice prodded again. It took Cal a long moment to reorient himself and realize that Vincent was obeying his last request.

"Okay. Okay. I'm awake." His head still hurt. He felt better though. "Thanks, Vincent."

"No sweat, no blood."

The room was faintly illuminated by a covered window set at an angle between the wall and ceiling.

A small lever moved easily under Cal's touch, and suddenly the interior of Daedalus was once again in full view. The vertigo he had felt when he looked at the two overhead continents was not as bad as before, perhaps because he was enclosed in a room. Wispy clouds had formed at scattered intervals over all three continents.

He closed off the view and briefly surveyed the darkened room. A door near the entrance could only be the bathroom.

Besides the bed, there were just three padded chairs and a desk terminal with a wall screen, which currently showed a Mars landscape. Cal moved to the keyboard and pressed the large ON switch.

Almost simultaneously a feminine voice said, "Hello. I'm ready to serve you. Which choice do you prefer?" and the screen displayed the same message with several computer menu selections, including live video news, text news, entertainment, communications, tourist information, Daedalus library, travel information, and several others.

Cal moved to one of the chairs and lowered himself carefully. "Let's try text news. Last twenty-four hours. Here on Daedalus. Crime or homicide, whichever has fewer entries. That should do it."

Two headlines came up on the screen:

1. WIFE KILLS HUSBAND—THEN SELF
2. UNIDENTIFIED BODY DISCOVERED IN DOCK AREA

"Show me number two," Cal said, his throat suddenly dry.

The requested article replaced the menu on the screen.

04:20 12 APRIL 2156 The body of an unidentified male in his early thirties was discovered in Daedalus dock area C5 after an anonymous early-morning tip alerted police.

No statement has yet been made about whether the death was accidental or deliberate. Authorities believe the severely battered body had been moved after death occurred. Little blood was found at the scene, inconsistent with the wounds to the victim's head and upper chest.

Undisclosed sources report that several capsules of Vital 22 were confiscated at the scene by police. Officials refuse to say if the restricted cell-regeneration stimulant may have been a motive for murder.

The victim's identity is expected to be disclosed this morning. Tips go to code D56-122.

Cal turned his head to stare out the window. What had he got himself into? He wasn't sure he wanted to know. Without standing, he retrieved the capsules from his pocket.

"Vincent, can you identify these?"

"They look like capsules to me."

"Thanks. Are you sure that's all you can deduce?"

"Sorry. You could take them to a pharmatique."

So what now? Maybe he should turn himself in to the police. Let them determine what had happened last night. He couldn't be guilty of a crime. Could he? Had the pressures in the last ten years flicked an internal switch? Something else bothered him; he wasn't even sure that on Daedalus one was innocent until proved guilty.

There were too many questions, too much room for error. The police would probably be just as likely to detain him as help him. He looked back at the wall screen.

"Let's see live video news, for here on Daedalus."

Next on the screen was a view of two young women standing in front of what must have been one of the crop fields on Icarus. As they talked about a new technique that might allow five percent more production, Cal realized he was thirsty.

Rising shakily, he moved from the chair, passing through the image of Icarus, since the hologram was particularly deep. In the bathroom he took a long drink. He could have been on Earth, except that next to the toilet was an arrow and a warning sign about Coriolis force.

The same familiar stranger's image in the mirror stared back at him with bloodshot eyes. He splashed some water on his face and pushed his brown hair closer to where he wanted it. The effort didn't improve his image much, so he returned to the computer.

The topic had changed. A woman was interviewing a man behind a desk. At first Cal was disinterested, but then he took a closer look at the man.

The man was perhaps in his early forties. His receding hair was space black. Curly chest hair poked over the low shirt-front. He scratched his closely cropped beard.

The man appeared calm. His eyes moved from the reporter to the camera to a screen on his desk. But beneath the calm seemed to lie rigid control. Cal had the impression that if someone came up from behind and put his hand on the man's shoulder, he would deliberately keep looking in the same direction for a moment before glancing to see whose hand it was.

But the submerged control was not what had drawn Cal's attention to the man. It was a dim recollection. Could Cal have met him, worked with him, or merely seen him in the media? He pulled, but nothing more would emerge from his memory. Maybe the video *was* a better idea than the text. Perhaps his memory would respond more readily to pictures than it did to words.

Cal realized that he had been staring, and again he heard the words being spoken.

". . . and what do you think you will miss the most when you're on the *Vittoria?*" the woman asked. Cal could have seen her face if he were interested, but it would have required him to move from the chair.

"The sun, I suppose. People laugh a little when I say that, but the *Vittoria* will have almost everything else." The man's level voice was as controlled as his facial expressions, but his speech prodded no further memories.

"Thank you for taking the time from your busy schedule." The woman turned to face the center of the audience, and added, "This has been Michelle Garney, speaking with Russ Tolbor, who is soon to be the commander of the generation-ship *Vittoria*." She wore her brown hair pushed back over her ears. She seemed quite attractive in a businesslike manner, but unfamiliar. Would Nikki be as foreign to him?

The hologram collapsed into a blank wall, and a new scene sprang from a pinpoint to form large block letters saying simply:

FORGET-ME-NOW
ERASURE PARLORS

Cal stared at the image, and a shiver passed through him. A moment later another news story began. "Computer, turn the sound off for now."

"Yes, sir," the computer said into the silence.

"Vincent?"

"Just a minute. I'm busy."

"You can tell me some jokes later. Be serious for just a minute, okay?"

"Okay."

"What are erasure parlors?"

"Memory erasure parlors."

"Right, but what do they do? Why do they exist?"

"If you want to forget a painful incident, you can go there and pay them to erase your most recent memories. You lose your life savings in a casino, your wife leaves you—you pay your money. 'Blank' is a better word than 'erase,' because, over the course of the next year or so, the memories eventually come back, slowly enough that you get accustomed to them more gently. That's the theory, anyway. You want some techified data?"

"Maybe later. Was I in one of those places last night?"

"I don't know."

"Could my symptoms be caused by a visit to one of them?"

"Possibly, but unlikely. They normally blank a year or so, not over a decade. You'd have to be fairly unsettled to want to lose a decade."

Cal thought for a moment. "So there are enough customers to justify a place like that. Lots of bad memories?"

"That's not the only reason. For some people it's a change of pace, a fad. And it's a convenient way to prevent the police from forcing a person to provide evidence against himself."

"You mean someone could commit a crime and temporarily erase the memory?" A second and a third realization hit him. "And the police have the authority to force you to testify against yourself?"

"If lives are at stake."

"And therefore it might be unwise to complain to the police that I've lost my memory."

"Too true. They might infer things you wish unmentioned."

Did a murderer think like a murderer if he lost his memories of the crimes? Or even with his memories, what was it like? Maybe he continually rationalized his activities, convincing himself that his victims deserved their fates. Was there perpetual guilt, or did a shifted value system alter the individual's perceptions? Cal didn't feel like a murderer, but he wasn't at all sure that how he felt mattered. Vincent's comment unsettled him.

"Computer, give me the main menu again." Cal reexamined the choices. "Let's give the Daedalus library a try this time. Daedalus itself. Construction."

Instantly a full-color scale model of Daedalus hung in the air before the screen. Glowing letters and arrows indicated tubeways, structures, power lines, plumbing, homes, businesses, and far more.

"Can you rotate the image the same way Daedalus acts?"

Obediently the cylinder slowly turned on its spin axis. As the three outside mirrors turned with the structure, their images almost reached Cal's chair. They were each joined to Daedalus on the left end of the cylinder, but they spread wide to catch the sun's energy.

Outside the left end of the living-area cylinder were two disks with the same diameter of the cylinder, aligned on the same axis. The one nearer the cylinder rotated with the same period. The far one, next to the outside parabolic power-plant mirror, hung motionless. Cal knew it was for zero-gravity manufacturing and research even without the label over it.

Filaments, tethers to Icarus, connected to the axis and stretched out into space, one from each end of the cylinder.

"Can you mark area C5 in the dock area?"

A light began to flash in the spinning disk. Cal looked more closely and could see concentric floors dividing the disk into an enormous number of levels. C5 lay near the outer edge.

"Can you also mark a point a couple of kilometers up the hill from this hotel?"

The second flashing light served only to indicate how short a journey he had made that morning. Nothing linked the two areas. The tubeways reaching from the "level" valley floors traveled up the hill to the axis, but there was no access to them anywhere near the point where Cal had woken up.

"Stop the rotation, please. Fine. Can you indicate where my house is?" Cal wasn't sure if the room computer had enough data available to make the link, but near the center of one of the continents, a third light began to flash. "Okay. Now highlight the transportation means from here to there."

Three tubeways passed between the village and the outer shell of Daedalus, apparently running through long grooves set in the rock that formed a cosmic ray barrier for the inhabitants. The center tubeway seemed to come within a kilometer of the light indicating his house.

That was where he must go. Visual triggers were working the best at jogging his memory. He had to know what was happening. Were the police even now trying to locate him? Maybe they already knew where he was, since the hotel's computer was tied in to all the others. When he opened the door to his room, would there be a policeman quietly waiting with a list of questions he might not even comprehend?

Cal turned off the terminal, and the image of Daedalus vanished. The dark gray of the room matched his mood. He rose stiffly from the chair and moved across the floor.

Cal touched the switch to open the door. As it slid far enough for him to see out, he caught a glimpse of someone moving away from the space in front of the doorway.

────── Chapter three ──────
Home

CAL'S heart raced, and his throat suddenly tightened. The door opened all the way. He stood motionless, afraid to leave. After a long moment he leaned forward to see that the hall outside his hotel room was almost deserted. No police lay in wait. Down the hall a man and woman staggered slightly, apparently on their way to their own room. Sheepishly Cal went through the door and tapped the button to close it, indicating that he was finished with the room.

Why was he so startled? Simply because of the trauma of memory loss, or because of submerged guilt? Maybe he had more to feel guilty about than he already feared.

The bar was still noisy, but he didn't venture near. Outside he squinted in the reflected sunlight for a moment as his eyes adjusted. Vincent confirmed the direction to the tubeway.

There were more people out now. Cal passed pedestrians and bicycle riders as he traveled deeper into the city. He watched faces, seeing mostly serious expressions, but no one who actually seemed familiar. A few people took two looks at him, probably because of the dirt on his clothes, but no one spoke. Casual glances at store windows revealed hand weapons, cinema notices, and home furnishings, none triggering new recollections. The store names were mostly Indian, ranging from Killapata Weapons to Mohican Moccasins.

He passed three more busy bars as he walked, but attracted no more solicitations. Sounds of singing emanated from a church along the way, the church incongruously located next to a drugstore that apparently specialized in recreational drugs. Not everyone he passed wore a wristcomp, but there were several people obviously talking to their own wristcomps.

"How much farther to the tubeway?" he finally asked Vincent. His feet were beginning to hurt.

"Microns. That's the access ahead."

Fortunately, the tubeway that ran nearest his house was one of the two closest to the hotel.

At the base of the building with a tubeway sign, Cal joined a few others as they followed the markers along a granite-lined walkway cut into the hillside. After twenty steps white indirect lighting took over from the sunshine. After twenty more he found himself on a fifty-meter platform extending between two darkened, empty track beds, each sporting a single large repulsion rail. His footsteps echoed off the walls.

Four gaping tunnel mouths, one for each direction on either side of the platform, emitted neither light nor sound. All the surfaces seemed to be cut from granite. One of two illuminated arrows indicated the tunnel that led toward home.

Home. It was a funny word, loaded with connotations. But now it summoned nothing of an earth-sheltered, rock and glass dwelling in the middle of a continent on Daedalus. The few images it did generate were all from Atlanta, of a sister calling to him in his room, warning him that he'd be late. Late. His sense of time was as disjointed as his feeling of home.

With no audible warning a brightly lit string of yellow cars emerged from the darkness of an uphill tunnel mouth. Cal followed three women into the vehicle and picked a seat away from other passengers. A slight murmur of ventilation air was enough to blanket most of the noise of soft conversations elsewhere. He saw no policemen in the car.

Cal rubbed his finger against a nearby panel that listed almost fifty stops, four of which were labeled "Greenwich." The car accelerated swiftly. Vincent told him which stop was best, and he requested it.

That done, he looked around the inside of the vehicle and caught the eye of one of the women who had entered when he did. He smiled at her. She returned the smile briefly before turning back to her traveling companions.

Snatches of sentences came to him as he sat. It was hard to make much sense of the fragments, but it seemed to him that the subject of drugs came up frequently.

Eight stops later Cal exited the car, puzzled by the apparent emphasis of the conversation. Daedalus seemed like a place where that kind of need wouldn't be so strong. He was the only one to get off, and he watched as the tube train sped silently away. A gently sloping ramp led to the surface.

The grass was thick and knee-deep, as it had appeared in the view from above Machu Picchu. Cal looked back at the city and was surprised to see how far away it was. He had known he was going to the midway point, but the trip had gone so fast, it didn't seem possible that he had come so far. From here the city was nothing more than vague striations across the hillside.

"Which way, Vincent?" Six paths led away at approximately equal intervals. Brief road names were inscribed in blocks set into the ground near each path. The paths themselves were smooth, dark brown, and just the slightest bit resilient.

"Longfellow," Vincent said.

Rolling hills broke up the monotony of the enormous valley and provided earth-shelter backdrops to the scattered houses. To his left he could see nearly the whole length of the edge of the continent as it joined the long window above it.

Ahead a young boy perhaps eight years old with a toothy grin rode a bicycle toward him on the path. The freckled child turned his bike to follow a bend in the path, overcorrected for the Coriolis force change, and almost rammed Cal as he raced by. "Sorry," the boy called behind him.

Cal encountered no one else before he reached the house that Vincent informed him was his. More anxious than before, he walked along the narrow walkway that joined the main path. The image of the house stirred a murky memory, as though he had seen it most often in the dark. Then the feeling passed. The house was much like the neighbors' homes. Rectangular windows lined the front and faced away from the breeze. Decorative rock covered the exposed surface.

Was Nikki inside? Cal stood before the door for a long moment, noting the now-familiar white square for a thumbprint. He performed the required ritual, and the door slid open.

The house was smaller than he had expected from the outside appearance. Two bedrooms and a modest bathroom were the only rooms divided from the sparse main area. A waist-high semicircular counter surrounded the kitchen space, while the rest of the room was given over to a table, some comfort-able-looking padded chairs, several large potted plants, and a desk computer. He was alone in the house.

He felt vaguely relieved. Now he could get cleaned up and have a chance to learn a little more before Nikki arrived.

He looked at Vincent's screen again. 11:00. Nikki would probably be at work.

In the main bedroom closet he found a fresh set of clothes. With them in hand he moved to the bathroom to take a shower. Muscles that hadn't bothered him for more than an hour involuntarily contracted as he took off his shirt and trousers. After a moment of standing still and letting his head clear, he tossed the old clothes into a bin.

The hot water felt remarkably good. What was left of the blood yielded to the steaming water.

Eventually he stepped out of the shower and began to dry himself. The mirror showed a view of the off-center bruise on his back. All dark and ugly purple, it was roughly circular, at least as large as a soccer ball impact.

With his clothes on and hair combed his image in the mirror looked much more like what he guessed was normal. Without forethought he abruptly smiled at the stern image. Had he smiled much lately? Somehow he couldn't believe he had. Enough of that, though. He wanted to investigate the house.

He left the bathroom, accidentally bumping Vincent into the door frame.

"Ouch," Vincent said.

"Sorry. You okay?"

"Right enough. But I must be a masophile to keep you."

"Oh, go plug yourself into a high-voltage line."

"Say, that's more like it. Maybe you are feeling better."

"Vincent, do you say that because of the way I've been act-ing the last few hours, or a much longer period?" Cal was in-explicably sure he knew the answer.

"Lately, in general." Vincent confirmed his suspicion.

"But you don't know why?"

"On the nose. I can see symptoms, but it's tougher to see the cause."

Pictures on the main bedroom wall attracted Cal's initial at-tention. The first few showed scenes of Daedalus's construc-tion.

Cal stopped in front of the next picture. Nikki. This time

there was a surge of memory. She had smiled the same way the time they had skipped a conference to spend more time together. Deep-blue eyes stared back at him from the high-contrast picture. Her black hair was straight, and her lips were slightly parted. He could imagine smelling her perfume. The lighting accentuated her cheekbones.

The picture suddenly reawakened the same feelings he had experienced as he'd watched the hiker depart earlier in the morning. But there was more, much more than just physical attraction this time. He had shared hard times with Nikki, and felt good at her side.

Then, as quickly as it had arrived, the pleasurable feeling faded, leaving behind only the objective memory. Cal stared at her picture, straining to remember more. What did she enjoy? What were her dislikes? How was she strong, and what were her weaknesses? Now the harder he tried to recall, the farther away he felt. All he could do was subjectively decide from her picture that she was intelligent as well as pretty. Sad that he could reach no closer, he moved to the next picture.

He stared at himself, smiling in the sunshine in front of the house. Apparently it had been taken several years ago. He was older than in his college days, but not much. How often had he smiled since then, he wondered again.

In front of the last picture, he felt the blood drain from his face. At first the brown-haired girl in the picture reminded him of his sister, Carla, but he knew exactly who she was. Lynn. So he had forgotten not only his wife, but also his daughter.

Several more memories dislodged from their resting places deep in the mire and floated to the top. Lynn. Cal had been afraid of having children, afraid he would not be a good father. It took so much patience, understanding, time. He had agonized over whether he'd be adequate.

And after all the doubts, he had done fine. Loving Lynn was as natural as loving Nikki, and Lynn had been a terrific child, always cheerful, asking all those happy children's questions. She was active, almost hyperactive, and wanted desperately to try hang gliding when she was old enough. They had been quite content, the three of them. But what about recently? As he tried to remember more, the flow of memories trickled off.

He remained in front of the last picture, not understanding

the lonely ache that the string of photos had created in him. There existed a barrier. All he could see was the outside. On the outside, Lynn was happy, as was Nikki. Was it the truth?

The contents of the closet told him little except that both he and Nikki apparently possessed conservative tastes in clothing. Most of the colors were subdued, containing a high proportion of somber blues, grays, browns, and charcoals. Only a few jackets were made of heavier material than what he was wearing.

Uncomfortable about searching Lynn's bedroom, he went instead to the desk computer. A push of the ON button caused a menu to flash onto the wall screen. He chose several successive menus and reached an entry labeled "Employment Data, Cal Donley."

He skipped over the first sections, stopping at the last item. So now he knew more about what his job involved. He was in charge of communications computer systems aboard the *Vittoria*. And maybe that explained the familiarity of Russ Tolbor on the newscast. The summary said he reported to someone named Tom Horvath and that he'd had his job almost four years.

Seconds later, data about the *Vittoria* filled the screen. None of it triggered any new recollections. The *Vittoria*, looking a little like a giant turnip, was intended to transport ten thousand pioneers to a planet circling Barnard's Star, or rather, transport their descendants, since the *Vittoria* was a generation-ship. The trip would take five hundred years.

Cal, however, was more concerned about the next few hours and days. The fleeting feeling of urgency had returned. He soon found a data base describing Nikki Nokoto. At first unable to avoid feeling like a trespasser, he selected a fairly impersonal choice: her employment history. According to the display, she was an M.D. with a specialty in transplanting artificial organs.

He was still absorbing information when the sound of a door opening behind him cut short his investigation. Guiltily, he fumbled for the CLEAR SCREEN key before he turned.

"Hello, Nikki," he said, facing the woman in the doorway.

She stood there, back to the doorway, for a long moment before she spoke. "I don't know whether I should be angry or relieved that you're okay." It was Nikki's cool, even voice that dredged memories to the surface.

Awareness of affection and respect joined the embarrassment Cal felt at almost being caught looking at her information in the computer, and it came to him that Vincent was still turned on. "You tried to call last night." He had intended a question, but it came out as a statement.

"Tried." The word hung there, waiting for a response. The door slid shut behind her, cutting off the backlighting that had made it hard to see her features. She was more beautiful than her picture, but distant.

Cal struggled to find an adequate explanation. If he told her about his memory loss, would she immediately sympathize, or would she call the police? He could sense her anger, but couldn't tell what loyalty lay with it. He thought for so long that Nikki herself saved him from answering.

"I know," she said. "I know. You'll tell me soon what it is you're up to. Where did you spend the night?" She moved to a nearby chair and sat, but she didn't look comfortable. She rubbed her thumb and forefinger together slowly.

Surprised by getting a question he could answer, Cal told her the truth. "I slept outside on the hill above Machu Picchu."

She turned her head and inspected him out of the corner of her eye. "You're serious, aren't you? Don't you think you're carrying things a bit too far? I was—I was worried about you." The reflected light from the window accented her blue eyes.

Cal wanted to move to her, to hold her, and he suddenly had no doubts about being attracted to her in the past. But he didn't move. He was an alien here. He said, "I'm sorry you were worried. But I am touched."

Nikki looked sharply at him, then blinked and rose from her chair. She moved behind it and rested her hands on the back. Cal had the strong feeling that she was struggling to maintain her self-control. There was apparent surprise on her face.

"You're touched. I want to believe that. I *need* to believe I can still touch you. But what can I do when you're so erratic? One day you're attentive, caring, feeling, and the next you're distant, cold, shut off." A wistful look of vulnerability reached her eyes, and Cal noticed, as though for the first time, that she must have a trace of Japanese ancestry. Her hair was longer in back than in front, apparently cut so no strands could reach her eyes in zero gravity.

Cal was puzzled. She had been hurt. He had hurt her. And yet he felt an overpowering urge to protect and help her. He knew somehow that beneath the quiet surface she was strong. With the feelings, however, came no tangible recollections to tell him what the feelings were based on. He wanted to be there with her, not one more obstacle in her path.

"I don't want to hurt you," he said.

"I know that. If I thought you did, I wouldn't be here. But I can't take much more."

"You won't have to, Nickname." The word came without warning. It seemed silly even as he said it, but the thought was too late.

"You haven't called me that in a long time," she said, a puzzled frown forming on her forehead. "I guess I associate that name with the more peaceful part of our marriage."

"The first years were good, weren't they?" he asked, sure that they were.

"You're always so good at understatement." She smiled for the first time. Her smile made his breath unsteady.

"It's going to be that way again. Trust me."

"Trust you. God, how I want to. Are you sure you're okay?"

"Yeah, fine. Why?"

"I don't know. You seem different somehow today."

"Maybe you're just paying more attention today. Why did you come home now?"

"The computer told me you were back. I wanted to talk to you, so I got someone to take over for me."

"And what do you want to say?"

"I don't know anymore," she said. "This conversation isn't going the way I expected it to."

"What *were* you going to say?"

Nikki straightened and rubbed her hands against her upper arms, as though to warm herself. "I don't feel like talking about it right now. You're *sure* you're all right?"

"I'll survive."

"How about if we eat some lunch while you tell me about last night?" She walked toward the kitchen.

"Could we talk about it later?" Cal still worried about her reaction to his amnesia. She might accept it, or she might feel he was covering up. Without knowing what strains had recently been applied to their marriage, he couldn't gauge her loyalty. He wanted to believe she would have faith in him, but didn't know if his recent behavior would merit that. It was the wrong response.

"Later?" Nikki stopped where she was and turned to face him, her voice suddenly hard. "Later, as in 'Not now, dear,' or in 'Some other time'? *Damn* it, Cal. How long are you going to shut me out? When are you really going to talk to me again?"

"When *I* know what's going on." What the hell *was* going on? Obliterated memories, inexplicable events, a dead man, and fresh bruises. "Maybe I'd be better off back in Atlanta."

"Atlanta," Nikki said, her face white. "Sure, that's the easy way out—to be dead with the rest of them. As it is, only your *feelings* are dead." With that, she turned to the door and left without another word.

Cal might have tried to stop her, but sudden fear pinned him to the chair and paralyzed his vocal cords. What had she meant, dead with the rest of them?

When he could move again, he turned back to the computer keyboard. He entered several menu choices before he remembered Vincent.

"Vincent," he cried. "What's wrong with Atlanta?" And why had he not thought about his parents until then? Was his mother still designing teaching aids? Was she alive? What about Carla and his father?

"Atlanta, Georgia, North America?"

"Yes, yes."

"I'm sorry. The population of Atlanta is zero."

"Oh, *God*." Sweat broke out on his forehead. "What happened?"

"The problem is not just with Atlanta. There is no one left alive on Earth."

———— Chapter four ————
Headline

THE room was as silent as hard vacuum. Finally Cal heard his own ragged breath, coming in gasps. His awareness of the room returned, with it coming puzzlement at the distorted view of the surroundings and the warm, moist feeling on his cheeks.

With no conscious thought, he rubbed his eyes and wiped his fingers on his pants legs.

"Everyone's gone?" Cal asked. After he spoke he was suddenly surprised that he had to ask. He knew Vincent had told him the truth, even though his memories couldn't tangibly support the belief.

"There was no warning," Vincent said. "They think a container in some hazardous materials dump must have given way about two years ago, releasing airborne bacteria. At first everyone thought there was a new mild flu going around. Then, after the initial mild symptoms, everyone died. *Evangeline,* the one ship that had left Earth after exposure, never reached Daedalus. Fortunately, it had been put in quarantine just in case. So the people on Luna are okay too. There's a team working on recovery, but no success so far."

"My parents were down there. And my sister." Cal turned in his chair so he faced the window. A moment later the Earth traveled past. Then again. "It attacked only humans, right?"

"Yes. I thought you didn't remember."

"Every once in a while, something jogs loose. So the memory blanking parlors started business shortly after that?" He also understood the bars, the drugstores, and the churches.

Cal slumped back into the chair. The Earth continued its cyclical journey past the window. Were the plant and animal kingdoms the true meek? The Earth crossed his field of view another ten or a hundred times.

"Vincent," he said at last. "I want to call Nikki."

"It's ringing now." Half a minute passed before Vincent said, "She's not answering. You want me to try periodically?"

"No. Let her be. I'll deal with my fears myself."

"You're afraid?"

"Damn right. Afraid of what's happened. Afraid of what I've been doing. I keep remembering fragments, but I can't remember the really important things."

"I don't suppose you're talking about music lessons?"

"No." A nervous laugh escaped. "I need to know what I did last night, what I've been doing lately. For all I know, I've been a little crazy since the accident. And I don't know where to start."

"You could try your bank records. They'll tell you some of what you've done."

"Great idea. My brain must still be a little run-down." Cal turned to the desk computer, and soon the screen showed a list of transactions in reverse chronological order.

"Talk about your good news and bad news," Cal said a moment later. "At least I know where I was for some of last night, but how could I *do* that?"

The top line of the screen showed a payment to Machu Picchu Forget-Me-Now, shortly after midnight. This time, however, no feeling of belief accompanied the new information. It made no sense. If he had decided to blank his memories, why not tell Vincent to do a quick reorientation when he woke up? Why didn't he remember the journey *up* the hill?

Then it hit him. Maybe he had not been a willing customer at the parlor.

"Vincent, I think it's time I visited Forget-Me-Now."

"Don't you think you've got enough problems already without forgetting everything again?"

"That's *not* my—" Cal paused. What if someone *had* forced him? Might they not just run him through again? He looked back at the screen, suddenly curious to see if there were other payments to Forget-Me-Now.

He relaxed after scanning the first two pages of transactions. There was one payment without a name, but no other entries mentioned the parlors. So he might not always keep his log current, but at least he hadn't been trapped in some bizarre cycle, returning to a parlor every day or week. Nikki would have known if something was severely amiss.

Lost in his thoughts, Cal shut off the desk computer and left. He retraced his path to Machu Picchu, where he followed Vincent's directions rather than squint at the map on the screen. The walkways were significantly busier than they had been earlier, but with fresh clothing on, Cal didn't worry about other people's reactions.

According to Vincent it was mid-afternoon, but the sun still hung centered in the overhead mirror. The clouds might have been slightly more substantial, but he couldn't tell.

Cal was passing a wristcomp store window when Vincent whistled.

"Look at that body," said Vincent.

Cal stopped by the window and peered in. There were more selections than on a multiple-choice ethics exam. "Which one are you looking at?"

"The one on the far right. It's got infrared sensors and twice my storage. And look at those diamonds. Wouldn't you like it?"

"Are you getting tired of me, Vincent?"

"No. It's for *me*. Just transplant me into it and you've got all the new features, but you don't have to start all over."

"I think you're fine the way you are."

"I think you're cheap."

Cal grinned and moved to the next store window. The Sterile Cuckoo carried everything from autoclaves to disinfectant. Everything you needed to be absolutely clean. Cal resumed his walk.

This time he had to climb stairs rather than descend, so he was relieved when he finally saw the Forget-Me-Now sign ahead. The small shop stood in a long row of others nearby. Thick closed curtains over the display window concealed the interior view. Between the dark curtain and the glass, a simple sign said, "Shed your painful memories, while you wait."

Cal stood before the window, wishing the mere fact of returning would dredge still more memories to the surface, but nothing new came. "Vincent, if I—if I come back out of here and don't remember you, will you recap the past day's events for me? I'm going to the police if I forget anything more."

"My pleasure. But I don't remember everything—I purge nonessential data periodically."

"But if I give you a few sentences I want you to repeat later, you can do that, right?"

"Sure. Anything you want me to remember, I will. Just think of me as an elephant."

Cal summarized what he had learned so far, then turned to the door. Under his touch it slid aside, revealing a conservatively appointed office with a desk and a few visitors' chairs. There was no one inside.

"Hello," Cal called. The door slid shut, sealing him into the office, which made him decidedly uneasy. He resisted the impulse to open the curtains.

Set into the gleaming desktop were a bank stick slot and a white thumbprint square. No doubt this was a cash-in-advance establishment. Still no proprietor emerged from the closed door at the back of the office. Were their normal customers so insistent that even a lengthy delay would not discourage them?

Cal moved to the back door and opened it. Beyond lay a slightly larger room reminiscent of a dentist's office, but more unsettling. Three reclining chairs on pedestals were positioned with their backs against one wall. Next to each was a curtain on a ceiling track. There were no trays of clamps and picks, but behind each headrest hung two parallel plates with wires running to short equipment racks. On shelves next to each chair were lightweight gas masks with straps. The equipment was much smaller than he had expected. Cal's uneasiness remained, and no sense of familiarity came to him. A second closed door was set into the far wall.

"Hello," he called again. Why was no one here? Had *he* even been here? He looked at the chairs again, but felt neither revulsion nor recollection. To see if he could trigger more memories, Cal sat down and leaned back into one of the chairs. The cushion and arms were cool against his flesh, and his body tensed. The headrest met the back of his head at just the right height. But he could summon no prior images of his presence here. He strained so hard he barely heard the soft noise of the back door opening.

"The business office is out front. You shouldn't be back here." Approaching uneven footsteps sounded. Embarrassed, Cal pushed himself quickly out of the chair and turned to face the proprietor.

The tall man stopped as he neared. "Oh. It's you."

As Cal stood mute, wondering what to ask first, the other continued. "Let me guess. You don't remember me."

"Well, no. I suppose that's normal." Cal read his name tag. In truth, the man was a total stranger.

"Except that most people don't come back." The proprietor had worried eyes, the kind that slant down on the outside, giving him a perpetually nervous expression, but Cal couldn't detect any actual signs of nervousness in the man. His voice was smooth and even. No telltale twitches or abrupt movements broke his calm.

"So I *was* here last night?"

"Of course," the man said impatiently. "Didn't you keep the brochure?"

Cal could imagine the man treating a shoplifter just as politely. "I didn't know there was one. I didn't see one when I recovered."

"Sure there was. I watched you read it when you woke up. And I told you to take it with you. The treatment scrambles your short-term memory, too, for a couple of hours." The man continued, apparently noting Cal's blank expression, "Most of your memories stay in a short-term holding area while the brain processes them for long-term storage. If it's not working, you don't remember anything except the immediate past. How far back can you recall?"

"Maybe ten or twelve hours."

"You're fine, then. What's the trouble?" The man gripped Cal's arm. Without obvious effort he maneuvered Cal toward the office.

"The trouble is I've lost my memories."

The man halted and gave Cal a hard look. "I can't help that. You paid me to do it."

"Okay. Okay. But was anyone with me? Did I act like this wasn't necessarily the right thing to do?"

"You must be joking. You were alone. You couldn't wait for me to start."

Cal slumped. "You're *sure* no one was with me?"

"Look around you. How big is this place? You think I wouldn't notice if someone followed you in?"

"I don't understand. I'm told the normal erasure is for about a year. But I'm missing more like a decade."

"Look, mister. I only work here. You came in here in a fantastic rush, told me you had to speed up the process, and you ignored my warnings. What do you want me to do?''

"I want my memories back." Frustration made Cal's voice harsh.

"You'll get them. Eventually. But it's usually a few months before they start, and it's a slow process."

"Is there any way to speed it up?" Cal didn't ask about the fragments that had already returned to him. Maybe only the most recent year was thoroughly erased. But without that year he was almost as bad off anyway.

"Sorry," the proprietor said, attempting unsuccessfully to move Cal closer to the exit.

Cal shook off the grip on his arm. "Do the police make restrictions on whoever uses this place? Do you need a license?"

"No."

"Did I say anything about why I wanted it done?"

The man merely shook his head, as if to say he didn't ask questions like that and didn't cultivate his curiosity.

"Can't you tell me *anything* more?"

The proprietor shook his head again.

"Well, do you at least have another copy of the brochure you gave me last night?" Cal asked.

In answer the proprietor opened the door to the office and retrieved a pamphlet from one of the desk drawers. Silently he handed it over.

"Thanks so much for your understanding," Cal said.

The man was still silent as Cal left.

Outside, Cal looked again at the two overhead continents, feeling highly annoyed, but much less nauseated than he had felt earlier in the day.

"I don't understand," he said.

"Why you came here last night?" Vincent asked.

"Right. Tell me what would happen if I overrode your instructions to purge most of what you see and hear. If this happened once, maybe it could happen again. And if you have as much data to work with as I get, you could help me more."

"How much would you want me to remember?"

"Use your own judgment unless I specify. You can erase anything that seems unlikely to have a bearing on the situation. For instance, what I eat."

"I can keep most significant events for a few months without overflowing, as long as you don't mind the privacy invasion. The police have the right to ask me anything I can remember unless you explicitly encode it."

"Okay. Any other problems?"

"My reactions might slow down a few microseconds if I have to search through that much data, but I don't think you'd notice unless you're awfully particky."

"Go ahead, then. If I want you to forget anything in particular, I'll tell you. For starters"— he looked at the brochure— "this guy's name is Paulo Frall. The shop is open twenty-four hours a day. If he's got a motive for lying, it's not obvious to me."

"Noted."

Cal started back toward the tubeway to Greenwich. He was silent during the journey until just before entering his house, when he stopped to say, "Nikki may be back. I'm going to shut you off for a while. Good-bye, Vincent." Cal waited a moment. "Can you still hear me?"

There was no response, so Cal unlocked the door and went in. The house was silent. He checked the living room and stood listening for a moment.

"Hello, Vincent," he said.

"That didn't take long."

"No one's here. Can you turn off when Nikki comes back home?"

"Si, señor."

"Okay. There should be some more news on the body by now." Cal quickly figured out how to bring up the live news on the desk computer screen. The default filter level was set to UNEXPURGATED, so he left it there and switched the video to the wall screen.

He had to wait through only a few unrelated stories before a woman he recognized as the same woman who had interviewed the *Vittoria* commander, Russ Tolbor, came on the screen.

"Authorities have confirmed that the man found dead in the dock area this morning was murdered," she said. "The victim was Gabriel Domingo, a construction worker." She continued with a recap of what Cal had read earlier.

The man's name meant nothing to Cal, but a moment later when the holo projector displayed a slowly rotating bust of the victim, Cal clenched his fingers onto the chair arms.

"Gabe," Cal said involuntarily. Then he wondered at his connection with the victim and felt the certainty he was beginning to recognize when he connected with an old memory. Despite remembering the shortened form of the man's name, he couldn't recall anything about their relationship. Coworker? Longtime friend? Accomplice? Cal couldn't believe he had killed him.

Domingo's level gaze bore into Cal as the image turned to face him. The unreadable look could have concealed defiance, curiosity, or perhaps a quiet self-confidence. Cal's memory did nothing to fill in the blanks. The man's hair was short and black, almost wiry, partly covering his ears. Although he seemed to be in his late twenties, his face was more wrinkled than Cal's, as though he had spent a lot of time under pressure or in strong sunlight.

". . . last seen at approximately seventeen hundred yesterday," the woman's voice continued, "leaving his job aboard the *Vittoria*. Police are investigating bloody handprints found on the victim's pants legs."

Cal took the revelation about the prints more calmly than he might have. Apparently he had been conditioning himself for the worst.

"Police say they want to talk to the owner of the handprints, not *necessarily* about murder accusations and drug trafficking." The reporter shook her head lightly and grinned the barest grin possible, but the message was plain.

"The police have also confirmed the discovery of Vital Twenty-Two at the scene. Health officials stress that this illicit cell-regeneration drug has *not* been adequately tested and carries the risk of severe, permanent damage to anyone who uses it. Domingo may well be one more victim in a series of drug-related killings. And this time it may have been for drugs to prolong life. This is Michelle Garney."

An unrelated story began, and Cal turned the sound down.

"This must be what they call overwhelming circumstantial evidence," he said.

"You mean because pretty soon this guy's going to be grinning at the daisy roots?"

"That's not all," Cal said. "There's the blood."

"Plus, you know the guy, right?"

"What do *you* know about him?"

"Nothing," Vincent said. "You said his name."

"Well, his face is definitely familiar, but I still can't imagine where I know him from."

"Can you wear a wristcomp if they lock you up?"

"Vincent, I think this is really the point where you say, 'Don't worry. You couldn't possibly have killed anyone.' "

"Don't worry. You couldn't possibly have killed anyone."

"Dammit. Can't you—Oh, never mind. There's no point in my trying to force you to be glum too. But I'm worried."

"It's spilt milk under the bridge, but I can do a good glum if you insist."

"No. Be yourself. I'll be all right." Cal hesitated. "What could be more normal than me telling a computer to 'be yourself'?"

"Maybe there's hope of salvaging your sense of humor even if they do lock you up."

"That's part of the worry. I still can't accept it, but if I get genuinely convinced that I murdered someone, then I'll have to turn myself in. But if I really did kill someone, then wouldn't it be more consistent for me to decide *not* to turn myself in?"

"I think you've got a no-win argument."

"Yeah, but—" Cal cut off, interrupted by the sound of the door opening.

It was Nikki. She walked in slowly and closed the door. "I didn't expect you would still be here," she said.

"Because of what you said earlier?" Cal stood up.

"No. Just because you're so seldom here." She put her jacket over the back of a chair and walked tentatively toward him. "I didn't entirely mean what I said."

"It's okay. I'm not entirely sure it wasn't deserved."

Nikki tilted her head fractionally, then moved to one of the other chairs and sat. "You haven't watched the news in a long time."

"I guess I've seen enough for tonight." Cal reached over and turned the display off. When he turned back, Nikki was watching him intently. What did she see in his face? Guilt? "You never did tell me what you wanted to talk about earlier."

"For a while after I got home, I didn't want to talk about it. And then I wanted to talk about it, but I was too angry."

"What was it?"

For a long moment it seemed she wasn't going to respond,

but then she took a deep breath and said, "You can't be blind to what's happening to our marriage. I need out."

Cal didn't know what to say. He wasn't even sure if he *could* say anything. Suddenly his mouth was dry and his body cold. The aches he had ignored before now all returned, and the worst of all was loneliness. "Too angry?" he said at last. "Too angry to talk about divorce?"

"I don't want to do this out of spite or anger, Cal. I've just been hurt too much. I need to step back and get a new perspective on my life. And I didn't want you to think I'd do something like that in the heat of an angry moment."

Cal wasn't sure which was worse—anger or cool restraint. "You're like that, aren't you?"

Nikki tilted her head again, questioningly, but Cal shook his head and spoke again. "I mean I understand."

Maybe his troubled marriage had contributed to the pressure that must have been building recently; but he still didn't know what had caused the tension. Was he simply too self-centered, or too busy, or what? He had wanted to confide in Nikki; to tell her about his amnesia, but now—now it would seem like a blatant lie, an excuse to hold on to her. What was worse, he couldn't convince himself that she would be doing the wrong thing. Maybe she would be better off without him. Who could say what he had been up to lately? And if he himself wasn't convinced he hadn't done anything wrong, he could hardly expect her to support him.

"How sure are you," he finally asked, "that it's the right thing to do?" Without forethought, he added, "I need you."

Nikki stared at him, her dark-blue eyes strangely luminous. "We don't talk like we used to. I'm no longer sure what I want."

"I'm not sure I see how being separated would help our communications a whole lot." He heard resentment in his voice and wondered how he could be resentful and sad with Nikki when he didn't even *know* her.

Nikki was thoughtful for a moment. "You haven't told me you need me in far too long."

"I suppose you're right." Somehow, without *knowing*, he had the feeling that she was telling him the truth. But how could he have been so blind? To have "lost" her and then "found" her only to lose her again knotted his stomach. Cal's guilt grew, and with it grew dislike of the man he had been. "I guess we don't always say what we feel."

"What do you feel right now?"

"Surprise, anger, nostalgia, loneliness. Love." Only after he spoke did he realize it was all true. He couldn't explain it rationally.

"It's not right that we should be together and both feel lonely." The highlights in Nikki's hair rippled as she moved her head.

Confusion tore at him. He had to talk Nikki out of her decision. The urge grew within him, but, again without *knowing*, he was convinced that he had talked her into or out of things enough times to make it a sensitive issue. He hadn't the slightest idea whether this was one of the rare times that Nikki *wanted* to be talked out of her decision.

"It doesn't have to be that way," he said finally. Was this why Lynn wasn't home? Maybe Nikki had already taken her to a new home.

"But it *is*. It has been."

"I don't seem to be able to change your mind."

Nikki fell silent.

"Let me be clear," Cal said, "about one of the few things I understand. I don't want you to leave." He swallowed hard. "But if that's what you really want, will you tell me your plans?"

"I'll get an apartment in Machu Picchu, near the clinic. In the next week."

So Lynn must have just been at school. But what were Nikki's plans for her?

"How does Lynn fit into all of this?" he asked.

Nikki's eyes had been lowered, but abruptly she snapped her gaze back onto Cal's face and her eyes widened. "What do you mean by that?"

"I mean who does she stay with?"

Nikki looked like someone had slapped her, her face going from shocked anger to hurt. Then the hurt expression was quickly replaced by a puzzled frown. "Cal, are you all right?"

"No," he said simply.

"Lynn is dead. Are you telling me that you don't—"

Even before Nikki had finished speaking, Cal felt the blood drain heavily from his face. His body began to shake. He shivered uncontrollably, and his mouth moved soundlessly.

He was totally unaware of Nikki's movement, but some seconds later he realized that she was embracing him, and that his arms were wrapped around her. Her arms reached tightly around his upper back. He tried repeatedly to speak, unsuccessfully, feeling dangerously short of breath, his pulse pounding in his ears. He held onto Nikki even harder.

Nikki squeezed his shoulders again, then slipped her hands down his back, and hugged him all the harder at the base of his spine.

He felt a blinding pain. In a final instant of consciousness, Cal heard himself begin to scream.

Chapter five
Hints

FOR the second time that day, Cal regained consciousness. Instead of dusty ground beneath him, however, soft carpet cushioned his body. He shifted slightly to get more comfortable, and grimaced. He felt worse than the first time.

"Cal, are you okay?" It was Nikki's voice.

What was Nikki doing here? He puzzled over the question for a brief moment before he found the answer. They had been talking, and she had told him Lynn was dead.

Still without being able to recall the actual event, he knew without doubt why Lynn was not at home. Nikki had spoken the truth. Cal felt sadder than he could ever remember feeling before.

"I'm okay," he said at last, and opened his eyes.

Nikki, kneeling beside him, took a deep breath. "What's going on? What happened to you?" She touched his cheek. Her gaze was softer than before.

Cal lay there weakly, and looked up at her. "I'm not the right person to ask. How did Lynn die?"

"You really don't remember, do you?" Nikki wiped her eye.

"Please tell me."

"She died down there, with all the others. On Earth. You remember that much?"

"I do—now. Why was she on Earth?"

"Cal, I don't think it's best for you to think about it now. You may be in this state because of your damned unreasonable guilt. I want to get you to the clinic."

"I need to know. I *have* to know. Just tell me."

Nikki leaned back. "She was there on a field trip."

"At my suggestion?"

"We both agreed that it was good for her."

"But I pressed for it, right?" Earth was his home, after all. He was sure that Nikki was a second-generation Daedalus resident.

"That doesn't make it your fault."

Cal struggled to rise. "Can you help me?"

"You stay put. You've done enough damage to your body already. It's a wonder you're not partially paralyzed from the impact." Cal raised his eyebrows, and Nikki added, "I saw your back while you were out. What the hell have you been doing?" The tenderness that had been in evidence while Cal was recovering faded.

It was a little too late to try to conceal some of the day's events. "I don't know how I got the bruises. Evidently I spent part of my discretionary income last night at Forget-Me-Now."

"Forget-Me-Now? What's going on?"

"I don't know yet. Can you help me up?"

"As long as you agree to let me get you into the clinic. Just for tests."

Cal propped himself up on his elbows and grabbed a chair arm to pull on.

"*Damn*, you can be stubborn." Once it was obvious that he wasn't going to stay still, she helped him the rest of the way. "Why Forget-Me-Now?"

"My very question. I don't have any idea why." Cal stood shakily, partly supported by Nikki's arm. "But I plan to find out. I think if I visit my office, maybe more will come back to me. Visual stimulants seem to work the best."

"Cal, did you—did you remember me?" Nikki was breathless.

"Why do you ask?"

"Why do you answer questions with questions? I don't know. You're different somehow."

"No, I didn't really remember you," he said candidly. "At least at first. I still don't *know* you, but things are beginning to come back to me."

"So all those words about needing me, wanting me to stay, they—"

"They came from the heart. That's all I can say. Feelings seem to come back prior to the actual remembrances." Cal saw the hurt in her eyes, and it tore at him. "I know it's damn little comfort, but it's the truth. And it's all I can offer. I didn't say those things to manipulate you. I said what I felt. It's obvious that I haven't done very much of that recently, or you might know what's been going on, and maybe I wouldn't have driven you away. But right now I've got to jog more memories loose—I've got to go to the office."

"But I want you in the clinic. You're under too much stress."

"I'm sorry, Nikki. I just can't. It's another feeling, without any hard facts to back it up, but something's wrong. More wrong than just my cracking under pressure and vacuuming my brains. I've got to find out what it is."

Impulsively Cal kissed her and turned to go. From the open doorway, as he looked back, he saw Nikki standing motionless. Her expression was unreadable.

"I'm sorry," he repeated softly. "I have no choice."

The door closed quietly, and he stood in front of it for a moment, wondering if he really was doing the right thing. Would she be there when he came back? With his recent history, would he even be able to find his way back?

He was almost to the tubeway before he said, "Hello, Vincent."

"Hello. Where are you going now?"

"To my office. Maybe I can learn more there."

"Which office?"

"You mean there's more than one?"

"Zacto. You've got one in Machu Picchu and one on the *Vittoria*."

"Let's try Machu Picchu first. I suppose the one on *Vittoria* is only temporary. I hadn't made plans to leave cn the *Vittoria*, had I?"

"Not to my knowledge."

As Cal descended into the tubeway station, he noticed a child's scrawl in chalk, saying, "Machu Picchu Choo Choo." For an instant he wondered if Lynn had written it. With an effort he forced the image from his mind.

According to Vincent his office address was not far from one of the tube stops. It was fairly easy to find. The building looked a lot like the hotel from the outside, except for the gold sign saying COMPUTER CONTROL SYSTEMS.

The receptionist's desk in the lobby was vacant. Cal was surprised for a moment, but thought to look at Vincent's screen. It was probably after quitting time, so most people would be gone by now. Next to a locked door leading to the office area was a thumbprint square. Cal tried it.

With a sharp *click* the door moved aside, revealing a long corridor lined with doors on both walls. Fortunately, the offices each had name tags adjacent to the doorways. Cal walked along the hall, looking at the tags on the right side more expectantly than at the ones on the left. Five doors down he found his office, on the right side.

The room was utilitarian, but amply equipped. Two large screens occupied much of the wall space. Dominating the room was a massive desk with a tilted screen set in one surface. The window gave him the familiar view angled toward the far end of Daedalus's cylinder.

Feeling like an intruder, Cal moved to the chair and sat. Flush with the front edge of the desk was a faint rectangle a different color from the desk itself. He pushed on it lightly, and it first moved in past the desk surface, then sprang back so he could grip it and pull it out, revealing a keyboard.

He pressed the white square with his thumb, and the tilted screen brightened. Shortly the image of *Vittoria* hung in the air above the desk screen. Cal's peripheral vision picked up a flicker of motion, and he realized that most of the switches on his keyboard now had new legends. He pressed LIVING AREA and looked back at the hologram.

The ship's image was reminiscent of a shish kebab skewer with one large turnip and two smaller cylinders impaled. One cylinder was separated from the other bodies by the length of the skewer. A wide band around the turnip's broadest contour turned orange to indicate the area designated for living space. So the *Vittoria* spun on the skewer much like Daedalus did. The sharp end pointed in the direction it would eventually travel.

The switch marked OFFICES AND LABS lit up the saucer-shaped area that covered the blunt end of the body and stretched to the living area. AGRICULTURE lit the final section.

Cal touched SPECIFIC and OFFICE, and a new set of key-top legends replaced the old ones.

"Vincent, what's my office number on the *Vittoria*?"

"Fourteen-twelve D."

As soon as Cal entered the number, a blinking red light lit approximately midway between the living area and the center of the office space. Uneasiness grew within him as he looked at the glowing image of *Vittoria*. He felt even more uncomfortable than he had in the Forget-Me-Now parlor. Had he had some painful experiences there?

He tapped several more keys, and a recording began an overview of the *Vittoria*. Cal settled back into his chair and watched as it began a summary of *Vittoria*'s design, propulsion, life-support, control systems, shielding, navigation, backup systems, communications, agriculture, living conditions, and history.

The information all seemed new, but he found himself absorbing much of it more easily than he would have expected for a first-time exposure. It was, however, not as good as actually being there. He still felt drawn to the *Vittoria*. But first, there were things to be learned here.

Maybe his phone list would tell him if Domingo, the murdered man, was someone he talked to. A moment later a column on the left showed full names and numbers that could have been personal ID numbers, or phone numbers, or both. In the center were addresses. To the right were short forms of the names, which had to be what he normally used to initiate a call.

The list included Nikki, several names of people with addresses near his, and a few he supposed were business associates, including Russ Tolbor. Cal stared at the list, wondering who, if anyone, on the list he could trust as a confidant. It was only then that he realized that the one name he had been afraid to see, Gabriel Domingo, was not there.

At the bottom of the screen was a message that said MORE. He hit the button marked NEXT PAGE, but the only change was that the bottom line now said MORE (PW). A help menu confirmed that the rest of the list was protected by a password. But why?

Abruptly his meager confidence in his own innocence dissipated. Domingo could easily be on the concealed portion of the list. But why would he password-protect just someone's name? Surely the mere fact of knowing someone would not be incriminating.

He tried a few obvious attempts at a password. It didn't respond to "Nikki," "Cal," "password," or any of several other possibilities.

"Vincent, do you know any of my passwords on this system?"

"Negatory, good buddy."

"How do you expect to help me when you know so little?"

"Wait. Don't tell me."

"Thanks, Vincent. Go take a nap."

Dead end. Unless he could remember more. Maybe his computer mailbox would yield a clue.

There were no incoming messages, but the last three messages he had sent were still stored in the computer. The first was a status report apparently sent to his boss. The destination field said TOM H, whose office was evidently just down the hall. The details meant little to Cal, but listed four final tests. Three were marked complete, leaving only a final communications test. At the end of an otherwise businesslike report were the lines, "I left another cutting for you. Don't mess this one up."

Cal's attention was momentarily diverted by the sound of snoring.

"Stop that, Vincent."

The second note was puzzling. "21:00. Tinsdale." The message destination said "Angel," but there was no Angel on his phone list. The real name must be in the password-protected section. Twenty-one hundred had to be a time, but what did "Tinsdale" mean?

Perhaps he could be seeing another woman. Was that why Nikki had been feeling shut out? That would certainly do it. Maybe she was just too polite or afraid to mention it, or she had no idea. But no, he couldn't accept it. The attraction he felt to Nikki was so strong, he could not believe he would do that to her, and no matter how much he had gone through in the last ten years, he couldn't see himself changing that much.

"What's 'Tinsdale'?" he asked.

"A twenty-first-century social revolution moving force, a park on *Vittoria*, and a brand of life-support suits," Vincent told him.

A park on *Vittoria* made the most sense. Was he to meet Angel at twenty-one hundred in Tinsdale Park? Tonight? Maybe it was last night. The message transmittal time was yesterday at 19:00. There could be an understanding that undated meeting times meant the current day, or prearranged meeting days might have been established. Then again, maybe his Tinsdale suit was due out of repairs at 21:00. But then "Angel" wouldn't be significant. Angel's Suit Repair sounded unlikely, and in any event wouldn't need to be password-protected.

He gave up temporarily. The last message was to "Jam," and said, "Hope to learn more about S & G tonight. Will report ASAP." But if the first message was to his boss, who was this one to? "Jam" wasn't on his phone list either. Some people had two bosses. But if he did, why would he be covertly communicating with one? Was he selling secrets? For all he knew, he had a lover and someone was blackmailing him. "S and G" meant nothing to him.

He cut off the speculations. He needed more hard information, and he would be better off going and getting it. Leaning forward in his chair, he pushed the OFF button and slid the keyboard back into the desk. He would have to move fast to get to Tinsdale Park by 21:00.

"Vincent, it's time I went to the *Vittoria*. Can you point me in the right direction as we go?"

"Does Daedalus spin?"

As the tube sped up the hill, Cal brought Vincent up to date.

Gravity slowly departing was the obvious signal that they were nearing the endcap of Daedalus, but Cal also felt a lateral force push him against the seat back as the vehicle lost angular momentum. The tube slowed to a complete halt. Only the seat belt held Cal in place.

He floated into the tunnel, his hands on a grip, his feet ever so slightly drifting to rest against the floor. Through a window in the ceiling he could see other spokes join a smaller disk at the center of Daedalus's rotational axis. The wide tubeways narrowed to smaller tunnels like the one he was in. A ring connected the tubeways so passengers could move from one to another.

He had been mistakenly expecting all the tunnels to merge into one main one, but instead his tunnel just curved so that it was aligned with Daedalus's axis, and the walls turned transparent. The junction between Daedalus and the adjacent industrial disk resembled a group of dozens of clear straws all parallel to one another, with one larger straw right in the center. A few people moved through the other tunnels.

Across the junction the tunnel walls were opaque again, and the tunnel curved into a circular room with two low-gravity poles. Cal moved to the one labeled DOWN and gently fell perhaps twenty meters, landing easily on the floor.

The floor was a strip about twenty meters wide, curving upward and out of sight on both ends. Elevators stood at intervals in the wall.

Cal bounced lightly as he entered the nearest elevator. His head bumped the padded ceiling just as the box began to drop to the outermost floor, because he forgot to use the handholds. He tried to think of what might have happened to Domingo at C5. He was tempted to go there, but the police might still be there.

The floor of the outermost level sloped upward much less noticeably. Immediately to his left, a sign said SHUTTLE, and an arrow pointed to a circular opening in the floor. More signs were visible in the distance.

A ladder led downward through a heavy airlock door, and the passageway widened into an area large enough for maybe twenty people to stand comfortably.

Inside the shuttle there was little more than chairs and two large shuttered windows. At one end a large DANGER sign warned about an emergency exit. A flight-suit locker stood next to the door. Cal sat. On the armrest were two switches. He set one to VITTORIA and the other to OPEN SHUTTERS.

Cal shielded his eyes against the glare and sucked in his breath at the view. Daedalus's outside cylinder wall extended overhead. The sun shone incredibly brightly below. Stretched away from Daedalus's body were two enormous mirrors. He moved his head to see out the window at an angle, and Icarus sailed into view, moving rapidly in a giant arc, followed by the Earth. A moment later *Vittoria* came into view.

A flicker of motion caught his eye, and he turned to look out the window behind him. Fleeting images of antennae and awkward shapes whirled by the window far too fast for him to distinguish. He was looking at the disk next to the one he was on, but it took a moment more before he remembered that *he* was moving. The other disk was stationary, for zero-gravity work. Beyond the disk lay the enormous curved mirror that drove the power plant.

He turned back to the first window just in time to see night fall on Daedalus, at least on the inside. The mirrors were angling back toward the surface, and moments later they slowed gradually until they just melted into Daedalus's hull.

"So Icarus gets to stay up later," he said. Icarus still had its mirrors extended. Vincent's screen said he had less than an hour to go. Would he reach Tinsdale Park on time?

"Icarus stays lit until midnight," Vincent said. "Crops don't have quite the same requirements."

"So now what?"

"We should be leaving anytime now." Almost as Vincent quit speaking, there was a muted *thud* against the top of the shuttle. "We're almost set. When we're aimed exactly right, Daedalus will let go."

Abruptly gravity vanished. At the same moment Daedalus started to move above and behind Cal's field of view. Icarus, *Vittoria*, and the Earth stopped in their apparent journey around Daedalus and hung where they had been at release. Cal experienced a moment of dizziness, but it soon passed.

"How long does this take?" he asked, watching *Vittoria* grow slowly larger ahead.

"About ten minutes. Let's just hope we're exactly on track, so *Vittoria's* magnet can catch us."

"Are there many misses?" Cal wondered if he should have asked more questions before coming this far.

"Never has been one, but nobody's perfect. My brother Harold on the other end is pretty sharp, though."

"Your brother?"

"Figure of speech. The computer controlling the receiver."

As they moved still closer to *Vittoria* a soft, deep grinding noise began, and the capsule began to rotate slowly about its direction of travel.

"What's going on?" he asked.

"Just routine. The shuttle can be caught in any orientation, but if it doesn't rotate, you'll be hanging by your belt when we stop. I can't imagine that would be real pleasant."

"I'm not complaining."

Vittoria grew in size, now appearing in the upper corner of the opposite window. What was there about *Vittoria* that disturbed him so? An overhead *thunk* sounded against the hull, and gravity pushed Cal back into his chair. A second distant noise apparently signaled that mechanical attachment to *Vittoria* was complete.

A near reversal of the procedure on Daedalus brought him to a low-gee passage into *Vittoria*.

Vittoria was as brightly lit as Daedalus had been, but the light came from a different source, a brilliantly lit tube along the rotation axis.

Being inside gave an impression more like clinging to the inside of a large ball than a cylinder. The scale was smaller than on Daedalus. Cal could make out large structures on the far side of *Vittoria*. On Daedalus he had seen nothing more than blurred smears of colors.

The transportation system was also modest in comparison. Above-ground rail cars moved from one end of the zero-gee axis to the other.

Vincent told Cal which track would take him closest to Tinsdale Park, and Cal boarded a car after a short walk. The slow-moving car looked as if it could easily be converted from passenger use to freight by detaching the open-air rows of seats.

It was minutes after the possible appointment time when Cal stepped off the vehicle and surveyed the park, which wound its way between irregular peninsulas of single-story town houses.

He wasn't alone in the park. Several other people relaxed on benches or rested in the grass, and he could see more in the distance. Was Angel here? Maybe he or she had left when Cal hadn't been there on time? For all he knew, this wasn't even the right day. He could have met Angel here yesterday.

"I don't see anyone coming over to greet me," he said, starting to walk with forced indifference through the grass.

"Maybe you don't look friendly," Vincent suggested.

"Maybe." Cal stopped. "This park goes around the whole circumference of *Vittoria*?"

"No. It looks like it, but every half-kilometer or so, the name changes. Ahead is Tandem Park. It's a bit more comforting to people to meet at a place with a name than at sector five, quadrant sixty-two and all that ap-cray.''

''Are computers always right, Vincent?''

''Invariably. After a long study one of my ancestors concluded that ashtrays cause cancer.''

Cal continued walking, still disconcerted at the even more pronounced curvature of the land as it rose gradually around him in all directions. No one he passed looked familiar. He didn't glance back to see if anyone was observing him. If only he had a tiny bit of data about Angel. Height, hair color, sex, age—anything to narrow the field.

The equation had too many unknowns. Ahead he could see a sign identifying the park boundary, and still no one had approached him. He turned to retrace his steps, but then stopped. A medium-size elm tree he had noticed earlier now seemed distinctly familiar. He had definitely been here before.

Cal looked at it a moment longer and said, ''You ready for another short trip, Vincent?''

''You promise not to bang me into anything?''

''I think I can manage not to.''

''Okeydokey. Where to?''

''My office here.''

The building looked much like the one on Daedalus except there was no lawn in front, and this one seemed much busier. *This* lobby was occupied.

The receptionist said nothing, merely nodding as the door slid open. At least he belonged here. Cal thanked him and moved into the corridor beyond, conscious of an increased noise level from fragments of conversations in the row of offices.

Cal tried to walk quickly, so he could find his office without exposing his condition. His luck didn't improve.

''Hey, Cal,'' a voice called from a doorway he passed.

Cal was already past the opening, so he could at least read the occupant's name tag without being conspicuous. Leroy Krantz, Communications Concepts.

''What can I do for you, Leroy?'' Cal asked, facing a man he had no recollection of. For a moment he wondered if ''Mr. Krantz'' was what he usually called the man. Leroy was maybe fifteen or twenty years older than Cal and had closely cropped gray hair. His eyebrows were so much darker than the rest of his hair, they almost looked dyed.

"We were supposed to meet this morning," Leroy said. After Cal remained silent, Leroy added, "To go over the final com control interface test."

"Some, ah—problems on the home front came up. Can we reschedule it?" Maybe by then he would have more of an idea of what the other man was talking about. This must be the one remaining test from his note to Horvath.

"Tomorrow morning?" Leroy said.

The feeling lasted only an instant, but Cal was sure the other looked relieved. But why? "Tomorrow afternoon?" he offered. So soon.

"Review the results at thirteen hundred, here?"

Review the test results? He wouldn't be able to make much sense of a few printouts. Maybe if he could get some visual cues, he would stand a better chance. "What about running through part of the test itself?" Cal asked.

"What? Oh, sure, sure. Whatever you want."

"See you then." Cal turned to leave.

"You okay?" Leroy asked.

"Fine. Why?"

"Nothing special. You just seem upset lately. You want to go out for a drink? Talk it over?"

Cal hesitated, wondering if he would learn more from Leroy if he opened up, or if he should keep to his plan and go to his office. Was Leroy honestly trying to help, or did he know more than he pretended and was just playing with Cal? Cal wavered for a moment, until the barest degree of unease seeped into him. "No," he said. "But thanks anyway."

"Maybe some other time." Leroy smiled as Cal turned again to go. Was he smiling *at* Cal, or simply being friendly?

No one else called to Cal before he reached his office. The room was much like the one on Daedalus, except for the view and a weak impression that many of the office furnishings were on wheels, ready to be removed when *Vittoria* was about to leave.

The desk itself, with the computer, could have been the same one as in his Daedalus office. Even the data stored in it was apparently identical. This time, however, inspired by Leroy, Cal called up his appointment log.

There it was: Leroy K, 09:00, today. Purpose: final acceptance test on control system interfaces to the communications system. Surely that wouldn't just involve Cal and Leroy. But apparently it did.

No other appointments existed in the log, so there were no clues from that source. Cal got up and shut the door.

"Vincent, what do you know about Leroy?"

"He has an office near yours, he knows you, and *he* doesn't miss appointments."

"In other words, all you know is what we both just observed?"

"You right again, Lone Ranger."

"I've got the law on my side."

"Say again?"

"The law of averages. After the early part of today, it's only natural that I get a few things right." Cal sat up straight in his chair. "I'm not making enough progress here. Are there any other places I frequently go?"

"The command center. Where the bus driver is going to sit."

"Where is it?"

"Ten minutes from here. It's at the same latitude as this office."

The command center was even busier than his office area had been. After passing another receptionist, he wandered in the interior corridors for a few minutes until finally he saw a sign saying OBSERVATION AREA. Successive arrows led to a dimly lit room with one glass wall. Beyond the window the scene below looked like a mission operations amphitheater he had once seen on Earth.

Three curved tiers of glass-enclosed cubicles contained the operations staff. Before them, on the opposite wall, was an enormous multisectioned display. One quarter of it currently showed a portion of the sky, with an image-enhanced magnification of Barnard's Star and the surrounding area. The stars forming Ophiuchus were out of the field of view.

Text displays with interspersed graphs apparently summarized power levels, navigation status, and subsystem conditions. At the upper right, large orange letters said, NOMINAL: 4D 9H 14M 47S. The seconds counted down. Cal's sense of urgency strengthened.

From his job description in the computer, he knew he had a hand in the foundation of all this: the computer control system responsible for linking all the subsystems together.

In the most recent hours his memory had been recalcitrant, offering little in the way of new insights. Maybe he had been hurrying so much that his subconscious refused to link to his conscious mind, or maybe being at the command center gave him enough new visual triggers to start his mind working harder again. Whatever the cause, he found that he was aware of more than a fresh visitor would be.

The time at the upper right of the screen was the remaining time until *Vittoria* departed. Less than five days. He hadn't realized before that the time was so short. He felt uneasy about *Vittoria* leaving.

He scanned the windows opposite the wall screen. Even without the glowing letters, he knew that the center office on the second tier belonged to Russ Tolbor. Cal could detect no motion within the cubicle, but it was too dark to see if Tolbor was there, motionless, silently watching the screen, or—or watching Cal.

That's absurd, Cal told himself. Paranoia was overpowering. Everyone he saw seemed to bother him.

As Cal stood, wondering what to do next, the contents of the screen disappeared, and a hologram larger than any he could remember materialized. It was the *Vittoria*, apparently color-coded to indicate how close she was to being ready for the journey. Almost the entire surface was green. Here and there, a few flakes showed yellow. A tiny handful of red regions blinked slowly. *Vittoria* was close.

Cal looked back at the center office. "What can you tell me about Russ Tolbor, Vincent?"

"Other than what was on this morning's newscast?"

"Yes."

"He volunteered for the job and met almost no opposition. He's in the Daedalus *Who's Who*. Forty-one, never been married. He's been responsible for charitable programs, mostly connected with the church he favors, Presodists, but he's also been involved with efforts to break down denominational barriers. His previous command experience includes a couple of Jupiter missions. His original technical field was the same as yours—computers—and he was responsible for several innovations before he moved into management."

Cal stared at the hologram. Memories stirred and shifted. Instead of feeling at a total loss, as he had when he woke up, he was beginning to feel more like the information was almost within reach, if he only knew where to look. But the almost-at-the-tip feeling was just as frustrating.

"I don't suppose you ever get tired, do you, Vincent?"

"Bored maybe. My first owner only wanted me to balance his financial log. But not tired."

"That's the truth?"

"No. You bought me new. But that's dull."

"Well, I'm getting tired, but certainly not bored. I wonder what Nikki's doing right now."

Cal left the observation booth and walked slowly through the corridors toward the exit. He was within sight of it when a side door opened, and he came face-to-face with Russ Tolbor.

"I thought you'd be here earlier," Russ said. "We've finished most of the final checks." He looked expectantly at Cal. In person, the commander looked darker, healthier than he had on screen. The several centimeters of height advantage he had on Cal made his oncoming baldness less noticeable than in the hologram and made his neatly trimmed beard more prominent. If the silver and gold finish on the man's compband was any indication, he wore a wristcomp like Vincent.

"I ran into some problems early in the day," Cal said. "I'm still trying to get caught up."

"Nothing you can't handle, though, right?"

"Right." Cal held back, again experiencing the same uneasiness that he had felt during the day's previous conversations. "You're really looking forward to leaving all this?"

"Yes. God makes demands of us all, and we need to accept them in good grace. I'm actually looking forward to this. Life's too complex on Daedalus."

"God told you to go?"

Tolbor laughed. "No. It's not like that. I'm surprised at you, Cal. God doesn't move so directly. But in the course of my life, I've felt the nudges in the proper direction at a few important intersections."

"Does that mean you were picked for the job because of your religious beliefs?"

"Hardly. *Despite* them is more like it. Religious freedom isn't entirely dead, though. But *you* don't look too well today. You've been pushing yourself pretty hard lately. Watch out for too much stress," Russ said. The intensity apparent during the interview was still in his eyes. "You take care of yourself."

"I'll do my best." Cal turned to leave.

It wasn't until he entered the lobby that he realized that his breath came more heavily than normal, and he felt a slight chill. But was it because of the commander? Maybe Cal became nervous whenever he was in the presence of people in power. He had no way to tell for sure, but it seemed unlikely.

Could "Angel" be Russ? There was no guarantee that a password-protected ID couldn't refer to someone Cal knew in public, someone with whom he had a different relationship in private.

But that could also be true of anyone on his list. Who else was a candidate? He could start down the list, talking to each person, working the word "angel" into the conversations. No.

He left the command building, aware again of fatigue. His eyes were dry, and his slight limp had returned. Maybe he should go home. Surely Nikki would be back by now. A talk with her and some rest might help.

Cal boarded an unoccupied rail car and started up the hill toward the low-gravity exit. He shut his eyes for a moment. "Vincent," he said. "Is it possible for you to monitor the newscasts and tell me if anything about Gabriel Domingo comes on?"

"Easy. But you're late. There's already been more. I've been listening."

Cal's eyes were open again. "So tell me. And keep me up to date if you hear any more."

"Your whim is my command. Just over a half hour ago, the news said that the police search of Domingo's apartment turned up some interesting information. Domingo apparently had met several times with someone, maybe a doctor, at the Taber Clinic."

"Taber Clinic. That sounds familiar."

"I'm not wildly surprised. It's where Nikki works."

———— Chapter six ————
Hospital

"WHAT else did the newscast say?" Cal asked. "That Domingo might have been selling drugs to a doctor who marks them up and resells them?"

"Near enough," Vincent said. "And they found more capsules of Vital Twenty-Two in his apartment."

The *Vittoria* rail car continued up the rise toward the exit.

"So there's a link between Domingo and the clinic where Nikki works. That doesn't mean there's a connection between Domingo and Nikki."

"Not necessarily anyway," Vincent said. "You sound defensive."

Cal paused. "Maybe I am. Wouldn't you be—in my place? Half of my memories snuck away in the night, and I may have killed Domingo. Obviously I haven't maintained a terrific relationship with my wife, and maybe she could be tied into this mess also. For all I know, she's got more than a doctor-deceased relationship with Domingo. Her specialty is transplants."

"But you don't really think that she has done anything illegal?"

The rail car reached the top of the hill.

"No, I guess not," Cal said finally. "But I don't like to take a chance on being wrong."

Quiet and thoughtful, Cal returned to Daedalus. He wondered why Nikki wanted him in the clinic. So she could keep track of him, or simply because she was worried about his health? Or sanity? He wanted to believe the innocent answer.

Cal thought briefly about examining the location where Domingo's body had been found, but decided against it. He was near exhaustion, and the police might still be watching the area.

He managed to stay awake on the tubeway. Along the path to his house he could feel his stomach muscles tense as he thought about Nikki. What more could he say to her without first learning more about himself? Nikki was still almost a stranger.

He had worried for nothing. Nikki was gone.

Cal wondered at first if she had moved out. He checked the computer for messages and found one from her, recorded about two hours earlier. The message was brief. She said simply, "I've been called in, Cal. I'm not sure how late I'll be." She hesitated for an instant, as though wanting to add something more. Then her face was gone from the screen.

Despite his fatigue, Cal replayed the message. He found the speed controls and paused Nikki's image. Her tired but quizzical expression held the suggestion of concern, her dark eyes looking straight ahead, focused precisely. Cal reached out to her image. Maybe she could help him discover what was going on. As he lost himself for a moment, staring at her, the distrust he had felt earlier dissipated. After a last long look he turned off the computer.

"Vincent, I'm going to bed. Will you wake me in six hours?"

"With soft music or a police siren?"

"How about a simple 'Wake up'?"

"Boring."

"Vincent, are there any newer models than you? Ones that might obey a little better?"

"There are several competitors on the market," Vincent said stiffly.

Cal settled onto the bed slowly. "Vincent?" he said a moment later. "Are you still awake?"

"You mean am I still talking to you?"

"I don't need a new model. You're doing just fine."

"Thanks."

"And Vincent. Anything but sirens."

"A-OK."

In dreams Lynn was not as far away as in the day. She was

alive and happy, playing nearby with a small gyroscopic toy, watching it rotate every two minutes, her expression animated.

"I've got another toy for you, Lynn," Cal said.

His daughter looked at him eagerly.

"It's down here," he added. "Come with me."

He took her hand. They left the brightly lit room and walked along a long, dark hallway toward a second room. Light shone from behind the partially open door. Cal opened the door wide, and they stepped inside.

"What is it, Daddy?" the girl asked.

It was a clear, shining, hollow sphere.

"Just watch," Cal said, and split the sphere into two halves. "Hop inside."

Obediently Lynn did so. Cal closed the two halves together.

"Now you can roll it wherever you like," Cal called, louder now to reach through the shell.

Lynn rolled the sphere, first one way and then the other, laughing as she tumbled unexpectedly. She rolled in a new direction.

For several minutes she laughed and played, but Cal could see that she was tiring. Why hadn't he thought of that? Soon she stopped. "Daddy," she said. "I don't feel well."

Of course. The air was getting stale. Cal would simply separate the two halves of the sphere and free her.

But where was the seam now? Cal's hands moved frantically over the surface, searching for the hairline gap. It *had* to be there.

"Please let me out," she said. Fear tightened her features.

"I'm getting it, Lynn," he said, trying not to let her hear the panic in his voice.

She fell back, her eyes beginning to lose focus. "I feel dizzy."

He had to hurry. But it was as though the seam had somehow sealed itself, and wherever his fingers touched, they felt only the smooth, unbroken surface.

Dear God, what could have happened? How could he have been so stupid? Lynn lay in the bottom of the sphere, breathing painfully.

"I'll find a way," he called. "Don't give up."

Where could it be? His fingers grew hot from moving so quickly against the surface. He thought for a moment that he'd found the seam, but it was just a hair.

He looked back at Lynn. Her face had darkened, her eyes closed. She stopped breathing.

"Lynn!" he screamed, and kicked at the sphere once, then harder, again and again and again. "Lynn!"

"Cal," a voice said. But from where? Out in the hall? Cal looked back toward the door and saw nothing. The voice called again. "Cal."

This time the walls faded from view, and the sphere with Lynn's body inside vanished.

"Cal," Vincent called again. "Wake up."

Cal bolted upright in bed. The room was dark and hot, but his body felt chilled, sweaty. He was alone in the bed. He shuddered violently and squeezed his eyes shut tightly against the pain.

"I'm awake, Vincent," he said finally. "Thanks." Cal's mouth felt as dry as his body was damp. "God."

"I wasn't sure if I should wake you, but you sounded terrified."

"You did the right thing. Haven't you—" Cal stopped, realizing that in the past Vincent would have been turned off while Cal slept.

"You dreamed about your daughter?"

"Yes." Cal thought a moment. "What time is it?"

"Oh five hundred."

There was no way he could go back to sleep.

A hot shower soothed the muscles that had stiffened during the night. It would have felt even better, but he still saw Lynn's eyes, imploring him to help.

His fresh clothes on, he discarded yesterday's. At first he thought nothing of the fact that the hamper was empty, but then he realized the implications. In all the activity of the day before, he had forgotten about the bloody clothes. And the capsules.

Nikki must have found the clothes. What would she think about the blood, and the capsules? Moments later he located the clothes in the washer, still bloody. Maybe he shouldn't have left the capsules in the pocket. He wondered about the penalty associated with them. Was it enforced for confirmed trafficking, or for mere possession?

"Nikki's still not back," Cal said. "I wonder where she is."

"You could call her."

"Maybe later." If Nikki was still out at 05:30, she probably didn't need a call right then.

The full weight of yesterday's experiences began to press in on Cal again. The nightmare with Lynn was a clear indication of at least one pressure he had been under: guilt. Was that the key to his apparently irrational recent behavior, or was there more to it than that?

There must be some way he could stimulate more rapid memory recovery. What other functions on the computer might help? He sat in front of the keyboard and paged to the general information menu.

"What does 'Earth Telescope' mean, Vincent?"

"There's a large telescope outside that's no longer in full-time use for astronomy. For five minutes at a time, anyone can use it. Most of the time the peek freaks point it at Earth, and it's equipped to track a point on the surface."

Could he bear to look at Atlanta? Would it be worth the pain to retrieve more memories that way? He hesitated only briefly before selecting the option. The odds that Atlanta was facing Daedalus right now *and* was clear of clouds weren't great. Maybe he could look elsewhere.

Atlanta was out of sight, so he arbitrarily chose Paris. The image from a spotting scope came up on the screen, showing an area of perhaps twenty kilometers in diameter. The air over Paris was clear, and by the westerly shadows, it was morning. To the left the Eiffel Tower caught his attention, so he moved the cursor to it and zoomed the image.

From this angle the Left Bank was on the right. The image grew, and the Seine moved off the screen to the northwest. The tower filled half the screen. It seemed to lean northwest because of the latitude and time of day. A flock of birds flew by, and as his gaze followed their course, he noticed a motionless shape on the ground.

It could only be a skeleton. The resolution of the image was not great enough to see the details, but the form was too narrow to be someone sleeping. Had the poor soul died right there with no notice, or deliberately gone there to die?

It was just as well that the telescope's resolution was apparently deliberately limited. He had seen enough. He knew that he had observed Atlanta before, looked at the campus, looked at the old apartment building where his parents had lived and died.

He remembered that last excruciating phone call, two minutes scheduled in the middle of the night, limited because of the overhead of calls going between the living on Daedalus and the dying on Earth. Everyone wanted to talk for the one last time. So each family got two minutes when the time came. How can a person say enough in two final minutes?

Only after he had been in college for a couple of years had he finally realized how much he respected his parents. Why hadn't he been able to talk to them sooner? It had taken him far too long to realize that his father's gruff manner was simply his manner of defense. Cal swallowed hard.

He looked back at the top of the tower. Since the image had first come on the screen, the tower had shifted with the Earth's rotation just enough to perceive. The tower now pointed closer to east-west vertical, but still leaned northward. The Earth spun slowly in its grave. As he watched, the image was cleared from the screen, replaced by a message saying his time limit had expired.

About to leave the console, Cal hesitated. Yesterday he had examined his financial transaction log to see if he had paid money to Forget-Me-Now any previous time. There hadn't been a prior entry during the last month, but what about earlier?

He recalled the log and began to search backward. Two months before, there was still no mention. None at three months, but something else puzzled him. There was another debit without a name attached.

Cal scanned several months, and the pattern became obvious. Near the tenth of every month, there had been a withdrawal from his account, every month for almost a year. The amount was always the same: a significant sum, but not enough to hurt him very much. This wasn't simply carelessness in keeping his log current. But he had no idea whom he had paid. Or why.

The most recent entries told him something else. It was approximately a month since the last payment. Was he making blackmail payments to an anonymous someone? Perhaps someone he knew but didn't want a public link with. If so, for what? Maybe he reached the state he was in *because* he failed to make a payment a day or two ago.

A second possibility chilled him. Suppose Gabriel Domingo was blackmailing him. It wasn't difficult to imagine the scene.

"You're not going to pay me?" Domingo would say.

"No."

"Okay. You had your chance. I'm going to have a short chat with the police. Nikki is going to be very disappointed." Domingo would begin to leave.

"No, you won't do that," Cal might say.

And now there was one explanation for a dead Domingo and a bloody Cal. It couldn't be possible. Or could it?

Cal forced away the disturbing possibilities. Maybe Angel, whoever he or she was, could help, if only he could locate Angel.

"Vincent," he said, reaching a decision. "Can I send a message through you to my work computer and have it relayed?"

"Shoot."

"The message is 'I need to talk to you.' " Cal explained about the code name.

"How do you want to sign it?"

"Don't. I'm not sure why I've been using code names, but I'd better play safe. If Angel gets so many messages with code names that he doesn't know it's from me, then he might not be much help anyway. I'm not going to know what Krantz is talking about this afternoon if I don't learn some more at the office."

Nikki still had not returned. Cal vacillated about leaving a message for her and decided against it. He didn't know what more to say.

Morning light that Cal hadn't noticed earlier streamed through the windows as he left the house. The light reduced his depression just a little.

Almost a third of the tube car seats were occupied, and at the next stop a few more people entered. A young man with a mustache took one of the seats beside Cal, but Cal made no effort to start a conversation. Cal wondered idly if he was snubbing people he normally rode to work with.

More passengers entered at the next few stops, and soon the tube car was almost full. Cal glanced at the status panel. What would Nikki be doing right now?

That was funny. The status panel turned red. Still puzzled at the color change, he became aware of the unexpected odor of mint leaves, and a moment later he was sure he smelled fresh rain.

His neck and shoulders began to tingle, and suddenly his face felt hot. The lights in the tube car flickered, or his vision was playing tricks on him. What was happening?

"Vincent," he began to say, stopping for no apparent reason. His vision cleared, and just as he thought he was all right, a burning pain in his chest made him cry out. He couldn't breathe. He needed air, but his lungs refused to obey him. Cramps in his stomach doubled him over, and he fell heavily to the floor.

His legs and body stiffened, and his face contorted in agony. Just when he felt as if his head would explode, he was able to suck in a large breath of air. Gasping, he felt his body begin to undergo rhythmic contractions. His outflung elbow hit a chair support so hard, he thought he must surely have cracked the bone. He felt pain in his mouth and a strong, liquid, salty taste.

He tried to call to Nikki or Vincent, but couldn't. Hands grabbed his arms, restraining him. Despite the help, his head whipped violently back, connecting with the floor, and mercifully he lost consciousness.

At first all he heard were fragments of a soft conversation in the background, most of the words unintelligible. "Idiopathic epilepsy," someone said, and the conversation faded again.

Cal tried to speak, but pain in his swollen tongue cut off his attempt.

"So you're awake," a soft male voice said.

Cal opened his eyes and squinted against the light.

"I'm Dr. Bartum," the voice continued, now associated with a round-faced, middle-aged man standing next to the bed. "You're in the Taber Clinic. How much do you remember?"

Cal choked back a laugh. So he was in the clinic where Nikki wanted him. "I remember being in the tube car," he said with difficulty. His tongue must be swollen. "And having some kind of seizure, I guess."

"Good. We could see no indications of brain damage on your scans, but you bit your tongue quite hard and knocked yourself around a bit. Your wife should be here soon. She went off duty about half an hour before we realized the connection."

"What happened to me?"

"Medical terms, all that kind of thing? Something rare, actually. Ever hear of epilepsy? I know your record says you have no history. No, I suppose not. You apparently experienced a grand mal, an epileptic seizure. Can you tell me exactly what you felt?"

"It's all a little confused, but I'll try." Cal told him what he could remember about the seizure itself and the sensory precursors.

Doctor Bartum grew thoughtful, no doubt curious about seldom-seen diseases, as Cal spoke. He seemed about to speak when the door opened.

"Cal," Nikki said. "I came as quickly as I could."

"Thanks."

"I'll leave you two for now," Bartum said. "But I'd like to talk to you before you leave, Mr. Donley."

Cal nodded, more interested in Nikki. She touched his hand, and Bartum retreated.

"How are you," she asked. She seemed genuinely concerned, not just pretending.

"Okay, I guess. But I feel a lot better seeing you." Cal heard the distortion in his voice, but his tongue was too sore to avoid it.

Nikki averted her gaze, as though she wouldn't have come if Cal's condition had been less severe.

"This has never happened to me before, has it?" he asked.

"Never. I checked on the symptoms on the way over. Attacks are sometimes triggered by strong emotions." Cal noticed her wristcomp for the first time. It was slightly smaller than Vincent.

"You don't look much better than I imagine I do," he said.

"Transplant operations don't always pick convenient times. I'm exhausted."

"Thanks for coming. At least I'm where you wanted me."

"I think you should stay here a few days and recuperate. I don't want you trying to get out of here by tomorrow."

"Tomorrow? What time is it?"

"A little before eleven. You've been out for a few hours."

"I've got an appointment after lunch."

"You can't be serious. After all this? Cal, don't push yourself so hard. You may be here because of that. Besides, you've still got some explaining to do."

"Such as?"

"Such as the clothes you left at home." She looked at him sternly.

"Oh." Cal was silent for a moment. "You took the capsules, right?"

"Yes. They're being analyzed."

"By someone you trust?" Damn. "They're probably Vital Twenty-Two."

Nikki sat down. "Maybe I can keep her quiet." Her dark eyes scanned Cal's face, her gaze shifting in small, rapid motions. "I want to know the rest."

Cal told her about waking up on the hillside above Machu Picchu wearing bloody clothes, and about the capsules in his pocket. He mentioned what Vincent had told him, and what he'd heard on the news. "But there has to be more to it than that. I can't believe I'm guilty," he finished. "Can you?"

"I don't know what to think. You've changed, especially since Lynn died. And the last couple of months, you've been tense and uncommunicative, snapping at me, gone at all hours. Maybe you've just given way under the pressure. That doesn't make it a crime. Just a sickness." Nikki's expression grew sadder as she spoke.

Cal wasn't sure that was a whole lot better. He sat up slowly. "I'm not sick, Nikki. There's more happening here than you or I understand. I just know it."

"Maybe the police could figure it out."

"That's the last thing I need right now, with all this circumstantial evidence dribbling over me. I need information—the kind that only I can get. Don't call the police."

Nikki's eyes searched his. "All right," she said finally. "Why didn't you tell me this earlier?"

"I was afraid. And I didn't want you to think I was making it all up to keep you from leaving."

Nikki said nothing, but walked to the window and stood staring for a moment before she said, "I don't suppose I could blackmail you into staying here at least overnight?" When Cal didn't respond, she sighed and said, "All right. Do what you want. I'm going home."

"Before you go, could you tell me where my clothes are?"

"I'll have them sent in," she said, and moved toward the door.

Cal called after her. "I'm not trying to hurt you. I just *have* to find out what's been happening. I've got to find out soon. I don't know why, but I do. Please understand."

She turned back at the door and looked at him. Finally she nodded in resignation and left.

Minutes later Cal was halfway down the hall to the nurses' station.

"I'm not sure it's wise for you to be up and around so soon," Dr. Bartum said from behind him.

"There are things I've got to do," Cal said simply.

"Nikki warned me you were stubborn. But—but come in here for a minute." He gestured at a small, empty waiting room.

Bartum shut the door. "Sit down a minute, Mr. Donley. I'm stepping a bit outside my normal professional boundaries, because I like Nikki, and because I'm bothered by something." He looked out the window for just a moment, and then turned back. "Do you have any enemies?"

Cal suddenly felt a draft. "None that I know of," he said truthfully.

"I'm not trying to alarm you. But one of the things you told me about your seizure bothers me. It could be a quite normal, although rare, occurrence. But I think you should know something." The doctor's eyes were unblinking. "The sensations you experienced, like the odor of rain, are typical for that kind of attack. But there's also a chemical—a gas—that can induce those same symptoms."

"Go on," Cal urged as Dr. Bartum hesitated again.

"Well, the reason I mention all this is—and it may be simply my overactive imagination—the gas smells like mint."

──── Chapter seven ────
Hoax

"You're saying my going through hell this morning might have been deliberately induced?" Cal asked, incredulous.

"*Might* be," Dr. Bartum said.

"But I was on a crowded tube car. Why wouldn't anyone else have succumbed?"

"There's a possible explanation for that. The gas oxidizes rapidly in air. If it were released quite near you, you alone might breathe it in its original state."

"But how—" Cal stopped. The young man with the mustache who sat down next to him on the tube car. All he would have had to do was run a flexible hose down one sleeve, spread his arm across the seat back, and turn a valve. "Okay," he said slowly. "I'll grant that it could be done deliberately. But why?"

"You're asking the wrong person."

"You're right. How difficult would it be to obtain this gas?"

"I'm afraid I don't know that either. You're outside of my specialty now. The gas is called Lendomen. I can tell you its chemical formula, its specific heat, its molecular weight, the effect it has on humans, and a few other details. But I wouldn't know where to start in buying it or handling it. And this could easily all be my imagination." Bartum stood. "I just wanted to let you know, just in case."

"Thanks. I appreciate it." He shook Bartum's hand and left. He could tell the doctor was still curious about why such a thing might have been done, but he couldn't help the man. Cal was just as curious. And worried.

Cal was stopped once again as he tried to leave, this time by a nurse seated at the hall station. She demanded that he sign a release to absolve the clinic and Dr. Bartum if there were any complications. She was painting her fingernails, a different color on each, so that her nails looked like a spectrum.

"This is a usual practice?" Cal asked.

"No. Only when a patient wants to leave before the doctor recommends it."

Cal flushed and signed the log.

Outside he found a bench and sat. The mild heat from the sun's rays felt good against his skin. It had been colder than he liked inside the clinic.

"I suppose you heard," he said. His tongue felt like an old sock.

"What?" Vincent said.

"Don't be cute."

"I heard. I'm glad you're feeling better."

"I hope I didn't knock you around too much."

"I'm getting used to it," Vincent said. "You're a regular bumpathon."

"You don't have any odor detectors, do you?"

"Nope. Video, audio, temperature. That's the lot."

"What can you tell me about Lendomen?"

"All that stuff the doctor mentioned. And that it's used in the assembly of lightweight solar panels. It's not an illegal substance. Why? Do you think he might be right?"

"I've never liked coincidences. What bothers me is *why*. Is there someone trying to get revenge on me, or does someone just plain hate me? I barely noticed that guy who sat next to me, but he didn't seem familiar. So does that mean maybe I killed Domingo, who was blackmailing me, and that guy was his partner, trying to even things out?"

"To quote Dr. Bartum, you're talking to the wrong person."

Cal stared into the distance. He missed the changing shadows of Earth. A flicker of motion high above caught his attention. There were a few tiny specs flying near the center of Daedalus's axis. An almost invisible net contained them.

"Has anyone ever fallen from up there?" Cal asked.

" 'Fall' isn't the right word. This isn't true gravity, so it's got some quirks. If you pushed an object with no wind resistance out from the center, it would just slowly keep going until it hit the ground as slowly as you pushed it. But the ground's relative velocity, because it's spinning, would do a lot of damage. If the object *had* a lot of wind resistance, it would gradually spiral down just because it was being pushed farther out by the centrifugal force caused by the wind."

Cal squinted into the light. Lynn had never been able to go hang gliding. Cal felt sad. There were so many things she'd never seen. So many first times he would never be able to share with her.

He watched for another moment before he recalled what he had scheduled. "Oh, no," he said abruptly. "I'm supposed to meet Leroy Krantz this afternoon. I'm almost late."

He felt weak and wobbly for his first few steps but ignored the discomfort. "Vincent, how much video can you store without cramping yourself too much?"

"At what rate and resolution?"

"Ten frames a second. Typical newscast resolution."

"Almost thirty minutes. Why?"

"I'm worried about future attempts. How about this? Can you continuously record, and save the most recent ten minutes, and keep portions of the oldest recordings? For instance, one frame a second for the previous hour, one a minute for the previous day? Or as close as you can come to that. If something happens to me, save as much as you can while adding a frame every ten seconds from that point? And can you save *all* the audio?"

"Easy. I'm starting now. Why didn't you think of this before?"

"I couldn't use my hindsight any earlier."

The trip to *Vittoria* seemed to take longer than it had the day before. Cal arrived fifteen minutes late at Leroy Krantz's office, not having had time to do the research he had planned. He would just have to fake it the best he could.

"Sorry I'm late," Cal said.

"What?" Leroy asked.

"I said sorry I'm late," he repeated slowly.

"You okay?"

"Fine."

"Don't worry about it," Leroy said, pushing aside what he

was working on. "Can I get you anything to drink before we
get started?"

Cal thought about his missed lunch, then considered the
way his body felt after the morning's activities. "Thank you,
no."

"Let's go, then," the older man said. "You want to sit at
the keyboard?" Leroy gestured at his desk and leaned back in
his chair. He grinned. "Don't be bashful, son."

Cal froze. Leroy couldn't know about his condition. But if
he did, was he teasing Cal? Cal looked at him closely. Leroy
seemed friendly enough. His hair was beginning to whiten
about the edges, but he still had almost invisible dimples as he
smiled. Cal decided that his problem was simply nerves. If
Leroy was so good an actor that he could know about Cal's
memory loss and pretend not to, Cal was at a strong disadvantage.

"Why don't *you* run through it?" Cal said at last. "I'm
content just to watch."

"Fine. Fine." Leroy rolled his chair to the desk and rubbed
his hands together briefly before he began.

The wall screen lit up with several long paragraphs of
legalese, headed by VITTORIA—DAEDALUS COMMUNICATIONS
CUSTOMER ACCEPTANCE TEST.

"Shouldn't there be someone else here?" Cal asked, thinking about how formal the occasion really was.

"Tolbor doesn't seem to be too interested. He's more likely
to spot-check the log than attend all the tests. I notified him."
Leroy looked up at the screen for a moment. "This is all
boilerplate material. Slow me down if I go too fast."

He went too fast, but Cal was too inhibited to tell him.
Pages of information flashed past. Skimming the green text,
Cal was able to verify that the test procedure was designed to
demonstrate satisfactory performance of the long-range com-
munication system that would allow the *Vittoria* to keep in
contact with Daedalus during the journey.

Performance criteria included transmission and reception
protocols, error-rate, redundancy, and power consumption.
This final test concentrated on reception quality. The flow of
text pages was interrupted by graphics showing antennae il-
lustrations and shots of the various items of communications
support gear.

"We're ready for the tests." Leroy shifted in his chair.

"The Jupiter bounce is complete. I didn't think you'd want to wait around for a few hours, so I ran it last night. Any problem?"

"That's fine." Cal didn't ask for clarification, but assumed there was a repeater in Jupiter orbit or on one of the moons.

"Great. Here are the reception results."

A multisectioned color display indicated performance characteristics in each reception mode. Green analog and digital indicators tracked instantaneous levels and showed minimum, maximum, and average values for signal-to-noise ratio, modulation percentage, signal strength, and other readings that Cal didn't have time to absorb. Leroy turned on the second wall screen for overflow.

The test transmission included audio, video, slow-scan video, and binary. Overwhelmed, Cal took a seat.

Cal tried to examine one parameter and then another, narrowing his focus. Everything looked reasonable to him. Each value he checked seemed to be comfortably above its minimum acceptable level.

Cal had looked at only a fraction of the measured parameters when Leroy said, "Okay. That pretty much finishes the Jupiter test. You satisfied?"

"Fine," Cal said, although he couldn't really say whether the equipment had passed every possible test. But surely this test was merely a formality, documenting officially what Leroy knew all along was a good product. Leroy seemed calm and honest.

"Let's see now." Leroy tapped a few keys, and a star-filled image came up on the screen. Slowly at first, then more quickly, the field of stars moved across the screen, until Luna entered the display. It was almost full. The moon moved to approximately the middle of the screen. Then the image began to zoom toward a spot midway between the center and the right edge.

Luna filled the section of the screen, and surface features continued to grow. Presently Cal was sure the focus of interest was in the crater at center screen. Seconds later the crater walls expanded out of view, and a dark dot grew into a black mesh cubic structure on the crater floor.

"That's the corner reflector," Leroy said. "Let's crank it up."

A new set of display inserts flashed on the screen.

"Okay," Leroy continued, more animated now, as though he had enjoyed zooming in on the reflector. "We're at point one percent power now. On the left we've got what we're sending. On the right is what we're getting back."

The left side showed a video of a moving test pattern, and then one of surf pounding on the rocks along an unidentified coastline on Earth. The right image was an obvious copy, delayed so slightly that it was hard to be sure there was a communications lag, with one significant difference: the picture was grainy and snowy.

The transmitter began a series of slow-scan, still-frame images, which came back perfectly clear, and then the dynamic video resumed. All level indicators were showing acceptable operation when the image faded for an instant. Cal might have not even noticed if he hadn't been transfixed, staring at the recorded view of traffic in some now-dead city.

Leroy sat at the keyboard and made no comment.

"What was that?" Cal asked.

"What was what?"

"We lost the image for a second, on the receiver display."

Leroy looked up at the screen, his face expressionless. "Oh, that. Just an automatic failover test. We're on the B transmitter now." He pointed to a section of the display: ACTIVE TRANSMITTER B.

"Oh" was all Cal could say.

"It's a normal part of the test. Didn't you even read the test procedure ahead of time?"

"It's fine, Leroy. No problem."

Leroy turned back to the keyboard and continued the test, which ran for only another couple of minutes. "Okay," he said finally. "Mark your approval."

Unsure of the proper procedure, Cal reached forward to the keyboard. Just as his hand brushed a key, the memory came back to him. He placed his thumb on the white square and looked up at the screen. There was his name and a flowery graphic symbol that obviously indicated he was a witness.

Leroy reached over to the keyboard, and his notation appeared below Cal's.

"Is that it, then?" Cal asked.

Leroy turned to him. He looked at Cal intently for a brief moment. "That's it," he said, suddenly brusque. "All complete. Thanks very much."

Cal rose to leave, puzzled. Leroy seemed anxious, almost imperceptibly unsettled. In his place, Cal could imagine being nervous at the start of an important test and relaxed at the conclusion. Why were Leroy's actions opposite? What guarded thoughts lay behind Leroy's brown eyes? Or was Cal merely imagining mysteries where none existed? Maybe Leroy was surprised that Cal hadn't known for sure that the session was complete.

Leroy busied himself at the keyboard, and Cal walked down the hall to his office. People in nearby offices must have been busy, because no one called to him. Drained, he dropped into his desk chair and let his hands fall limply to the sides. After a moment he rose to shut the door and then sat again.

"Vincent, has he always been that inconsistent?"

"Leroy Krantz?"

"Yeah. Last night it was 'Let's go for a drink.' Today it's 'Thanks a lot. See you around.'"

"All I can remember about Leroy is last night's conversation and the one now. That's not enough for me to pronounce him manic-depressive."

"It's not quite that bad," Cal said. "But it's enough to worry me. I'm suspicious of everything right now. Leroy could have paid that guy this morning."

"Or you may have so many enemies that Leroy had to pay him not to do anything worse. As the actor says to the director, what's the motivation?"

"As the doctor says, you're asking the wrong person. It wouldn't be so bad, not knowing who the right person was, if I at least knew the right questions." Cal leaned back and shut his eyes for a moment, visualizing Krantz's office. "You're recording now, per our talk?" he asked.

"I've got more pictures than a baby photographer, but they're pretty dull."

"Let's look at them anyway—the ones from about fifteen minutes ago, when the picture faded during the test. Can you transmit it to the desk computer so it can use the wall screen? I don't need eyestrain on top of everything else."

The wall screen flickered, and the image of Leroy's office appeared.

"Great," Cal said. "Now can you blow up the section that shows his screen? And rotate it so it's level?"

His arm had been lying on the armrest during those minutes, so the angles were distorted, but the picture was clear.

"Let's try some image enhancement," Vincent said, and the bottom of the picture shrank slowly until the relative dimensions made it seem as though Vincent had been directly in front of Leroy's screen. Cal's screen looked like the original, except for a little graininess.

"Vincent, you're terrific." The echoed video was just starting to fade, or was about to recover. "Go forward a frame."

The echoed picture had recovered. "How about back two frames?" Cal asked. Again clear. "You're saving a frame a second for this interval, right?"

"Yeah. It's so cluttered in here, I hardly have space to sit down."

"If you don't shape up, I'll start storing all my old school records in there too."

"They're already down in the basement. You did even better in college than you did in high school."

"Okay, okay. Can you expand the upper left quadrant? It's a little fuzzy."

"Picky," Vincent said, and the magnification doubled.

"Fine," Cal said. "It says 'active transmitter equals A.' Now forward three frames. Okay. Now it's B. So Leroy was telling the truth. Was he bothered by something else?"

"I think you should listen to your doctor."

"You're right. I want to save this sequence for a while, though. Can you store the frames we've looked at just now, and one every ten seconds for the whole time we were with Leroy? Label it and don't overwrite it as you keep recording."

"I obey even as you speak. What's next, boss?"

"What was Leroy doing all this time? Show me the section with him in it, in real time, starting a second before the cutover."

Leroy's only reactions during the interval were a brief compressing of his lips and a glance at Cal. Cal inspected the image a moment longer before he gave up. There was nothing obviously sinister about Leroy's behavior.

"Maybe it's time I sent *my* boss a status report," he said. "Tom Horvath is on my phone list, and it seems I report to him."

Aided by computer prompting, Cal prepared a message that

said, "Communications test with Krantz passed." As he finished and started to sign off, he noticed an information block that said, "One message waiting."

Depressing two keys brought the message up on the screen. "I missed you last time" was all it said. The originator block, rather than containing a name, said, "Monthly."

Cal thought a moment longer before he made the connection. It had to be a message from the person to whom he paid monthly payments. But it still didn't explain *why*. If the message referred to a meeting, then Cal had no way to tell what the meeting was. If it referred to the incident on the tube car, then "Monthly" hadn't missed him. Unless the gas had been intended to be fatal.

"I'm spending too much time in front of computer terminals," Cal said abruptly. "I need more direct exposure. Is the news station open to the public?"

"Yes. But most of their data is available at any terminal."

"That doesn't matter. It seems that I recall more when I'm dealing with people."

"It seems you also run more risks."

"Something's wrong. I can't find out what it is by ignoring it."

"You're not worried about joining Domingo in the marble orchard?"

"Let's go, Vincent."

"I don't have a whole lot of choice, do I?"

"About as much as I have."

Cal kept a watchful eye for anyone coming too close to him on the way over, but saw no one. The news station was in Machu Picchu, near the center of the city. The facilities available to the public were similar to Cal's desk computer, but there were no thumbprint squares. The terminals were always on, available without specifying an ID.

Cal studied the lineup of screens in small cubicles, wondering if the trip had been worth the effort, when a calm voice sounded behind him.

"Not sure how to use the system?"

Cal turned and found himself facing the reporter he had seen on the earlier newscasts, Michelle Garney. Her vivid-green eyes hadn't shown up well on the video.

"I think I can figure it out," Cal said. "But I'm a little tired of dealing with machines." No offense, Vincent.

The woman smiled and nodded understandingly. "It's hard to avoid. What were you looking for?"

Cal hesitated. He didn't want any links between himself and Gabriel Domingo, but the woman appeared friendly and willing to help. "I'm investigating drug-related killings. And the death of the fellow on the news yesterday."

Michelle gave him a brief appraising gaze and said, "Why don't you join me in the break room? Maybe I can get you started."

They exchanged first names, and Cal followed her to a nearby room equipped with a few tables, chairs, and vending machines. Michelle smiled. It was a welcome change, and it felt good to sit down. He looked up and found her watching him.

"Hard day?" she asked.

Cal smiled. "Perhaps I'm just out of shape."

She raised her eyebrows, as if to disagree, but said nothing.

"Have there been many killings lately?" Cal asked.

"I guess that depends on what you mean by 'lately' and 'many.' Quite a few in the last year. But Vital Twenty-Two hasn't been linked to any before."

"So maybe this last murder wasn't a typical case?"

"I don't know that there is a typical case. But, yes, it's a bit unusual." Michelle looked thoughtful for a moment. "The body being moved, that particular drug, the injuries . . ."

"What about the injuries?" Cal tried to keep his voice calm.

"Messy. Crude. I guess it's a little more typical for the victim to end up with a laser hole or a knife cut. Domingo was—well, it's more like a whole gang beat him to death, or he fell a long way. His injuries were massive." Michelle shivered almost imperceptibly.

"So you saw the body?"

"Pictures. That was enough."

"Any chance they were faked?"

"Not any. He was way past hope. Some of my more morbid friends call a case like that a sidewalk soufflé." She leaned forward. "Why? What reason would anyone have for faking a murder discovery?"

"None that I can think of. Just curious."

"And why do *you* ask that? I thought maybe you were the police." A small frown wrinkled her forehead.

Cal was nervous. "I'm sorry. I didn't mean to pretend to be the police." He put a hand on the table and began to push himself up. "I apologize for giving you the wrong impression." He was halfway through his motion when she put her hand on his.

"Wait," she said. "I didn't mean to chase you off."

Her hand was cool and firm against Cal's. He looked at it for a moment. His hand tingled where she touched him. Her eyes were bright, alert, questioning, but still friendly. She didn't remove her hand until he sat down again.

"I guess it's my day for overreacting," he said, guiltily wishing she hadn't taken her hand away.

She said nothing, but watched him closely.

"Where did Domingo live?" he asked.

"An apartment here in town—on the west side." She gave him the address.

Cal didn't know how compass directions had been defined, but decided to ask Vincent later. "Is there anything you know that hasn't reached the public?" he asked.

"No. I'm not with the police either."

"Is that supposed to make me tell you why I'm interested in all of this?"

Michelle smiled quickly, but was silent.

"You know," Cal said, "you're not as opaque as we'd all like to believe we are. Your curiosity must be on full alert, but you're hoping I'll answer your unspoken questions."

She nodded and grinned again.

"You really enjoy your work, don't you?" he asked.

"You're right again. Why? Don't you enjoy yours?"

"Let's say I'm undecided. Look. I can't tell you the reasons for my interest. I'm just looking for the same thing you are: the truth. If I find it, I'll tell you. Fair enough?"

"You realize the information flow in this conversation is all backward?"

"Michelle, I—thanks very much. I enjoyed talking with you." Cal rose to leave. This time she didn't stop him.

"You really will tell me what this is all about sometime?"

"Yes."

"Don't go and get yourself killed."

Cal stopped. "Whatever makes you say that?"

"Like I said, I enjoy my job. I'm good at it. I trust my hunches. You didn't saunter down here simply to gather data.

You've got a personal stake in this.''

"You know, you're right.''

She raised her eyebrows.

"You *are* good at your job.''

Michelle smiled once more as Cal left. This time, however, he thought he saw worry mixed into it.

Out on the street Cal asked, "Which way is west?''

"The side of the continent opposite the direction of rotation,'' Vincent said. "North is the sun end.''

"So I'm walking west right now?''

"Right.''

"You heard Domingo's address, I assume. Want to give me directions?''

"It'll be a long walk without a bike. If you take the tubeway up the hill and switch to one that runs on the west side, you'll save some steps.''

"Up the hill is up to the south pole?''

"Correct.''

A half hour later Cal was on the streets of Machu Picchu's west side. There were no nearby businesses, only apartment buildings and occasional town houses, all with bicycle racks near the doors.

Domingo's address was a large building containing perhaps twenty units. Cal walked by it without entering.

The building was typically long and narrow, lined up east-west, with all the units on one level. Each had a window overlooking the valley to the north. Oak and pine trees provided a modest amount of privacy to the areas near some of the windows. Cal could see only two main doors, one at each end of the building.

Some of the windows were open. The apartment number Michelle had told him was eight. If the units were numbered sequentially starting at one end, there was a fifty percent chance that Domingo's was open.

Cal entered the building and found himself in a tiny, deserted foyer tiled in red and black. Without hesitation he continued into the long hallway beyond, until he came to the first apartment door.

Number sixteen. So the numbering started at the other end. Which meant—he did a short calculation—none of the open windows belonged to number eight.

He kept walking. Maybe, against all odds, the police had

left the door unlocked. He didn't believe it, but he was halfway there already, so he might as well continue. Fortunately, no one was in the hall.

Domingo's door looked like all the others: closed and locked. No notes marred the solid brown surface of the door. Disheartened, Cal was just about to give up and leave, when, struck by a sudden idea, he reached up and pressed his thumb against the white square.

The door to Gabriel Domingo's apartment slid silently open.

——— Chapter eight ———
Hologram

SURPRISED and apprehensive, Cal hesitated before the open doorway. He licked the ball of his thumb and cleaned the thumbprint square outside Domingo's apartment. The hall was deserted. He entered.

The door closed behind him. The apartment looked as though Domingo might have just gone out for a quick meal. Apparently his personal possessions hadn't been confiscated. There was a risk that the police had left behind a hidden video camera, but Cal had to find out as much as he could.

"You know anything about police procedures, Vincent?" he asked. "For instance, do they leave a deceased's home intact for a week or anything?"

"Sorry. You could be right, but I have no way to confirm or deny."

Cal took a long, slow look around. He had been here before. What things he had done, what conversations he might have had, were lost, but he knew he had been here before. Maybe if he saw Domingo sitting in the empty rope chair-hammock, more would come back to him.

All the furniture except the hammock and a desk chair was built in. The outline of a foldaway bed showed under the window. Dresser drawers came flush with the wall. The desk computer sat on a fold-down support. Shelves set into the wall held a small hologram and other knickknacks. The guilt of trespassing, as when Nikki had found him looking at her file, came back stronger.

Cal searched the drawers, finding nothing out of the ordinary. He was about to examine the closet when instead he went to the window and slid it open, noticing with surprise that it had been unlocked. Vincent's compband came off his wrist, and he hung Vincent from a nearby tree branch.

"Vincent, can you see both ways from there? I want you to warn me if anyone starts in either door."

"No problem."

It was only after Cal started searching the closet that he unhappily realized how natural it had been for him to use Vincent as a lookout. Maybe all this wasn't as unusual for him as he wanted to believe.

The closet held mostly clothes that seemed to have been bought for durability. Work clothes, heavy materials, patches on elbows and knees. With them were exactly what Cal would have expected to find in a construction worker's closet: a hard hat, tool set, reinforced-toe boots, an empty Thermos, and not much else.

Most of the items on the shelves meant nothing to Cal, but he found himself going back for a second look at the hologram. It wasn't a professional job, merely a do-it-yourself in a cheap backlit frame. But the view was what had inexplicably drawn Cal's attention. The hologram showed the outside of a church with a large gold starburst on the wall in front.

Maybe Domingo had been a religious man. Perhaps that explained why the hologram was there. But nothing else Cal had uncovered in his search fit with that hypothesis. There were no other holograms, and no other objects that implied anything more complex than the normal possessions of a construction worker. The police could have removed items, but that made no sense.

Still not knowing why the holo of the church attracted him so strongly, Cal had an idea. He found a pair of scissors in the desk. Taking apart the holo frame, he removed the film and cut it in two. One half he replaced. The edges of the frame slid closer together to block off the space now uncovered, and Cal put the other half in his pocket.

Back on the shelf, the hologram generated by the remaining film half showed a graininess not noticeable earlier. Other than that, it looked as though it had never been touched.

By the time another minute had elapsed, Cal had examined everything of interest in the apartment except the desk computer. He started to retrieve Vincent, but then thought back to the way the door had responded to his thumb. He touched the desk computer square.

The screen lit. Green letters said, "Gabriel Angelo Domingo. Personal."

Cal drew in his breath, looking at Domingo's middle name. It had to be. A minute later his suspicion was confirmed. Still stored in Domingo's message file was the note Cal had sent yesterday to "Angel."

He shivered and erased the message. Angel was past responding.

So there was far more to his relationship with the dead man than simple recognition. Sending coded messages to each other wasn't the hallmark of casual acquaintances. Or of people with nothing to hide. He understood now why he hadn't met Angel at Tinsdale Park.

Cal tried to ignore the building fear. So much for the easy explanations. The biggest questions were ones like *why* Cal knew Domingo. Learning more about the nature of his relationship with Domingo generated even more unknowns.

"See anything yet, Vincent?" he asked.

"Not a thing."

Cal turned back to the computer. It took him only another few moments to realize that Domingo's stored information was as sparse as his apartment. There were almost none of the indications of personalization that had shown up on Cal's home computer. There was no bank transaction log, no summary of employment or personal history. Other than the standard data base, there were only a couple more entries in his acknowledged message file.

The first one said, "Investigated comments overheard at Galentine's. Read S and G 1:19:24 before Tinsdale. Imperative."

Was this message from himself? Cal frowned. Galentine's was a bar he had passed earlier in the day. But what about the phrase? He tried to make sense of the number series as a date or a time, but failed to see any significance. "S and G" made no more sense than when he had seen the phrase in his own computer. He would have to go back to it later. He shouldn't stay here any longer than absolutely necessary.

The last file provided one more filament in the web. It was a message to "Jam": "Not sure about tonight's plan. Got a crazy message from my associate today. Will tell you more later."

Cal was just about to print the screen contents when Vincent's voice made him change his plans.

"Someone just started in the door. Couldn't tell if it was police or not."

An instant later Cal had Vincent snapped back on his wrist. He moved toward the door but checked his motion and instead took a quick glance outside, then scrambled over the windowsill. He slid the window closed.

Cal crouched, partially shielded by an oak and a couple of pines. His breath came heavily. No one should find him here. He had to get away fast. He tried to decide which way to run. Whomever Vincent had seen could simply be a neighbor of Domingo's, or there could be police on both ends of the building.

An upward glance decided him. The oak was just tall enough to reach the roof. Cal climbed, the exercise bringing back aches that had begun to fade. The tree's branches provided ample concealment from the view of pedestrians on the terrace above. He pulled himself into a position where he could stand on a limb and wait for the area to clear.

Come on, he thought. One lone walker passed by in front of the tree, and then he was gone. Cal jumped lightly to the roof of Domingo's apartment building. That maneuver should confuse any follower. No one seemed to notice that Cal had stepped out of the tree. He briskly walked until he came to a break between buildings and began to jog up the hill, trying to appear casual, but making occasional backward glances. No one seemed to be following.

He didn't relax until the tubeway had carried him well away from the area. He stayed on the car all the way to the south pole.

"As long as we're this close already, Vincent, I think it's time to visit the place they found Domingo. By now it should be safe."

"Famous last words."

As Cal moved into the docking disk, an image of a criminal returning to the scene of the crime bothered him. Shortly an elevator deposited him at his destination.

The room labeled C5 was nothing more than a large storage

bay. Rows of crates, protected by motion sensors, lined the walls. The floor in the center was scrubbed clean. Cal walked to one end of the room.

Maybe Cal had pushed Domingo off the top of a stack of crates, intending to disable him. Domingo could have landed on his head, making the fall fatal. But no, the police had said Domingo was apparently brought here after death.

"I don't get it," he said at last. "Almost everywhere I've been, I've gotten twitches, or small fragments coming back to me. But here I get nothing. Just a complete blank."

"So you did remember Domingo's apartment?"

"Enough to convince me I've been there before."

"And you didn't learn anything there either?"

"On the contrary," Cal said, and told Vincent about the message and the hologram. "And save that message."

Cal walked back to the center of the room. "What's in these boxes?"

"According to the part numbers on the labels, hardware. Nuts, bolts, washers."

"No drugs?"

"Not if the labels are right."

"I have to assume they are. Surely the police would have searched the place carefully." Cal sat down on the clean floor. "You know, I really don't think I was ever here. Vincent, what does that message mean to you? I know Galentine's is a bar, but what about 'one nineteen twenty-four' and 'S and G'?"

"Numbers could be almost anything. Dates, times, account numbers, passwords, codes, coordinates, angles, hat sizes. I could keep going for months, and it's already crowded enough in here. For 'S and G,' I could list all the businesses with names like Sand and Gravel, or all the couples with names like Susan and George."

"It may be pointless, but when we get back to a computer with a printer, I want you to make as complete a list of possibilities as you can in, say, an hour."

"Do I get overtime for this?"

"Guess."

"Chronologically, I'm a minor. Do you have any idea how many child-labor laws are still on the books?"

"Don't tell me. I think I need a drink."

•　　•　　•

It was after dinnertime when Cal saw Galentine's bar ahead.

"Vincent, can you display a picture of Domingo?"

"To hear is to obey."

Inside, the crowd tried to compete with the raucous noise radiated by a four-person group. It wasn't much of a contest; the group was equipped with high-power amplifiers and speakers. The long room held the bar and the band at opposite ends, as if management were employing the group to drive patrons back to the bar for more drinks. In the middle lay a haphazard assortment of tables and chairs, most occupied by people trying to shout over the music or apparently too drunk to care.

Cal picked a stool at the counter and punched the call button to order a drink he didn't want. When the bartender paused to deliver it, Cal shouted, "You ever see this guy in here?"

The bartender, a short, stocky man who gave the impression that he was also a bouncer, looked briefly at the image on Vincent and said, "Nope."

The man started to move away, but Cal called, "Wait. Have *I* been in here before?"

"Yep." This time the bartender gave Cal a piercing look before he busied himself again.

Cal got the feeling he wouldn't learn much more from a man who gave binary answers, so he found a two-person table as far away from the light and noise as possible. He rested his chin on his hand.

"I don't know about you," he said, "but this is not music to *my* ears."

"I can't understand a word they're saying," Vincent said, just audible over the din.

"You're not meant to. If they knew how to write lyrics, they'd be proud of them and *want* you to hear them."

Cal said nothing more for several minutes, sipping his drink and watching people come in and out.

"Why are we here?" Vincent asked at last.

"That's a pretty cosmic question to answer on only one drink."

"And you call *me* a smart-ass."

"We're here because I want to find out more about Domingo. If I knew what he really did, or what our relationship actually was, maybe I could find out what I've been doing, and why. But this seems like a waste. I'm—''

"You're what?" Vincent asked when Cal didn't finish.

"I'm surprised to see Russ Tolbor in here."

The commander had entered and was pushing through the crowd. He gave no sign of seeing Cal. Without speaking to anyone, he went directly to a door at the back of the room. Now that Cal looked more closely, he realized there must be a quieter section in back.

"Why are you surprised?"

"No particular reason. He's entitled to a drink just as much as anyone else. But I don't like coincidences. Or, more accurately, I don't always believe coincidences are actually coincidences."

"Run that by me again?"

"I don't think it's random chance that I just saw Tolbor. Galentine's bar was in the message at Domingo's. Tolbor visits Galentine's. There's a link there—not coincidence," Cal said. "I want to see who he's with. Are you ready with your camera?"

"Ready and willing."

Cal strolled leisurely, looking for the men's room. The door Tolbor had used did indeed lead to a second, secluded lounge with a few doors along its back wall. Besides the doors to the rest rooms, there were another three doors, all apparently connecting to private booths.

Back at his table Cal reviewed the images Vincent had captured. He looked at the groups at each table, magnifying the faces when necessary, but he didn't see Tolbor.

"He must be in one of the booths," Cal said. "When he comes back out, let's take some more pictures."

As Cal watched, trying to block out the music, he thought about Nikki and Lynn. The longer he waited, the more he wanted simply to go back to the house and talk to Nikki. If she were there.

Either the noise must have gradually numbed him, or his thoughts provided ample isolation. He realized that someone was talking to him.

"I said, are you waiting for someone?" The speaker was a fair-haired woman in a turquoise party dress cut so low that Cal didn't need to stand to enjoy the view. She had her hand on the back of the other chair at Cal's table and leaned toward him, looking at him expectantly.

"I'm awfully sorry, but yes, I am," Cal said, retreating to the literal truth.

The woman grinned briefly before turning her palms up and shrugging her shoulders. She moved away with what Cal thought was a trace of disappointment.

He was still wondering what to say to Nikki, when Tolbor finally came out. There were two other men who seemed to be with him. They were both older than Tolbor, perhaps mid-fifties. Clean shaven, both were lean men. The one in front never took his eyes off the door ahead of him as he weaved his way through the crowd. The other tried to continue a conversation with Tolbor as they moved through the bodies, but Cal could tell that the foursome with the power amplifiers were still winning. And then the three were gone.

"You got pictures, Vincent?"

"Right."

"Save a couple of views of each and erase the rest." Cal walked to the back room, where he saw the door to booth number one lay open.

Cal bought another unneeded drink and asked the bartender, "Tolbor comes in here every night?"

"Yep."

Cal left the drink on the bar, thinking about the myth of talkative bartenders, and walked out into the evening air. He hadn't realized how stuffy it was in the bar.

Tolbor and his companions were not in sight. That was just as well. Cal had felt a faint urge to follow them, but he didn't know what he would have done.

He started toward home, wondering if Nikki were there.

The house was dark. Disappointment came to him far stronger than he realized it would. And loneliness. He tried to think of something else. Maybe at least he could find a meal in the kitchen. He was starved.

As he passed the bedroom doorway on his way, he saw a dark form on the bed, on top of the covers.

He came closer. Nikki. For no reason he could explain, he suddenly worried that she might not be alive. Cal paused just inside the bedroom door, inexplicably nervous. She couldn't be dead. It wasn't possible. He broke away from his thoughts and moved quickly to the bedside.

Unthinking, he grasped her wrist, feeling for a pulse.

"Nikki," he said, his voice ragged.

Her arm moved. "What are you doing?" she asked, apparently waking from a light sleep.

Cal pulled his hand away abruptly, as though her skin were white-hot. "I was—this will sound really stupid, but I was afraid for a moment that you might be dead."

Nikki sat up slowly on the bed and switched on a reading light. "Maybe not stupid," she said. "Maybe bizarre. Do you still think you did the right thing by leaving the clinic?"

"I had no choice." Cal sat on the bed beside her and put his chin on his hands.

"Don't you think you're exaggerating?" Nikki pulled her knees up and wrapped her arms around them. Her eyes were hard to see in the dim room.

Cal looked at her for a long moment, reviewing the day's events, sifting through his feelings and trying to resolve them with the information he had learned since he woke up on the hillside. He had to trust someone.

Making a decision, he said at last, "Nikki, I realize I've hurt you quite a lot. I don't have any defense, any excuse. But I need you now. Things I don't understand are happening, and there's more to it than my overactive imagination. I'm asking you to call a truce for a few days. I'm not trying to say you can't move out. Obviously that's your right. But would you talk to me and help me?"

Nikki was silent for a moment, her face unreadable. "I don't know. I don't understand."

"Something bad has happened, or is going to happen. I don't know which. Ever since my memory was blotted out, I've felt a sense of urgency, a compulsion to do *something*. But I don't know what. Today I started acting like a spy and broke into an apartment. And I still don't feel all that much closer to knowing what the problem really is. This morning I almost got killed, and—"

"Wait," she said, sitting up straighter. "You said 'killed.' That's a pretty specific word, with distinct implications. Are you using the word loosely, or do you mean that?"

"I mean precisely that." Cal rose and paced lightly to fight off the nervous tension. "Dr. Bartum told me about a substance called Lendomen. It's capable of inducing a seizure. And its odor is like something I smelled just before the symptoms began. Bartum didn't strike me as a guy who'd suggest something like that unless he felt pretty confident. What do you think?"

"I think Bartum's competent, but so unimaginative that he probably did his thesis on why yawns are catching. He wouldn't mention anything he had doubts about. Whose apartment did you break into?"

"Domingo's. Except I didn't literally break in. The door was coded to accept my thumbprint. As was his computer." Cal told her about the rest of his day.

"But you don't think you actually killed Domingo?" she asked.

"I can't be totally sure about anything," Cal said, totally sure that he didn't want to lose Nikki. "But I don't see how I could have. If I said to Vincent, 'How could I have done this to you,' it has to have a context that . . . explains it. I'm not a killer."

"I know that." Nikki's voice softened. "Whatever has happened, I believe that. You still have the holo?"

He took it out of his pocket and handed it to her. "We should have a viewer somewhere, shouldn't we?"

Nikki rose and retrieved one from a shelf. "Will you turn the light on?"

Cal did so and sat back on the bed while she removed the original hologram and inserted the one from Domingo's apartment. She snapped it on, and they could see the church.

"It's the Presodist church in Machu Picchu," she said, and handed it to Cal.

Now that he had more time to look, he realized there were people in front of the church, on their way out. "Do we have a magnifying glass?" he asked.

Nikki retrieved one from the desk.

With its help, Cal could see slightly blurred faces. He wished he'd taken the entire hologram, but he found that by turning the hologram as he watched, letting his mind form the composite, he could more easily distinguish the people.

"One of the two guys with Tolbor tonight is here," he said after a brief inspection. "And there's—there's Tolbor and the other one."

"But you have no idea what the link is between Tolbor, Domingo, and the church?" Nikki asked.

"True—other than that Tolbor is a Presodist."

Nikki shook her head. "I don't see how you can hope to piece all this together in a few days, assuming it does all fit. You're sure you're not just trying to keep me off balance long enough that I'll forget about a divorce? That's not the way I am."

"I know that," he said truthfully. "If I thought for a moment that I had any chance at all of persuading you to stay, I'd probably do anything I thought I could get away with, maybe even lie to you. But this isn't fabricated. It's possible that I'm misinterpreting some of the things that have happened to me, but they're all real. And I'm convinced that something is very wrong here. Help me, Nikki."

She looked at her hands, making a minute inspection. "Cal, I can't," she finally said softly. "I think the stress has been too much for you lately. You need a different kind of help."

Cal said nothing for a moment, feeling like the world was washing away from him and the only thing he could grasp was silt. "Nikki, if that's what you think, then I understand. But do one thing for me now. Look in my eyes when you say it."

Nikki looked up. She seemed about to cry.

Cal gave her a level gaze and said, "But I really need *your* help, not a doctor's."

"All right," she said at last. "For a few days. Then I'm leaving."

Cal realized he had been holding his breath, and he breathed out heavily. "You've got to do whatever you feel you have to."

"Where's the message you found at Domingo's?" Her decision made, Nikki didn't hesitate any longer.

Cal wrote it on a piece of paper. "I know what 'Galentine's' means. But the 'one nineteen twenty-four' and 'S and G' are still a puzzle. I'll have Vincent print a list of possibilities."

"I wonder. Maybe they tie into the church."

"How so?"

"Just a few minutes. Let me try some alternatives." Nikki walked to the desk computer and started typing.

Cal watched the back of her head as she worked. He was grateful for her help, realizing that Nikki didn't do anything in a mediocre manner; if she agreed to help, she would do her absolute best. The sense of loneliness grew larger within him. How could he have been so stupid or preoccupied as to force her from him?

"Come here a minute," she called. "I think this is it."

Cal stood behind her and looked at the screen. The top row said, "Genesis 19:24."

"The church *was* the link. Presodists use the Bible. If you assume a biblical reference, this is where it takes you. There were three numbers instead of the usual two, so I assumed the first one meant the book: Genesis."

A cold feeling passed through Cal as he read the balance of the text: "At the same time, the Lord rained down sulphurous fire upon Sodom and Gomorrah."

"That's it," he agreed. "It has to be." His knees felt weak, so he pulled up a chair. "What's the context?"

"Genesis nineteen talks about the destruction of Sodom and Gomorrah. It says they were places of lust and evil, and God destroyed them just after an innocent man left. Cal, you don't suppose—no, that couldn't be."

"Suppose what?"

"No, it's too incredible."

"Come on, Nikki. We've got to share all our thoughts. We'll throw out the unlikely ones later."

Nikki's voice was husky. "Well, it's a pretty large jump just from reading this passage, but it made me wonder if what happened to Earth was really an accident."

———————— Chapter nine ————————
Housecall

HORRIFIED by Nikki's suggestion, Cal reviewed what he knew so far. "I wonder too," he said grimly.

"But if the disaster on Earth *wasn't* an accident, that would mean someone is unbelievably mad," Nikki said, looking back at him from her seat at the desk terminal. She was obviously worried, but there was no hint that she was regretting her decision to help.

"History's littered with instances of millions of people being killed in short lengths of time. It might only be a matter of degree. Is there any more to the chapter on Sodom and Gomorrah?"

"Not much. Abraham implored God to search for innocent men. He supposedly couldn't find enough innocents to justify saving the cities—only one man: Lot. On the way out, Lot's wife looked back, disobeying God, and was turned into a pillar of salt. Zoar, the last city of the plain, was spared."

"That's all?" Cal asked.

"There's a good deal of repetition in the Bible. In the previous chapter, while Abraham's arguing with God about how many innocent people it takes to justify saving the cities, he goes through almost the whole argument with the number fifty, then forty-five, forty, thirty, twenty, and ten."

"So, if this possible nightmare is true, Daedalus may correspond to Zoar, as the city that was spared," Cal said. "But it just seems too monstrous."

"Maybe so. But the parallels are scary. For instance, the passage says 'rained down sulphurous fire.' The bacteria caused a strong burning in the lungs before death." Nikki moved to a more comfortable chair. Her face was pale.

"Okay. We can't tell yet if this is our imagination, but if it isn't, why have I felt this strong urge to hurry? As though I have to do something before *Vittoria* leaves?"

"You tell me," she said.

"Well, if we assume Tolbor is the person responsible—he figures in this, he's a churchgoer, I'm sure of it—then maybe I was afraid he would get away."

"That explanation has a problem. All we'd need to do is call *Vittoria* and tell them what happened. He would still get caught."

"There's still a chance that, without sufficient proof, we couldn't justify sending the message. I don't know. There are still too many ifs."

"But if this is mostly true," Nikki said, "what was the justification?"

"Who says he has one? Maybe he's simply crazy."

"Even crazies have justifications. They just might not make sense to you or me. Maybe he was punishing the population of Earth for their sins."

"But Earth wasn't any different from here."

"Maybe to him it was. Maybe Earth was tainted by dirt or some other nonsense that makes sense to him."

Cal rose and walked slowly in a large circle. "I wonder if that thought is what pushed me over the edge earlier. I know how guilty I was feeling about Lynn." He saw the quizzical expression on Nikki's face. "The nightmares have started up again. But what I was saying was, if I felt this guilt over Lynn's death, and then I found out someone might have *deliberately* caused it—"

"But why wouldn't you have told me?" Nikki's pain was obvious.

"I wish I knew," Cal said, looking at her. "God, I wish I knew. Maybe the fact that I didn't means this whole theory is worthless. The real problem could center on Domingo, whoever Jam is, and me. For all I know, the three of us were doing something we shouldn't have, and there was a falling out. Jam could be responsible for my visit to the clinic this morning. Or it could have been engineered by whoever I've been paying monthly payments."

"What monthly payments?"

"About the tenth of every month lately, I've sent money to someone whose name I don't know. I've gone over all the possibilities I can think of, including blackmail, but nothing seems to make sense. I didn't make the last payment. Do you have any idea who they might go to, or why?"

"No. I don't suppose it ties in with the capsules?" Nikki asked.

"I don't know. Why? What did you find out about them?"

"You were right. Vital Twenty-Two. I *think* my friend in the lab will keep quiet for now. But how do they fit in?"

"I've got absolutely no idea," Cal said. "What I do know is, I'm tired." He sat down heavily in a chair.

"You've had a long day."

"We both have. Nikki—thanks for helping. I'm sure you're right about the biblical reference. I really needed someone to talk to. Vincent's a help, but he has a lot of built-in limitations. And I feel better after talking to you."

Nikki had been seemingly relaxing, but now she tensed, as though Cal had said the wrong thing. "Maybe it's time to quit for tonight," she said.

"Sure," Cal said, wondering what nerve he had scraped. But he was too exhausted to try to recover. He pushed himself out of the chair and began to place several cushions on the floor.

"What's that for?" Nikki asked.

"I'll be fine out here. Maybe you won't feel pressured to move out so soon."

Nikki said nothing but went to the bedroom and shut the door behind her.

Cal was sure she was irritated, but he was so tired that he couldn't figure out whether he would have made her more angry by assuming he could share the bed after she had announced her decision to leave.

He twisted and turned, trying unsuccessfully to get comfortable on the cushions. "Anything new occur to you, Vincent?"

"Nope. Is this what they mean by sleeping around?"

"Good night, Vincent. Wake me at oh seven hundred, okay?"

"You got it."

During the day Cal had forced his thoughts away from Lynn, but in dreams he had no control. At least once he saw

Lynn walking away from him, and Nikki following after her and not looking back.

The sound of a chime interrupted a dream, and despite his tiredness, he was glad to be awake.

"Okay, Vincent. I'm awake."

"That's nice, but it's not me. You've got company."

Cal opened his eyes and tilted his head to hear the sound better. It came again from near the door.

He struggled to his feet and hastily returned the cushions to their normal locations. The bedroom door was still closed.

The time was a little before 07:00. Cal pushed his hair off his forehead and opened the front door. His stomach tightened, not from hunger.

A uniformed policeman stood there. "Mr. Cal Donley?" he asked.

"That's me," he said. "What do you want?"

"I'm Lieutenant Dobson with the Machu Picchu Police Department. I need to ask you a few questions." The man was younger than Cal, but quite muscular. A badge lay in his hand. He watched Cal out of half-open eyes. Dobson had recently started a mustache, or it just didn't grow well.

"Come on in."

Both men took a seat, and the policeman unfolded a clipboard terminal. "I'm investigating the death of Gabriel Domingo, the construction worker found dead the day before yesterday," he said. "Could you tell me where you were from midnight to oh six hundred that day?"

"Sure. I was right here." Cal began to sweat. "Why?"

"Someone said they saw you near the murder location and wearing bloody clothes."

Cal fought the urge to fidget, forcing his hands to relax. He watched the man as he calmly entered Cal's claim into his terminal. The policeman's face betrayed no emotion. His next sentence could just as easily be "That's not what they say at Forget-Me-Now," as "That will be all."

"Did you know the victim?" was next, as it happened.

"No, I didn't. Surely there must be a fair number of people who look like me."

"I'm sure you're right, sir. Would you mind if I have a look around?"

"Not at all," Cal was compelled to say. "But my wife's still sleeping. I'd hate—"

"It's all right, darling," came Nikki's voice from behind him. "I woke up even though you tried to get out of bed quietly." She sounded nervous to Cal. He thought about the clothes he had worn that night. Maybe Nikki had washed them. Or washing clothes could be his job. Whatever happened, he couldn't afford to deny access to the police.

"In that case, help yourself," Cal said. "We'll wait right here." Cal sat in a chair, thinking of the hologram in the bedroom, wondering if this policeman might be the same one who would have gone through Domingo's apartment. "Have a seat, Nikki," he said, trying to keep his voice casual.

She took a chair near him and gave him a sleepy smile, evidently for Dobson's benefit, but Cal could tell she was nervous too. He was almost glad. If she had been expecting this visit, the situation was even worse than he thought.

Cal listened to the policeman as he went through the rooms. He made soft noises as he pulled drawers out and opened the bathroom cabinet, but Cal worried most when he heard no sound. Finally the man sat down in a chair near Nikki and Cal.

"I'm sorry to have bothered you so early," the man said. "I've got more people to talk to, and it makes for a long day."

Cal wondered if the man was seeming slightly more friendly because he hadn't found anything, or because he was trying to lower their barriers before the final questions. Maybe it was neither. The policeman left as soon as he finished another entry on his terminal.

Cal exhaled deeply when the door was closed. "Thanks, Nikki. You were perfect."

"You were too perfect. I didn't know you could lie so well." Nikki's level gaze bored into him for an instant, and then she rose.

"Wait a minute. If you're thinking that because I lied to a policeman, I must be guilty—or that it means I must have been lying to you, you're wrong."

"Okay," she said, but it was too casual.

Cal started after her but changed his mind. What more could he say than he had last night? If she doubted his word, there really wasn't much he could do about it.

Frustrated, he cleaned up and put on a fresh set of clothes. He found a banana in the kitchen and ate it.

"I'm going back to Machu Picchu," he said at last. "But let

me leave one thought with you. I think there must be more to the policeman's story than he told us. If it were that simple, he would have been here earlier. I think someone told the police about me specifically. Someone who wants me out of the way. Go ahead and tell me I'm imagining things.''

Nikki said nothing.

As Cal took one last look at her before he left, he realized that she probably hadn't slept any better than he had. ''Nikki—thanks for supporting me just now. Regardless of what you think, I appreciate what you did.''

''Where are you going?'' she asked as he opened the door. She seemed to have softened a bit.

Cal thought for a moment before replying. ''Maybe I feel a little religious. Going to church might help.''

On the way to the tubeway Vincent checked the public service data bank for information on the Presodist church in Machu Picchu. There were services every morning, afternoon, and evening.

The tube station was empty. Cal let one car go past on its way to Machu Picchu before he pressed the panel to indicate he wanted the next car to stop for him.

''Why did you skip one?'' Vincent asked.

''No good reason. As I was walking here, it just occurred to me how easy it would be for someone with a small telescope on one of the other continents to watch me walk from home to here. I'm not sure I want to see my friend from yesterday again.''

''Unless you want to follow him.''

Cal hesitated. ''Vincent, am I always this stupid in the mornings?''

''I really couldn't say when you hit your peak.''

Cal reached the church shortly before a service was scheduled to begin. The building was larger than he had expected from the hologram. The starburst out front glittered brightly in the sunlight. Whether it was a regular church ornament or a throwback to the original Machu Picchu, he couldn't say. He worried for a moment that he might not be suitably dressed, but after he saw three people in heavy-fabric work clothes enter, he followed them in. He got no feeling of being here before, only the memory of the hologram.

Signs inside made it easy to find the sanctuary. Cal wouldn't have been too surprised if the ushers at the door had recognized him, but they gave no sign. The pews were already half full, and the hushed sounds of whispering and people fidgeting and settling came diffusely from all directions.

Cal picked a seat near the rear, only then letting his gaze wander. The ceiling hologram was exquisite. The exterior of the church had been single-level, like all the other buildings, but to the eye the sanctuary had an arched ceiling that went up and up and up. Apparent stained-glass windows were enormous. The builders had even dealt with acoustic realism, because when Cal listened carefully, he could hear echoes and reverberations that had to be the deliberate result of using electronics with microphones, speakers, and delays.

Cal watched the other churchgoers as they chose seats. He saw no one he recognized until the church was almost two-thirds full. Paulo Frall. The proprietor at Forget-Me-Now. Frall was dressed in a conservative blue suit, moving to the center of the room before sitting down, apparently without noticing Cal. So there was a stronger link to the church. Cal finally gave up speculating when the service was about to begin.

In a small rack on the back on the pew ahead of Cal's there were hand-size terminals decorated to look like old hymnals, except for the screen and thumbprint square inset in the front cover. The screen indicated that the hymnal was set on manual. Cal picked his up and touched the AUTOMATIC choice. Information for visitors replaced the previous screen contents. Cal declined the offer of contact.

Moments later the service began, and Cal followed the text on the hymnal. Only after singing several hymns did he realize there wasn't a priest or minister, or whatever the Presodists called their equivalent, in sight. The scripture readings came from a disembodied voice, as though God Himself were on the staff and enjoyed responsive reading. Finally it was time for the sermon. A gracefully aging woman in a deep-blue robe appeared behind the pulpit, her gray hair confined in a bun. Her sermon was calm, her voice rising only a time or two. She never mentioned Sodom and Gomorrah.

It was not until she finished speaking that Cal realized that the large hologram behind her, depicting Christ lying dead on top of a marble slab, was actually an ultra-slow. Now Christ's eyes were open, and there were wrinkles in his brow not visible earlier.

The woman, identified in the hymnal as Pastor Welden, began what had to be the precursors of the collection. Jesus's hand slipped to the edge of the slab.

The hymnal screen displayed the church's version of what contributions were typical, depending on one's income, family size, and other factors. Cal inserted his bank stick in the hymnal and donated a small amount. As he watched the screen, it began to register statistics on the contributions. Cal's donation was about the lowest. The highest was nearly five percent of the total, which was more than Cal made in several months.

The larger-than-life Jesus had swung his sandaled feet over the side of the slab. As the last chorus filled the room with voices in song, Jesus finally reached his feet. Cal almost expected him to smile and wave.

Cal stood and waited as the front rows and Paulo Frall exited before he turned to leave with the rest of the throng. After a brief double take, he continued out, passing through an overpowering motion hologram of the Red Sea being parted. He felt a nonsensical urge to hurry and not step in the puddles. Outside, the corridor seemed drab in comparison.

The pastor was shaking hands with exiting congregation members. "You're new here," she said when Cal reached her.

"Yes, I am," Cal said. "Could you tell me if you have any midnight services?"

The woman shook her head. "Sorry. Just Christmas and Easter. Normally nineteen hundred is the latest."

Cal thanked her and left, faintly surprised to notice that she was wearing makeup and sandals. Paulo Frall was gone.

"Well, brother, are you saved?" Vincent asked when they were well away from the church.

"Maybe, maybe not. At least I learned something."

"What? That you know the head clerk of doxology works?"

"Nope. That I haven't been inside before. I'd remember, believe me. Let's try a change of course. Is there a public office for tracing financial transactions or getting help with communications problems?"

There was. It was a lackluster facility after the Presodist church, but it seemed functional and not too busy. In a few minutes he had described his request to the blemished young man behind the counter.

"Let me make sure I've got this right," the man said,

scratching his nose. "You've made payments to someone anonymously, and you want to trace the payments to find out who you paid. You don't know who it is."

"That's essentially it," Cal said.

At least the man didn't laugh at him or press him with questions. "It's possible. You have to waive your privacy rights temporarily, but we can do it."

"Let's go."

The clerk typed a few commands, and an official-looking document came up on the screen inset in the countertop.

Cal read it quickly and thumbprinted it.

"Okay," the clerk said, recording the last two bank transaction numbers. "The tracer should be finished in a few days. Check back with us then."

"A few days? I need to know soon."

The clerk raised his eyebrows. "Sorry. That's how long it takes. Official channels run deep."

"Can you at least call me as soon as it comes in?"

Automatic call-back was an extra-cost service, so Cal paid for it. On his way out he noticed a still video on the wall, showing a small child on a toilet. The caption said, "No job is complete until the paperwork is finished."

Cal wandered aimlessly outside for a few minutes, unsure whether to put in an appearance at his office. He could easily be fired if he didn't start paying more attention to it, but right at the moment he wasn't as worried about that as maybe he should have been. The only feelings he could summon about his boss, Tom Horvath, seemed to be good ones. Tom wouldn't fire him. He hoped.

More important than work was finding out who Domingo was. There had to be more information on him than Cal had been able to find in the man's apartment. Cal thought of another possible path to learn more and considered taking a risk.

At the news station he asked for Michelle Garney. A secretary told him he could wait in her office. She should be back in a few minutes. He ignored the request for his name.

Michelle had a modest desk with three empty cups waiting to be recycled. Green plants lined the windowsill where a small mirror reflected exactly the right amount of light to make them thrive. Cal was staring at a hologram of the *Vittoria* on the wall when Michelle came in.

"Oh, it's *you*," she said, sounding surprised yet friendly. "I didn't think you'd come back. How's Nikki?"

Cal sat up straight, feeling suddenly wary. He had been about to say "I didn't either," but instead said "You *are* good at your job. How did you do it?"

Michelle grinned and elaborately gestured, indicating nothing up either sleeve. Then she patted her desk terminal.

"Surely you can be more specific than that," he said.

"I'm good with faces." She tapped a few keys and motioned for him to look at her desk screen.

Side by side were two color images. One was Cal, taken within the last couple of years. The other was a strangely characterless, smooth-skinned, vacant-stared *representation*. A column of parameters indicated everything from eye color and earlobe shape to contour of cheeks.

"I'll be damned," Cal said. "How long did it take you?"

"Half an hour. There aren't very many more than a million people. I would have started with just 'Cals,' but I didn't know if you told me the truth. Fifty-two percent of the population are male. Under fifteen percent of them are in their thirties. Add brown hair, brown eyes, nice bones, height one-eighty centimeters, and you're already down to about a thousand. Start adding ear shape, nose type—well, I'm sure you understand."

"The half hour is what I don't understand. You must be a busy lady without taking up your time like that."

"I love a mystery," she said simply.

"What makes you think there's a mystery?"

"I think it was you who told me I'm good at my job," she said. "I'm also surprised that you didn't know about Faceup. Especially with your computer background."

"You *have* been busy."

"You were easy. You've been in the news a few times. Your picture makes me think the last year has been a rough one."

"I think you must be right."

"There you go again, being mysterious."

Cal was silent. He had come in with the idea of his anonymity protecting him while he solicited her help. The protection was gone, but he was impressed with her ability to make deductions. She obviously had a large information pool available, and she knew how to use it quickly. She could be a great ally, if only he could trust her.

But if he couldn't trust her, he was already at an overwhelming disadvantage.

"How much can I tell you in private?" Cal asked, arriving at a decision.

"As much as you want."

"You know what I mean."

"I can't make any guarantees. You'd better not tell me if it's illegal."

Cal studied her eyes for a long moment before he took a deep breath. "I paid Forget-Me-Now for their services the night Domingo died. When I woke up, I had blood on my clothes and Vital Twenty-Two in my pocket. But I don't think I'm guilty. If I find out I am, or if I find out what really happened, you'll be near the front of the line to be told."

"Whew."

"My sentiments exactly."

"Will there be any newspeople closer to the front?"

"No. You have my word."

"You want something in return," she said.

"Information. You seem to have wider access than I do."

Michelle leaned back in her chair. "So the mystery gets deeper. Exactly what kind of information?"

"I want to know who Domingo really was. I'm not convinced he was a simple construction engineer. And I want to use your talents with Faceup. Someone tried to kill me yesterday morning. I'd like to find him and say hello."

"Cancel all my calls," she exclaimed. "You're serious, aren't you?"

"Maybe too serious." Cal caught her questioning look. "Nothing. That's a different problem."

"How about something to drink?" she asked.

As they went to the station cafeteria, Cal filled in more of the details, stopping whenever someone else came near. Cal was talking about Forget-Me-Now when he smelled an odor that scared him badly. Mint.

He backed away too fast, almost losing his balance. And then he realized where the odor came from. Michelle's tea.

"Do you have mint leaves in your tea?" he asked shakily.

Michelle was speechless, obviously confused. She nodded quickly.

"Let's go back to your office and I'll explain."

She nodded again, probably wondering if she had agreed to

help a maniac. "You must have a hell of an allergy," she said, trying to make a joke out of it.

On the way back Cal told her quietly why he had reacted that way.

"You had me really worried there for a minute," she said, holding the office door open for Cal. In the office Michelle sat at her desk and motioned Cal to come and stand behind her.

"Okay," she said. "Some of the parameters, age for example, won't show up on Faceup. They're just for the search once we're done. He was about twenty-five?"

"Right. This is going to be hard, though. I paid almost no attention to him."

"Maybe as we get a picture started that will help jog your memory. Hair?"

"Black. It hung over his forehead, cut all about the same length." Cal watched as the blank head-shaped form on the screen sprouted black hair. "A bit shorter. And I think it lay against his head more. Longer over the ears. That's it."

Michelle continued, explaining the choices as she went. Slowly the mannequin head looked more and more like the young man with a mustache.

"That's it," she said. "But I don't think it will let us narrow it down to fewer than maybe twenty-five to fifty people. Not unless you can remember more specifics."

"That's as good as I can do. Even looking at it now, I can't decide if it's him or not."

"Okay." She tapped another few keys and drummed her fingers on the desktop. "This will probably take an hour or two at least, depending on priorities of whatever else is happening today. We'll get pictures of every match unless they find over a hundred. What next?"

"Domingo. Can you look him up in your data base? See what his history is?"

She tapped at the keyboard for another moment. When she stopped, on the screen was a short summary of Gabriel Domingo's vital statistics. Born twenty-eight years ago, on Earth. Died two days ago. Unmarried, no living relatives. There was a brief description of his employment history: eight years in construction. There was almost no other information. It seemed to Cal almost obscene that there was so little record of the dead man.

"I see what you mean," Michelle said. "I've hardly ever seen one this short. Usually children have longer summaries."

"How about Leroy Krantz," Cal asked.

Leroy's summary was significantly longer than Domingo's, but held no obvious clues. He was one half of a two-person company specializing in communications systems. The other half was a man named David Ledbetter. They had been in business almost six years with no complaints.

"Could we look at someone else, as long as we're here?" Cal asked.

"By all means." She looked up over her shoulder, and the excitement was unmistakeable. "Who?"

"Russ Tolbor."

This time when she looked up, it was a slow, deliberate motion. Then she swung back to the keyboard without a word and typed some more.

Tolbor's file was long. Born on Earth, in London, forty-one years ago. The file traced the highlights of a man who had to be brilliant and motivated. He had received a loan from his parents before college, and while he was one of the youngest ever graduates from the Astronautics Academy, the licensing fees from the patents his loan had paid for covered all his expenses.

He hadn't shown much interest in the church until after his mission to Jupiter. Tolbor had lost a brother and sister on Earth, as well as his parents. Other details matched what Vincent had already told him. The wealth of praise shook Cal's feeling that the man might somehow be doing something he shouldn't.

"Care to explain?" Michelle asked.

"Maybe it's nothing. But I still have the impression that this involves him. It could be only peripherally, but it seems he's a factor. Can you get reports on institutions as well as individuals?"

"Try me."

"Let's see what you have on the Presodist church."

"You must be joking."

"I'm deadly serious."

The summary told Cal nothing he could see was valuable. Dry details included dates of the most recent changes in policies, and short descriptions. Church officers were listed, but none of the names were familiar.

"I think it's time you told me some more," Michelle said accusingly.

"I'm afraid it'll all seem too bizarre. And I don't *know* anything. It's all guesses."

"Give. I'll worry later about whether I believe it."

"This is only a faint possibility. I don't have a shred of real data that supports it—"

"Okay. Okay. Disclaimers accepted."

"Well, there's a chance, a tiny one, that the disaster on Earth two years ago wasn't an accident. It could have been the result of someone's badly warped idea of making life imitate the Bible." Cal gave her a few details about the Sodom and Gomorrah references.

Michelle said nothing when he was finished. She just got up from her chair and walked to the window, where she could watch the Earth in its silent journey.

"I could easily be wrong about this," Cal said. "There are lots of other explanations I could invent to fit what I've learned so far."

"What else are you holding back?" Michelle asked finally, her cheerfulness gone.

Cal knew that nothing less than complete honesty could keep Michelle helping. "My wristcomp tells me that the night Domingo was murdered, I said something that implies I might be guilty of his murder." He waited until Michelle turned back to face him. "But I think there must be more to the situation that I don't know yet. I'm not a murderer. I think my wife believes that."

"I think I believe it too," Michelle said slowly. "All right. Whatever help you need, I'll give. I want the story first, but that's no longer my main reason for helping. But I swear to God, if you're lying to me, I'll roast you. You'll wish you were on Earth."

Cal didn't ask her who she had lost on Earth. He said, "I won't conceal anything from you. But I need your commitment not to go to the police if you find out something that incriminates me. If I've done something wrong, I'll give myself up and let you have the story, but I've *got* to have time to find out exactly what's happened."

She nodded. "Let me do some more checking on Domingo and get those pictures of people who might have sat next to you on the tubeway. I'll call you when I get anything."

"Michelle, I appreciate this."

"Just don't be lying to me."

"I'm not."

"I knew you were in trouble when you came in here yesterday," she said. "I'm not sure whether or not to be happy that my instincts are still working."

"Be thankful. We'll probably need them again."

Chapter ten
Hardware

MICHELLE was still in a sober mood when Cal left the news station. He couldn't tell how good a judge of character he had been before, but he felt Michelle was honest.

He had been intending to go to work, at least briefly, but along the way he noticed a store named Big Ears. It sold items that looked quite useful in his current search for information.

Inside the showroom was a wide variety of elaborate electronic products, but Cal approached the display showing the item that had caught his eye from the window. He was reading the advertising literature when a plump, middle-aged salesman came up.

"Those are the best pickups you can buy without a license," the salesman said, handling a tiny microphone-transmitter combination. It was minuscule in his pudgy palm.

"What's the range?"

"Half a kilometer, line of sight. Ten to twenty percent of that through walls."

It might be revealing to be able to hear what was going on in Tolbor's apartment, or in the meeting room at Galentine's. "What if I need a longer range?"

"Simple. You buy one of these—a repeater. It can be set to call directly in to your wristcomp."

"These things are rather expensive. What about a lease plan?"

"Sorry. They have a way of getting damaged." The man gave Cal a sidelong glance.

"I see what you mean." Cal asked several more questions

and in the end bought three pairs of listeners. He had been about to buy a device that would eliminate periods of no noise before he realized that Vincent could probably do that and five other jobs concurrently.

"What about door locks?" Cal asked finally. "My door at home has been acting up. Do you have anything that might help?"

The salesman gave Cal a knowing grin. "If you don't mind a temporary loss of privacy, you can use one of our high-tech specials." The man led Cal to a nearby shelf and handed him a small package.

Cal examined the unit, trying to determine what it did. It consisted of a small flat pad with what looked like pressure adhesive and a short lever on a spring.

"It works like this," the man said, demonstrating. He pulled the lever back and held the base near a door mockup. As the door slid open, the lever sprang into the doorway. As the door closed, the lever blocked the last few millimeters of travel. "Once the lever has flipped, the latch can't properly seat. After you get your door fixed, you can remove it. And in the meantime, it's small enough that it's not likely to tip off your visitors that your door isn't really locked."

Cal purchased one of the lever devices. He was tempted to buy a couple, just in case, but then he couldn't have maintained the facade that it was for *his* door, even though he was sure the salesman wouldn't care. He paid a slight extra fee for a bag without advertising on it and left.

"No messages yet, Vincent?" he asked once he was outside.

"Negative. I'll tell you if anyone calls. What are you going to do with all the stuff you bought?"

"I don't know about all of it, but right now I've got this silly urge to see what kind of place *Vittoria*'s new commander lives in. You understand me?"

Tolbor's apartment was less than half a kilometer from where Domingo had lived. The only outward sign that Tolbor's apartment was more expensive was that the doors along the hallway were almost twice as far apart as they had been in Domingo's building. Tolbor's name was engraved on a metal plate on his door.

As Cal slowed for a close examination, a man came out of an apartment down the hall. Cal resumed his pace, feigning nonchalance. Once the other man had left the building, Cal backtracked. Curious, he touched his thumb against the white square, but nothing happened.

Cal quickly positioned his new purchase in the lower corner of the door and pressed. It stuck. A sideways push met strong resistance. Satisfied, Cal straightened up, thinking about how awkward it would have been if Tolbor had opened the door while Cal was kneeling in front. But he should be at work at this hour.

From a standing position Cal could barely detect the device, and *he* knew it was there. Perfect.

Cal couldn't keep postponing going to the *Vittoria* office. He skipped lunch to conserve time. The hallway in his building was noisier than the last time. Maybe last-minute preparations were running late.

He glanced in at Leroy Krantz, thinking back to the test. Leroy was apparently engrossed in the contents of his desk screen and didn't even seem to notice Cal. It was just as well.

At his own desk Cal sat down and started to see what incoming messages had been sent to his office. But his keyboard failed to respond to his thumb.

"Vincent," Cal said, starting to worry that someone might have found a way to lock him out of his desk computer. "My keyboard's dead. Any suggestions?"

"I can call maintenance. This is funny. Usually some small component fails and the diagnostics find it, report it, and you never even hear about it. It's odd to see one completely off."

"Wait a minute," Cal said. "You gave me an idea." He stood and leaned forward, trying to see behind the desk. "I see it. The cord just fell out of the wall. Maybe the cleaning staff moved the desk out too far."

Cal shoved on the edge of the desk, but it was far too heavy to move easily. There was just enough room to squeeze between the metal desk and the wall, and he started to do so before a sudden observation stopped him abruptly.

From there he could see the power cord coiled behind the desk. It was a long cord. There wouldn't be much excuse for a cleaning crew to have pulled out the plug. Cal felt a tickling at the back of his neck, and he thought about his tubeway ride yesterday morning. Something felt decidedly wrong.

"Vincent, I've got another request."

"Ready."

"Take a look back here and turn on your magnification."
Cal moved Vincent to get a clear view.

"That's a pretty dull picture." But Vincent's screen now
displayed a section of the desk and the wall, including the electrical outlet. "What are you looking for?"

"Maybe nothing. Blow up the wall socket."

The image grew slowly until Cal said, "Hold it there." Cal
moved Vincent slightly, and the angle changed. He moved
Vincent a bit more, and a shadow he hadn't seen before was
visible. "Blow it up a little more. Fine." Cal drew in his
breath. "Do you see what I see?"

"The tape?"

"Right." A short piece of tape, the same color as the wall,
ran from just below the outlet down to the floor. Nothing was
visible on the floor, but as Cal panned the view along the
baseboard, farther away from the outlet, he saw a faint glint.
"Blow up the bright point there."

The bright area was about a centimeter long. It ran from the
baseboard out from the wall, where it was covered by another
piece of tape. At the desk leg there was another small portion
of shiny narrow surface visible.

"Focus on the plug," Cal said, and on the screen was the
image of the end of the coiled cord and the plug. This time Cal
didn't need to enlarge the image. Looking like silver ornamen-
tation on the plug, circling the portion he would have to hold
when he put the plug back into the socket, lay what he was
now convinced was wire. Wire fastened to one of the power
connections.

Chilled, Cal closed the door to his office and sat in the
chair. "Who the hell am I playing with, Vincent? All I needed
to do was wedge myself between the desk and the wall, grab
hold of the plug, insert it in the socket, and I wouldn't be a
worry to anyone."

"I don't have any more clues than you do. But maybe we
should take separate vacations this year."

"They shouldn't have done this," Cal said, unhearing. "Or
they should have made it more foolproof. Given enough time,
I might have been able to convince myself that the incident on
the tubeway was a genuine medical rarity. But not this."

Anger displacing the fear, Cal pulled violently at the desk.
At first it moved only a centimeter, but on the second force-
ful try it moved almost enough. A final shove gave it a good

safety margin. Wondering if somehow a second booby trap were lying in wait, Cal tried not to touch anything more than necessary.

The wire unwrapped easily. Once it was dangling, a few twists took it all the way off the plug. The other wire came free from the wall socket with the aid of a nonconducting ruler he found in his desk. Cal pulled up the length of wire running to the desk and threw the wire and tape into the trash.

After one last check he tentatively pushed the plug into the wall socket. An all but inaudible whine sprang up from inside the desk. Satisfied the sound was normal, Cal pushed the desk back into place.

Everything seemed okay at the keyboard. There were no messages waiting. Cal sat before the desk a moment longer, trying to recall what his job required him to be doing, but it was useless. Finally he picked up the shopping bag and selected one of the listening devices.

Making sure no one outside his window was looking in, he ran his fingers around the window frame. The top seemed ideally suited and out of sight. He placed the pickup down softly so the adhesive wouldn't set.

"You're bugging your own office?" Vincent asked.

"Bugging?"

"Monitoring."

"Right. After this little incident, I'd like to know when anyone else comes in here. Bugging?"

"The early models of microphones and transmitters had sections of wire sticking out. Maybe for antennae. They looked almost like insects. You've got a call coming in. Michelle Garney."

"Thanks. Answer it." An instant later there was a new sound, as though Cal's wrist were next to a small opening between his office and a room next door. He could hear light breathing and, much more faintly, an assorted ambience that came from the tiny reflected sounds in the other room. "Hello," he said.

"Your pictures are ready," Michelle said.

"Terrific. I'll be over shortly. You'll be there for a while?"

"No doubt about it."

Cal thanked her and prepared to leave, wondering briefly what his boss must be thinking of Cal's recent attendance record. He'd get his boss's reaction at the same time he gave him an excuse for his recent behavior.

Tom Horvath's office was in the Daedalus building, so Cal used the desk screen and turned on the video.

"Hello, Cal," the smiling stranger said. "I haven't seen much of you lately." The man gave no outward sign of being surprised that Cal was alive. He seemed genuinely happy that Cal had called. Tom looked about five years older than Cal. His dark curly hair was cut short and neat, with long sideburns. Bushy eyebrows framed warm eyes.

"Well, I'm afraid you won't see too much more of me today, either. I'm not feeling very well, so I'm going to take the rest of the day off."

"Thanks for letting me know. I hope you feel better. And don't worry about the office. All the reports I get say the system is hanging together perfectly. You really did your homework on this one too. Say hi to Nikki. Oh, before I forget. I appreciate the cutting you left. I'll be more careful this time. And I'll bring you back a new plant to say thanks."

Cal thanked him in return and hung up, left with the strong impression that Tom was exactly what he had seemed to be: a concerned ally. Cal felt guilty telling the man he was sick, but in truth he didn't feel too well. Like finding part of a worm in an apple, learning about a foiled murder attempt was only half good news.

He had only one more thing to do before he left. He took a repeater from his shopping bag and stuck it to the back of the desk. In a normal speaking voice, he said, "Vincent, can you hear me from the transmitter?"

"Loud and clear."

Cal picked up his shopping bag. It was time to go to Galentine's.

On the way down the hall, following an impulse, he said "Hi" to Leroy. Leroy seemed calm as he returned the greeting, but he didn't invite Cal in or try to start a conversation. Maybe it wasn't the behavior of a murderer, but it did seem cold after the invitation earlier. It could be as simple as the fact that now the test was over, Leroy had no need to coddle someone who had the authority to demand a retest if all wasn't right.

Galentine's was busier than Cal had guessed it would be in mid-afternoon, but it was calmer than it had been last night.

Cal bought another drink he didn't need from a different bartender, one who was as reticent as his evening counterpart.

The private booth Tolbor had occupied was fortunately empty, so Cal casually wandered in and sat. After a few minutes with no interruptions, he impatiently pulled another transmitter from his shopping bag and pushed it against the bottom of the table, where it stuck tightly.

Minutes later the repeater lay concealed in the men's room, and Cal was on his way to the news center.

Michelle was in her office when Cal arrived. She closed the door behind him. "I've got forty-two possibilities." She motioned him toward the desk screen.

Cal sat down at the desk and looked at the first image. The man matched the general description, but without knowing exactly why, Cal was sure he wasn't the man he was looking for.

"You okay?" Michelle asked.

"Huh?"

"Are you all right? You seem jittery. When you came in, you looked behind you like there might be someone following you."

"Maybe I *am* jittery. I found a lethal booby trap in my office an hour ago." Cal explained about the rewiring.

"Now that I think about it," he continued, "I guess there's something else that's bothering me now. Maybe I didn't really think about it until I found the wire, but I can't ignore it any longer."

"And what's that?"

"Someone is trying to kill me. By asking you to help, I'm exposing you to the same risk. I'll look at the pictures you got and take some names. I really do appreciate what you've done so far, Michelle, and I'll still—"

"Shut up!"

The loudness of Michelle's outburst seemed to startle her as much as it did Cal. She took a couple of deep breaths in an obvious effort to calm down, and said, with what had to be admirable restraint, "That's the very last time I want to hear you talk like that. I volunteered to help, knowing what had already happened. This is more important than some damned story. So I'm in it, and I'll *stay* in it. Is that perfectly clear?"

Cal studied her for a moment, seeing that her breath still came heavily. "Like I was saying," he resumed patiently, noticing her eyes begin to narrow. "I'd really like to get on with looking at these pictures if you'll let me."

Michelle grinned broadly, with obvious relief. "Okay. Hit this button when you're ready for the next one."

Cal reached to do so, then paused. "Michelle, I'll try not to overdo this, but thanks."

She simply nodded.

The next two faces were discards also, but Cal paused at the one after them. "I don't know," he said. "The first ones I could almost certainly say weren't the guy, but this one I just don't know about."

"Use *this* button here. We'll come back to anyone who's questionable."

The balance of the images fit in the same two categories: rejects and don't knows. No picture jumped out at him as being *the* person. "So what do we have?" he asked finally.

Michelle tapped a few keys before she said, "You identified five candidates." She touched a few more keys, and the screen displayed the five choices, all reduced in size to fit.

"If only I had paid more attention." Cal looked at the images. "It could be any one of them or none of them. I just can't tell."

"Let's look at their files. Maybe if one has been in the hospital for two years, we can rule him out."

They were able to eliminate two of the five. One was halfway through with a six-month stint on board an exploratory spacecraft. The other was on Luna.

"Let me transfer the information on the other three to my wristcomp," Cal said. "Listen up, Vincent."

"I'm warning you," Vincent said. "I've got so much information piling up in here, I'm going to explode soon."

Michelle raised an eyebrow.

"Call it a personality quirk," Cal said.

"Yours or its?" she asked.

"If he gets too wild, I can always reprogram him," Cal said, not answering her question.

"You and what other ten guys?" Vincent asked.

"Relax," Cal said. "You're ready to send?" He looked at Michelle.

She suppressed a smile and touched more keys on her console.

"Okay," Vincent said. "They're all here."

"I guess that does it for now."

"You're not getting out that easily," Michelle said, leaning forward in her chair. "You heard what I said earlier. That extends to just going away with no new requests for information."

"Okay. You're still looking for data on Domingo?"

"Right."

"Is there any more information available on these three guys than what I already have?"

"I can try to find out if any of them have had run-ins with the police."

"Great. That should do it." He looked at Michelle, who now sat tapping her fingernails on the desk, looking sternly at him. "Well, there is one more little thing. I've put a pickup in the bar where Tolbor and a couple of friends usually meet. And while they're there, I plan to put another in Tolbor's apartment."

"My, you *are* full of surprises. How big are they?"

Cal showed her the remaining pair from his bag.

"That one is all you've got left? Give me the model number."

"Why?"

"I'll be in Tolbor's office tomorrow. He's big news. *Vittoria* leaves in three days now."

"So you're—" Cal began.

"Exactly."

"I don't suppose I could—"

"Absolutely not."

Cal gave her the model number. "I wonder if my wife is going to be this stubborn."

"You mean about wanting to help?"

"Right."

"Why shouldn't she be?"

"Well, for one thing, she wants a divorce."

Michelle was silent for a moment. "I suppose you just found that out too?"

"Right again. I thought bad things were supposed to be limited to threes."

"I take it you don't want a divorce." Michelle seemed unhappy, but Cal couldn't tell if it was because she empathized with Cal, or if she saw in him more than just a friend.

"It's hard to explain rationally, since I have only a few days of current memories to go on, but I love her. I'm not saying it's a product of these last three days. The blanking didn't wipe feelings so much as actual events.''

"You don't have to tell her everything. That way she can make her mind up without feeling forced into helping."

"That's tempting. But I think that's part of the problem. Whatever I've been doing lately has caused me to keep a lot of information bottled up. I think maybe that's one reason why the barriers started. Whatever I do now, I have to be open with her."

"Even if the truth drives her away?"

"It's a risk I have to take. Thanks again for your help, Michelle." Cal rose to leave.

"Where are you going now?"

"Two of these guys live in Machu Picchu. I've got time enough to visit one of them before I go back to Tolbor's place."

"Maybe you should let me know before you do anything critical, so I can call the police if you disappear."

"Good idea. I'll give you a call."

When Cal glanced back on the way out, she was watching him, looking concerned.

The first man on Cal's list lived in the middle of the south edge of Machu Picchu. The houses thinned out as they rose to the green hillside where Cal had awakened. When Cal was within sight of his destination, a house that was almost all windows and with a deck out front, he called Michelle and gave her the name of the occupant.

"Vincent," Cal said. "Can you turn on your magnification and show me what you can see from here—in that house?" Cal turned Vincent so he had a clear view.

Vincent's screen showed nothing at first, but as he scanned the portions of the interior visible from where Cal stood, someone seated with his back to Cal showed in the image.

"I can't tell from this view," Cal said, and began to approach the house. He was still trying to think of the right excuse for knocking on someone's door when he got there.

There was just silence after his initial knock, but then the door slid open. In the doorway was a dark-haired man in his mid-twenties, in a wheelchair.

Cal suddenly felt tired. "Sorry to bother you," he said, "but my dog ran away. Have you seen one around? Miniature collie, big white spot to the left of her nose?''

The man in the wheelchair politely denied seeing such a dog, so Cal thanked him and left.

''Michelle?'' Cal said when his call to her connected. ''False alarm. He's in a wheelchair.''

''Maybe he thought you might check up?''

''Maybe the real guy would, but this wasn't him. I don't know exactly what features are different, but it's not the same guy.''

''Cal,'' Vincent interrupted. ''You wanted to know when there was activity on your bugs.''

''Bugs?'' Michelle said.

''The pickups. I'll tell you about it later. Vincent, would you record everything you hear? And in the meantime, why don't you let us hear the first couple of minutes?''

''You're going to have to call a collection outfit to get rid of all the excess data when you're finished, but okay. This is coming from Galentine's.''

The sounds of a conversation started from Vincent's speaker, interrupted once by a deep thudding sound. ''I shouldn't have put it on the table,'' Cal told himself, and began walking.

After a moment Cal was able to identify one voice as Tolbor's. That was fortunate. He had been worried that they might have picked another booth, or not gone there tonight.

''I used to be able to sway you,'' said the voice Cal had identified as Tolbor's. ''Why won't you let me convince you to join us on the *Vittoria*? It's going to be an exciting time.''

''You used to know when to quit,'' an unidentified voice said, using a laugh to take the edge off the comment. ''I like it fine right here. Maybe I'm getting too sentimental, but I'm happy here. It's home now, and we've not been here all that long.''

A third voice made a murmur of assent.

''Vincent, turn it off for now,'' Cal said.

''They didn't sound exactly like coconspirators,'' Michelle observed.

''I'd have to agree. Maybe they aren't. In any event, I've got to get to Tolbor's before they finish.''

''Watch yourself,'' she said.

After Michelle hung up, Cal said, ''Vincent, would you keep monitoring their conversation? Tell me if they mention

Sodom and Gomorrah or anything you feel ties into things that don't sound quite legal.''

"You got it."

The conversation at Galentine's was still underway when Cal reached Tolbor's building. His apartment door looked just the way Cal had left it. But this time when Cal tried to slide it sideways with pressure from his fingertips, it moved with little effort. Cal went inside quickly and slid the door shut.

The interior was luxurious. There was real wood furniture, an expensive sound system along with a color holo recorder, and what looked like real glass tabletops.

"They're still talking, right, Vincent?" Cal asked, looking around for a good place to hide the pickup.

"No change."

Tolbor's desk computer was next to a curtained window. Surely that would be the most likely location of any conversations that would interest Cal. Remembering the extraneous noises that came from having the transmitter at Galentine's under the table, Cal placed this one under the molding that ran around the window and pressed it into place.

The repeater he placed on the rear side of one of the desk legs.

"Okay, Vincent. Listen to this one for just a minute. Testing, one, two, three, four."

"Perfect."

Cal started for the door, but changed his mind and halted. He made a token attempt to access Tolbor's computer, which didn't respond to Cal's thumb. A quick tour of the man's apartment told Cal that Tolbor was extremely fastidious. Not one item seemed to be out of its place.

The apartment also seemed to contain fewer belongings than Cal had expected, until he realized that within a few days the *Vittoria* would be leaving, with Tolbor on it. Probably the rest of his things were already on board in other quarters.

Tolbor's wall held only two pictures. Side by side hung the Earth and Daedalus. Cal was surprised to find no pictures of people and decided that if Tolbor had any, they must already be aboard the *Vittoria*.

In Tolbor's desk drawer lay a few supplies in orderly bins, but a page of paper torn from a small notebook caught Cal's attention. He picked it up, trying to avoid leaving fingerprints.

The note was not at all what he had expected.

"Maybe I'm not on the right track, Vincent," he said.

"Because of the note?"

"Right. It's a list of names, and I'm on it. But it doesn't look like an execution order. It's a list of people to receive commendations for getting the *Vittoria* operational."

"Congratulations."

Cal began a search of Tolbor's bedroom, but still had found nothing of interest when a chime sounded. His heart accelerated. He frantically looked for a hiding spot.

———— Chapter eleven ————
Homicide

CAL held his breath, seeing no good place to hide. The chime sounded again, and he realized that it was the phone, not the door. It rang six more times, echoing in Tolbor's apartment, before the caller gave up. So no one would be waiting outside for Tolbor to return.

Just as Cal began to relax, Vincent warned him that the conversation at Galentine's was breaking up.

He was two blocks away from Tolbor's apartment before he asked Vincent what else they had talked about in the bar.

"Nothing that sounded suspicious. They never mentioned murder or Sodom and Gomorrah. I can play it back for you or print a transcript once we get back."

"When we get back is soon enough."

There were lights on in his house when he arrived. Nikki was sitting at the table in the kitchen when Cal entered the house.

"Hi," he said softly.

"Hi." Nikki said nothing more, but watched Cal as he approached.

He remembered then how quiet she had been when they first met. All he knew for the first week he was acquainted with her was that she worked at Taber Clinic. Only later, when she finally opened up, had he found out she was an M.D. He felt their communications had been good then, until whatever pressures that existed began to exact their prices.

Cal opened two cabinets before he found a glass and poured some water into it. He suddenly realized how tired he was.

"Habits are funny things," Nikki said at last. "I was worried about you today, especially when it started getting late and you hadn't called.''

Cal decided to wait before he mentioned the faulty wiring in his office. "I don't have many conscious habits yet. Maybe they'll come back eventually. Maybe not. I didn't know whether I *should* call. I made you angry this morning. I thought about calling but figured I might just do it all over again."

"Just don't try to tell me what to do. I've got to make my own decisions, without you complicating things."

"Does that extend to talking about my feelings for you? Or is that manipulative?"

"I can't believe you have feelings."

"You mean because I've lost some memories, or because I'm unfeeling?" Cal looked into Nikki's eyes and saw they were bloodshot.

"I can't imagine you could feel for me without remembering our wedding, Lynn's birth, the trip to Luna."

"I remember Lynn's death—and some of the time we took off together that first year."

Nikki cocked her head.

"It's still just bits and pieces. Enough to know that losing you will be just as bad as losing Lynn."

"Don't you dare start on me with guilt when you don't even—"

"Okay. Okay." Cal held up his hand. "I won't talk about it."

Nikki simmered for a moment, but then seemed to calm down. "I found out a little about Gabriel Domingo today. But you're not going to like it."

"You what? How?" Cal sat up straight.

"I looked up his medical record and started asking questions." Nikki looked slightly happier now that she was on a different topic. "Treska Palmer was his doctor. She said he didn't seem to be a regular construction worker. She didn't think he was honest."

"Why does she say that?"

"For one thing, he hinted, not too subtly, that he'd rather pay for the services with some home entertainment items or kitchen appliances."

"I don't suppose he got bonuses where he worked."

"That wasn't the impression she got."

"How perceptive is she? Is she one of those doctors who never even looks the patient in the eye?"

"I believe her."

"So, what does that make me?" Cal asked. "A criminal too?"

"I don't know what it means. I said I'd try to help, and I'm telling you what I found out."

Cal took another drink of water and looked at Nikki closely. She claimed not to be swayed by the news on Domingo, but she seemed subdued, more distant than when they had last talked.

"Are you having second thoughts about helping?" he asked finally.

"Sure. But I'm not about to renege."

"That's what I thought. But I need to tell you—"

"You've got a call," Vincent said.

"Who is it?" Cal asked.

"Michelle Garney."

"Who?" Nikki said.

"I'll tell you in a minute. Put her on, Vincent."

"There's a news release you should know about," Michelle said as the call connected. "The police issued a bulletin, just a little while ago, saying that Domingo was using an assumed ID. He was wanted for numerous theft charges on Earth. They say they still don't know how he successfully altered the records."

"This is my night for bad news," Cal said. "I got the transmitter in Tolbor's apartment, but he must have another apartment on the *Vittoria*."

Cal noticed Nikki's head come up sharply, but didn't say anything to her. "Vincent, while I'm thinking about it, feed the transcripts to the desk unit."

"You think we're looking at the wrong person?" Michelle asked.

"I don't know. I think maybe we should keep on him. You can get into his office tomorrow?"

"I've got an interview scheduled already. Oh nine hundred."

"I'll call you after that unless anything comes up sooner."

Michelle acknowledged and hung up.

"Where were we?" Cal asked. "I think I was saying I had some more to tell you before you decide if you want to keep helping."

"Still the master of understatement," Nikki said, the surprise on her face still not completely faded.

"That was Michelle Garney," Cal said. "She's a reporter."

"I figured out that much after I asked. Tell me why she's helping. And about the transmitters. You sound like a regular spy."

"I went over to the news center yesterday and said a little too much about Domingo. I went back today, to ask another question. I hadn't given her my name, but Michelle had already figured out who I was. She seemed to be a good investigator, and she already knew an uncomfortable amount, so I told her the truth."

"What about the transmitters?"

"Oh, those. I bought them and installed one at Galentine's, one at Tolbor's apartment, and one in my office."

"You broke into Tolbor's apartment?"

"Well." Cal grinned. "I didn't actually break in." He explained about the door.

"Okay," she said. "I understand Galentine's and Tolbor's. What about the one at your office?"

Cal took a deep breath. "Ah, that one. That's another matter. Someone played junior electrician with my desk computer while I was out."

Nikki's face paled as Cal told her about the incident in his office. "And that's why you weren't sure if I'd keep helping?"

"Yes."

"What would you do in my place?"

"I'd help," Cal said instantly.

"It's not very flattering to think you would believe less of me."

"It's not a matter of what I thought. It's a matter of being honest with you."

"It's about time," Nikki said forcefully.

Cal's forehead tightened. "I said—"

"I'll help. I'm just sorry it wasn't obvious to you that I would."

"Thanks, Nikki. Just try to remember that very little is obvious to me lately. Want to look at some pictures?''

Nikki gave him a questioning look, appearing to soften slightly.

"Vincent, let's have the pictures I got from Michelle. I don't care what order."

"Here they are," Vincent said. "Sorted by birth date." The first picture came up on Vincent's screen. Cal's eyes were so tired, he invited Nikki to join him at the desk computer and had Vincent transmit the pictures there.

"These are possible candidates for the guy who gassed me yesterday. Tell me if you see anyone you recognize."

At the end Nikki shook her head and said, "They're all strangers to me. What are you going to do?"

"Visit at least two more of them—the two who seem the closest to being the right one."

"Two *more*?"

Cal explained about the first man, the one in the wheelchair.

"My friend at work is getting more nervous about those capsules," Nikki said after a moment of thought.

"How nervous? Can she wait a couple more days?"

"I don't know. You're still sure that it's important to find out what's been going on that soon? I mean, I know the sooner the better, but you—"

"Yes." Cal called up the transcript and briefly looked through two screens of innocuous conversations. He went back to the kitchen, aware again of having eaten less than he should have during the day. "You hungry?" he asked.

"Food is about the last thing on my mind."

Cal found a large cluster of green grapes in the refrigerator and ate them as he thought. He was tempted to read more into the fact that Nikki was still here than he could rationally justify. Probably she would be in her own apartment within another day or two, but, remembering her reaction the last time he had brought their relationship up, he remained silent.

Nikki was still sitting at the desk computer, apparently lost in her own thoughts. He watched her, feeling the loneliness grow stronger within him, until she looked back and caught him looking, and he turned away.

"What next?" she asked.

"I've got to have some sleep," he said, moving to the couch.

"Me too. But you'll sleep better in the bed."

"With you?" Cal asked, so tired that he grinned before he could control the reflex.

"Side by side, not top and bottom." Nikki's face was unreadable again, neither angry nor cheerful.

Cal agreed, feeling uncomfortable. What could be more natural than husband and wife sharing a bed? Except when the husband could hardly remember the wife.

They took turns in the bathroom, changing clothes. Cal found Nikki in a nightgown that gave him the impression of being conservative for her but was still revealing. He tried to keep his eyes off her, because he was still uncomfortable, and he wanted to make her more at ease. He found no pajamas among his clothes, so he went to bed in his shorts.

"Good night, Cal," came Nikki's voice in the darkness.

"Good night. And thanks."

Cal lay there, trying to be quite still so he wouldn't keep her awake while he thought. He found rational thought hard to come by, his thoughts returning to Nikki time and again. He hadn't been as sexually aware of Nikki earlier, but just now she had looked so damned appealing out of her business clothes.

After a long tug-of-war between Nikki and the day's puzzling revelations, he finally slipped into a fitful sleep and began to renew his acquaintance with Lynn.

At least once during the night Nikki woke him from a screaming nightmare as he was crying out for her. As he lay awake, he thought he could feel the bed vibrate almost imperceptibly. He thought Nikki might be crying softly, holding it all in, but he couldn't be sure, and he didn't know what to say. Guilt grew within him as he finally drifted back to sleep.

The next dream he remembered was not about Lynn. He was walking along a long, twisting corridor lined with doors. Each time he came to a door, he was compelled to enter it. Some of the doors were unlocked. Others he had to smash in with his feet, or cut with a laser. Once he used a small mechanism to tamper with a door lock. Each room was empty, but he had to search them all.

While he searched one of the rooms, he heard footsteps along the corridor outside. He pressed himself against the wall the door was cut into, and listened. The footsteps slowed, then halted nearby but, after a brief interval, resumed only to diminish in the distance, leaving fading echoes in their wake.

When he finally awoke, he lay with his eyes closed, trying to make sense of the dream. He gave up and opened his eyes to find that Nikki was watching him from her side of the bed.

"What were you thinking about?" she asked, her voice a little husky in the morning. Cal liked it.

"I was wondering if, assuming the Earth disaster was deliberate, I had thought that finding and punishing the person responsible would stop the nightmares of Lynn."

"If you'd been spending all your spare time trying to find that out, why wouldn't you have told me about it?"

"I don't know," Cal said. He had asked himself the same question. He looked back into Nikki's eyes, feeling less strange than he had the night before, sharing a bed with her. Despite all the hurt she had received, she still seemed to keep a reserve of compassion.

Nikki changed the subject. "I may be able to check on Tolbor's medical records today, but I'll have to be more cautious."

"I'd appreciate that, but I'm still wondering if I'm watching the wrong person. Vincent, have you heard any more since last night?"

Nikki wrinkled her nose as Cal asked the question, as if to say, "Do you have to use that here?"

"I heard several good jokes at Galentine's after Tolbor left. Have you heard the one about the agriculturalist's daughter and the spacer? She's—"

"Shut up, Vincent," Nikki said.

"Do I have to take this, Cal?"

"Afraid so. Back to Tolbor."

"Very well. Still no mention of Sodom and Gomorrah or murder. He was up early this morning, making noises in the kitchen, but as far as I could tell, he didn't talk to anyone or make any calls."

"Okay. Put the transcript up on the desk screen." Cal got up and put on a light robe. He glanced back at Nikki as she put on a robe over her nightgown. She looked even more desirable than she had the night before.

Cal and Nikki scrolled through the text on the screen. "I feel uneasy about all this," she said.

"So do I. I was surprised at how easy it was to get the equipment."

"I just had a nasty thought. Suppose someone has already planted a device like that here?"

"I worried about that too. But I checked the door closely and didn't see any signs of a gadget like the one I bought. I've showered and changed clothes since I got home, so if anything had been concealed on me, it should be gone by now. If I decide to tap Tolbor's *Vittoria* apartment, maybe I could see if that guy also sells detectors. Hell, Tolbor could have one. Maybe that's why all this looks so innocent."

They ate breakfast without saying much at all. When Cal had put on a light jacket and was ready to leave, he asked, "Are you going to be at the clinic today?" Actually he wanted to know if she was going to be out apartment-hunting, but couldn't ask.

"Most of the day."

"I'll see you tonight, then," he said, wanting to kiss her good-bye.

"Right." Nikki had withdrawn again, her features noncommittal.

He went shopping again that morning. When he emerged, he tightly gripped a small package, carrying it until he entered a public bathroom a few blocks away.

Inside he carefully unwrapped a small pistol. For just a moment it felt awkward nestled in his palm, but then abruptly a feeling of déjà vu came to him. Somehow he felt comfortable with the burnished shape. It no longer mattered that almost all the weight was in the grip, leaving only a lightweight pair of sights above the trigger. If the feeling of experience hadn't been so strong, he might have wanted to test the gun on something and watch the bright light as it burned.

The feeling that he knew how to use the weapon was both comforting and disquieting. How had he come by the knowledge? Maybe he and Domingo had been involved in something illegal after all.

Cal walked back out to the street, wondering suddenly if he had ever used a gun on a man. And, if he had, could he again?

A twenty-minute journey brought him near the address of the next man on his list. According to the information he had got from Michelle, Fargo Edmund lived in an apartment building just ahead. The building held smaller units than Domingo's or Tolbor's.

Not having thought of any more devious a plan than the one

he had used the night before, Cal walked down the corridor, looking for apartment number fourteen. He drew in a deep breath and stood before the door for just a moment before he rang the bell.

At first he thought there was no one home, but then he heard quick footsteps on the other side of the door. The door slid open, revealing another young, mustached man of the same general description. Cal faltered as he began his question about a dog. He was just starting to think Edmund might really be the man he was looking for when he hit Cal hard in the stomach.

Edmund caught him totally unprepared. The man had used not a fist but his extended fingers held together to form a narrow focus. The blow instantly knocked the wind from Cal. Even as he doubled over, he was aware of Edmund pushing past him and running away down the hall.

After a long, painful moment Cal was able to gasp in new air and get back on his feet. He ran as quickly as he could in the direction Edmund had fled. Outside he hesitated for a moment, trying to decide which way the man had run.

"He turned left," Vincent said. "I saw him through the door glass."

"Thanks." Cal began to run in the most likely direction, which also took him toward one of the busy shop areas. He reached the edge of the activity but saw no sign of Edmund.

Abruptly he thrust Vincent over his head. "See him anywhere?"

"He's at thirty degrees right, walking real fast. About a block ahead."

Cal began to run again. By the time he saw Edmund ahead, he had closed the distance to half a block. At that moment Edmund took a quick glance back.

He obviously realized that moving with the flow of people hadn't worked. He began to run.

Cal's breathing deepened as he raced after the fleeing man, but he felt better than he had just after he woke up three mornings ago. The aches had gradually diminished.

He weaved through a larger crowd in the next block, gaining slightly on Edmund, because the other broke holes in the crowd that took a little while to close back up. Cal noticed a few people as they stopped to watch Edmund and him rush past. No one tried to stop them.

Cal was gaining now. He was sure of it. He could see panic in Edmund's expression each time the man looked back. Was he panicked because one of his targets had found him, or did he have particular reason to fear Cal? Cal thought again about how natural the gun had felt.

Ahead of Edmund were a couple of bicyclists approaching, riding perhaps a meter in from the lip of the street. In the same instant that Edmund took his next backward look, Cal had an idea of how to slow him down still more, and as Edmund's head was still turned, Cal lifted his fist high in the air, as though signaling to a partner.

It worked better than Cal had hoped. Or worse. Edmund held his backward glance longer than his last, probably looking for a second runner, or puzzled by the gesture. That extra time took him even closer to the outer bicyclist. By the time Edmund looked back, he was right in the bicyclist's way.

The young boy on the bicycle seemed just as surprised as Edmund must have been, but he had slightly more warning. He turned slightly in from the short rock wall at the lip of the street.

Edmund careened into the boy and his bicycle, bouncing off him and toward the wall. For an instant Cal thought the man could regain his balance. He was wrong.

Edmund first flailed his arms, then grasped at the rock wall, which hit him at the knees. But it did no good. He was unable to recover his balance.

It was all over too quickly. Edmund's body was visible for only another second before he fell over the edge, out of sight.

Cal was astonished. He had never intended to cause Edmund to fall. He had wanted only to slow him down. He cut his run to a jog to avoid standing out and kept on moving, past the point where the man had fallen.

Cal took the next set of stairs down two at a time and doubled back. By the time he neared the terrace below, a couple of people were already kneeling by Edmund, trying to help him recover.

At least that's what Cal thought at first. But as he slowed and came closer still, he realized that Edmund seemed to be unconscious.

Cal waited several meters away, watching the woman kneeling next to the body make a call on her wristcomp. Even at that distance he heard her words clearly. "He's dead," she said.

Cal's stomach suddenly hurt as disbelief and guilt rose up within him. He had never intended this. Edmund must have been the man on the tubeway, but still, Cal hadn't ever thought about doing any more than turning him over to the police.

Cal tried not to panic and began moving again, through the small crowd that had begun to form. The farther away he got, the faster he moved, jogging and then finally running. He couldn't change what had happened, but he could at least try to learn something from the man's apartment before the police arrived.

He slowed again as he approached Edmund's building, not wanting to attract attention. The apartment door was still open, so Cal hurried inside and closed it.

The apartment was filthy. Encrusted food lined the sink. Used cups lay everywhere. Dirty handprints marred the wall surfaces around all the light switches.

It took Cal several minutes to find anything other than dirty clothes and discarded packing cartons with the name Fargo Edmund scrawled on them. In the bottom drawer of a file were items that would seem innocent enough to the police if they looked, but meant more to Cal.

Along with wire cutters and a screwdriver lay two rolls of tape. One was standard electrical black, and the other was tan. Some of Cal's feeling of guilt dissipated right than.

Cal continued his search. He didn't worry about fingerprints. The police shouldn't have any reason to think that Edmund's death was any more complex than the accident it was. In another drawer he found a long, narrow gas canister labeled LENDOMEN.

A moment later Cal whistled softly and said, "Well, reverse my charges."

On Edmund's desk, in the middle of a stack of unrelated papers, was a picture of Cal. It wasn't a very good picture. It had been taken outside. His face consumed most of the picture, but the background made him think it had been taken near his *Vittoria* office.

It had been taken within the last few days, but he couldn't tell when. The bruise over his eyebrow was there, and the scene was in daylight, but that's all he knew. Almost anyone could have taken a picture like that from a distance without him even noticing. Edmund himself could have taken it.

But Cal got the distinct feeling that it hadn't been Edmund who had taken the picture. It was more likely that someone else, perhaps Tolbor, had taken it to give to a hired hand who had no grudge of his own.

Cal idly wondered how much Edmund had been paid. And if he had been paid in advance. At least this should stop the attempts, for a while.

A closer look at the picture revealed a feature he hadn't noticed before. In the upper right of the picture there was a small defect in the image. Three closely spaced dots marred the otherwise acceptable photo. They could have been introduced by small imperfections in the digitizing element in the wristcomp of whoever took the picture, or in the reproduction process. There was no way to tell more just by looking.

"You've got a call," Vincent said, startling him. "Michelle."

Cal thought about ignoring it but decided he couldn't risk it.

"News flash," she said when Cal answered. "One of the guys on your list just died."

"I know. I'm in his apartment, entertaining myself. Can I call you back in just a few minutes?"

"What? Ah, sure."

Conscious of the time, Cal pocketed the picture and hurried to complete his search. Unfortunately, he found another half a worm.

It was a partly used container labeled CAUTION—EXPLOSIVES. The canister was underneath Edmund's bed. Cal couldn't tell how long it had been there. If only he knew if it had recently been used.

Two failed attempts certainly implied the possibility of a third, but had Edmund already known the second attempt was unsuccessful? It was possible that he set up numbers two and three without waiting, to maximize his chances.

Cal found nothing more in the balance of his search. He closed the door behind him and hurried away, seeing no signs of the police yet. From a bench eight blocks away he called Nikki.

"Do something for me, will you?" Cal asked. "Be careful. Very careful. I don't want you hurt." He explained about the possibility of explosives and told her about Edmund's accident.

"But can't you go to the police now?" she asked. "Maybe they could help."

"No, I don't think so."

"Why not? That's their business."

"I think they'd be much more interested in asking me about my purchases yesterday, or about breaking into people's apartments. For all I know, they might think I killed Edmund. The other problem is that the trail is cold. With Edmund dead, I don't have a link back to whoever hired him."

"I still think you should talk to them, but okay. You don't have any idea whether he's already put explosives somewhere or not?"

"No," Cal said, watching Nikki's worried face on Vincent's screen. "So be careful."

"You too."

Cal hung up. No one seemed to be taking an undue interest in his activity. "Vincent?"

"At your service. Today has sure turned out busy, hasn't it?"

"Have you picked up your ability of understatement from me? Never mind. I want you to save some of your video from around the time Edmund opened his apartment door until he fell. Let's say one frame every second. I may have to prove I didn't kill him if this gets much more complicated."

"I'll vouch for you."

"Would that help?" Cal asked.

"Only your feelings."

"Call Michelle, would you?"

When Michelle answered, she looked concerned. "I suppose I heard you right a few minutes ago?"

"I imagine so." Cal repeated most of what he had told Nikki, including a caution about watching for indications of explosives.

"Well," Michelle said, once she had heard his story. "I've been busy too. I had another interview with Russ Tolbor this morning."

"And?"

"And he now has some extra equipment in his office." Michelle was smiling again, apparently recovering from the jolt of the new information.

"Have you heard anything interesting yet?"

"Not yet. He seems to be more quiet than I had expected. He's talked to four people with quick status reports on the final preparations for *Vittoria*, but nothing else so far. I'll call you if I hear anything that seems important."

"Great. Before you go, can you tell me how to find Tolbor's *Vittoria* apartment?"

After a short search she gave him an address. Cal was saying good-bye when Vincent told him he had another message coming in.

"Let's have it."

"You're not going to like it, but here goes. It's text, without identification of the sender. It says, 'Stay home for a week, or you'll be dead.' " Only after the silence lengthened did Vincent add, "There wasn't even a complimentary close."

────── Chapter twelve ──────
Hypnosis

"STAY home for a week, or you'll be dead?" Cal repeated finally. "It all seems a bit superfluous after the gas on the tubeway and the rewiring at my desk."

"Maybe someone doesn't like you," Vincent said.

"Perhaps. Or maybe someone is panicking, and he or she doesn't know I had anything to do with Edmund's death."

"You didn't."

"I mean he doesn't know I saw Edmund, and doesn't know I searched his apartment. And if he believes I'm all that oblivious, then he figures I need it spelled out for me. But it still doesn't explain *why* I'm supposed to stay out of the way." Cal realized he had raised his voice, and promptly lowered it. No one near seemed to be paying him undue attention, but if someone were, he wouldn't want to advertise the fact.

"So, what are you going to do next?" Vincent asked.

"Well, I'm damn well not going to stay home for a week playing solitaire."

"You're right. There's bound to be a few two-handed games we could both enjoy."

"That's *not* what I meant. Vincent, I *have* to force my memories back faster. There has to be more I can do. Show me the directory of places advertising anything memory-related."

A directory came up on Vincent's screen. "Forward," Cal said a couple of times. "Wait."

"Which one are you looking at?"

"Hypnotism. Maybe that could help."

"Or maybe it could make it worse. Those people are a little like witches and warlocks, aren't they?"

"You're thinking of astrologers."

"Now *there's* a group that's taken abuse. Did you know that they accurately predicted the personality types of—"

"I don't have time for that now. Can you tell me who's closest of the people listed in this section?"

Vincent did so. A few minutes later Cal entered a modest-looking building that housed a few professionals and several paraprofessionals. A Dr. Thacken was almost at the end of the carpeted hall. Next to his door was a notice that said his doctorate was not a medical degree.

Dr. Thacken was his own receptionist. He was also immediately available.

Calmly Cal allowed himself to be ushered to the inner office. It was more somber than the waiting area, and Cal felt soothed almost immediately. He settled into a comfortable chair.

"Now, sir. How can I be of service?" Dr. Thacken asked. He was a man whose age was hard to gauge accurately. Initially he had seemed to be in his forties, but now Cal revised his estimate up into the fifties. The man's forehead sloped gradually up to wispy, swept-back hair that curled behind his ears. He had better eye contact than Cal was used to in medical doctors.

Cal began to feel he had done the right thing in going there. He introduced himself. "I'd like to prod some memories loose, if I can. I thought perhaps some regression might help."

"I hesitate to voice the thought, but have you been to Forget-Me-Now?"

"So I'm told."

A pained expression came over Thacken's face. "I'll do my best, sir. I just wish I could deal with the problem rather than the symptom."

"Meaning you don't like the erasure-parlor concept."

"About as well as an M.D. likes applying a bandage to a chest wound."

"Well, at the moment, I'm not one of their strongest supporters either."

"But you say you paid for their services?"

"I'm convinced I went through the process. I've yet to

satisfy myself that it was voluntary."

"My, this *is* interesting. You're suggesting that your session was against your will?"

"I don't know," Cal said. "I do know that I don't recall anything immediately after waking in the parlor."

"Very interesting. Why do you suppose that is?"

"The attendant attributed it to scrambling of my short-term memory. He said it was typical."

"He was ill-informed."

Cal looked at Thacken questioningly.

"The process has an effect on short-term memory," Thacken said. "But the effect lasts less than an hour. By law, Forget-Me-Now is required to keep you under observation until your retention is back to normal."

"If that's so—" Cal began.

"You have been lied to," Thacken finished. He waited a moment and then said, "You don't seem too surprised, I must say."

"Strangely enough, I don't *feel* too surprised. It seems there's a lot of that going around."

"Well, sir, I want to warn you up front that the likelihood of my being able to help you very much is not great. But I am intrigued. I would like to try. There aren't too many people I see who activate my curiosity this way."

"You've already helped me. I now know at least one person who has lied to me. Also, that helps me resist the urge to write off some of my recent experiences to paranoia."

Thacken smiled. "Paranoia perceived, at least in my limited experience, is seldom true paranoia. Would you like to begin?"

"I've got a question first. Are you bound to any particular code of ethics?"

"Regarding professional confidences?"

"Exactly."

"None except the ones I build. But I believe them to be adequate. You need not fear that possibility."

Cal believed him. He hadn't much choice anyway. "All right. I'm ready."

"I might be able to work better with a focus. Rather than simply trying to find a key to unlock *all* your memories, I could concentrate my efforts in a critical spot."

Cal thought for a moment. "How about starting with the

recent past? Three nights ago, when I went into the erasure parlor.''

Thacken agreed and settled back into a large, comfortable chair. He swung a small keyboard over his lap and said, ''Ready, Mr. Donley?''

When Cal nodded, Thacken pushed a key, and one wall turned into an enormous motion view of Jupiter. The speed was adjusted to make the scene seem leisurely. ''Watch the red spot for me, will you, Mr. Donley?''

The red spot drifted laterally as the whorls and swirls slowly distorted it, and still it kept returning to its initial appearance. Cal was vaguely aware that the magnification of the view was increasing. The red spot slowly took up more and more of the wall, and Cal began to feel that it was pulling him in, as though it were a giant whirlpool, turning around him slowly, inexorably. Drawn in, Cal began to lose interest in his surroundings.

The spot grew larger, broiling with increasing movement. Now Cal heard the sound. It was like the distant rumble of a storm. The sound intensified. Roaring winds whipped at Cal, and the storm rose in a crescendo about him.

Some time later, without remembering a lag, Cal found himself reclining in a comfortable lawn chair. He seemed to be on the beach, and it was calm near him. Off shore in the distance, as though a hurricane spun around him, giving him a wide berth, winds carried debris aloft in constant motion, with him at the center.

Dr. Thacken was beside him now, in a similar chair. He looked relaxed, as if the raging force of the nearby hurricane held no interest for him. Like the eye of the hurricane, he was calm.

''I think we should talk,'' he said at last.

Cal said nothing.

''I think we should talk about the other night. The one when you visited Forget-Me-Now.''

''I didn't kill him,'' Cal heard his voice say.

''You didn't kill who?''

''Angel. Domingo.''

''The man they found dead? That was the night you lost your memories?''

''It's not just my memories,'' Cal said.

''What do you mean by that?''

Cal said nothing.

"What else do you have to lose?" the older man asked.

Nikki? Lynn? No. He had already lost Lynn. He'd probably lost Nikki long ago, without even trying. What *had* he meant?

"You're going back in time. You're going back to the evening before you lost your memory. What do you see?"

Cal screamed. A moment earlier he and the doctor had been alone on the beach. But now there was a body lying at Cal's feet.

It was Domingo. A river of blood flowed from a large wound over one ear. The blood gushed into the sand and was totally absorbed. The shiny red blood kept flowing, kept streaming into the sand, yet the sand around the body remained white and clean.

"What do you see?" Thacken prodded.

"Gabriel's dead." Cal looked at the horizon, to the edge of the storm, averting his gaze from Domingo's battered body. Against his will, he looked back. This time Domingo had a gaping chest wound. It looked as though his thick chest had been crushed to half its normal thickness, with bloody ribs protruding. "Gabe, don't die," Cal cried. "Damn it all, don't die. I did this to you. This is all my fault."

Cal was on his knees, Domingo's bloody head on his lap. The next thing he knew, he was dragging Domingo through the sand.

"Where are you going?" Thacken asked.

"For a doctor. Why do you ask such stupid questions?"

"To find out the answer," the older man said patiently.

"He's hurt. He needs attention."

"Isn't he beyond attention?"

"That doesn't matter. It's all my fault. I've got to do *something*." Cal stopped, puzzled. Domingo's heels lay stretched out where they had cut twin furrows in the sand. But the furrows extended through a doorway Cal couldn't remember. An airlock door stood there on the beach, looking as out of place as Domingo's body. The furrows went just through the open doorway, as though Cal had dragged Domingo's body through it, but he hadn't noticed it earlier.

"So you don't remember the door, or where it might be?"

Cal shook his head.

"What about her?" the older man asked.

Cal looked behind him and saw Lynn playing with a large

beach ball. Cal began to cry. A hand touched Cal's shoulder, and he spun to face Nikki.

When she saw it was him, she turned away, walking slowly down the beach, toward the windswept ocean. The surf pounded, and Cal could hear the distant cries of gulls.

"Don't go," he called out after her. But she kept walking. Cal stood where he was, unable to follow her. In the distance palm trees bent under the wind.

She continued walking, not looking back. Shortly a robed man appeared strolling on a path toward Nikki. She stopped as he came near, apparently waiting for him to speak. He never did.

What he did instead was draw a huge knife from his belt. Not even noticing, Nikki turned to leave him. Cal's heart accelerated. Nikki took a step away. The man waited no longer. With a strong, vicious motion, he thrust the knife into Nikki's back.

"No," Cal screamed. He ran toward where Nikki had fallen, his feet throwing the sand behind him.

Inexplicably she lay face up when he got there, and the robed man was nowhere to be seen. The tip of the knife had reached all the way through her body. But there was no blood oozing from the wound. Instead, a glistening mustard-colored fluid seeped from her opened ribcage.

Cal silently sobbed. He fell to the sand, kneeling before Nikki. As he stared blindly into the sand, he was aware of a word written there, as a child would write it with a stick: DEPARTURE.

Once again he felt a hand on his shoulder. He quickly rubbed his fists into his eyes and turned.

"Mr. Donley," Thacken said. "It's time for you to wake up."

Cal was back in the man's office. Once again the wall was a plain cream-colored surface. Cal shook his head to clear it and realized he was still sitting in the chair he had originally picked.

"How do you feel?" Thacken asked. His eyes were worried.

Cal realized he was trembling. He willed himself to calm down and slowly began to recover. He looked at Thacken and saw his concern. "I'm fine. Fine."

The older man seemed slightly reassured, and he sat back down in his own chair. "You're an unusual man," he said. "I wasn't able to go as deep as I had intended. You don't make it very easy. I couldn't do a normal regression, because you wouldn't let go. So I had to do a relational probe. Apparently it was fairly painful. It does indeed seem to me, however, that you do have psychogenic, selective, retrograde amnesia, the variety temporarily induced by the blanking process."

"But you found out something else?"

"I'm not sure I learned any more than you did."

Cal blinked. The afterimage of the red spot seemed to hover in front of his eyes. "I'm not sure how to interpret what I saw. Oh, some of it was obvious, but not all."

"You love your wife very much. At least I assume that was your wife."

Cal nodded.

"But you fear for her life."

"That's one of the parts that doesn't make sense. She's not in any danger that I know of."

"Maybe not anything you're consciously aware of," Thacken said. "Incidentally, I'm not sure I've ever seen so much pent-up guilt in a person who seems to have so little to feel actually guilty about. Guilt over the little girl, your daughter maybe? Guilt over your wife, and the man who died."

"Maybe I just have a lot to hide."

"I don't think that's it. There's a small chance I'm making a mistake, but the indications I saw are far more commonly associated with *misplaced* guilt."

"I'd like to think you're right, but it's difficult. Whatever the reasons, it's obvious to me I've made my share of mistakes lately."

"What are you searching for?" the doctor asked.

"I don't know. The key to some damned puzzle."

Dr. Thacken thought for a moment. "I guess the only other observation I can make is that you didn't receive the regular treatment at Forget-Me-Now. I know that's already obvious because of the length of blanking, but there's another reason. A typical session is slow and fairly precise. The result is like carefully cutting out the last few pages of a book. What has happened to you was a hasty, careless process, more like tearing out *most* of the last third of the book, leaving dangling, frayed edges. That may be why your memories are returning faster than normal, but I can't add any more."

"It's still a help. The door I saw was familiar. I don't know where it is, but it ties into the night I lost my memory. I'm sure of it. I don't know about the word in the sand, but it has to be important. I've been worried about the *Vittoria* leaving— maybe that's it." Cal paid Thacken his fee, thanked him, and left.

Outside, Vincent informed him that Michelle had been on two newscasts while he had been occupied. "I thought it could wait. I'm not sure there's any new information."

"You did fine," Cal said. "You have them recorded?"

Vincent did. Cal sat on a nearby bench and watched them. The first was a report on Domingo, repeating what she had told him earlier about the man's alleged criminal background.

The second report was the interview with Tolbor. Michelle looked the faintest bit nervous, which must have been because of planting the transmitter, rather than the presence of Tolbor. Michelle certainly had already done enough interviews to have got over being nervous. Cal wondered where she had left it. Perhaps under the chair she sat in while interviewing.

Despite his tension he smiled while he watched her interview the man she was planting a transmitter on. She didn't stir the same ache that he felt when Nikki wouldn't leave his thoughts, but he had to admire her. Whatever her own reasons for helping, he appreciated her efforts as much as if they were solely on his behalf.

The interview itself was interesting. Tolbor seemed even happier now that the start of *Vittoria*'s voyage was closer. He was more animated than during the earlier interview Cal had seen. His casual manner renewed Cal's fear that he was looking at the wrong man.

A couple of Michelle's questions about Tolbor's new lodging on *Vittoria* reminded Cal that he should try to get in there also, but first he had business at his own *Vittoria* office. He had an idea about the word he had seen scrawled in the sand. He rose and started for the office.

"Has there been any activity in my office?" he asked Vincent when he was almost there.

"I don't think so. I noticed sounds from other offices a few times, but I don't think anyone actually came in."

When Cal arrived, the room *seemed* untouched. He looked around thoroughly but couldn't see anything that felt out of place. The desk computer responded to his touch normally.

After shaking off a queasy feeling that someone could have

done something in his office that he couldn't detect, he sat down in his chair and started on the computer. He quickly found the first request for a password. He typed DEPARTURE.

The status line on the top of the screen changed to PRIVILEGED MODE. Cal was elated.

The first item he came across was confirmation of what he had already found out. Angel, on his phone list, was indeed Domingo.

The second item the computer revealed was the name of the person he had been making monthly payments to: Jerry Lopez.

The name meant nothing to Cal. "Vincent, does the name Jerry Lopez mean anything to you?"

"No. I'm always the last to know."

"What do you do all day that fills your time?"

"I'm watching an old movie on channel C right now. It's one of Marlo Tingotil's first starring roles. On channel F there's a serial I never miss."

"I never know when you're serious."

"This is all true. I learn all kinds of interesting things from broadcasts."

"And you're always receiving?"

"Sure."

Cal turned his attention back to the screen. A few more minutes of investigation revealed one last item: another report to Jam. But there was still no link from the code name to a real name. The message was apparently sent earlier than the other message Cal had seen, and it said: "Have decided to scrap original plan for tonight. Want to find out more about something else. Will proceed without Angel if he doesn't want to go. I'll explain later if I find anything."

Cal leaned back in his chair. He wondered what it was he had found out that made him change plans. Or what his plans had originally been. If he just knew who he had been reporting to, maybe that would make more of the rest clear. So who was Jam?

"Jam" didn't mean anything to Vincent either. Cal tried to think of all the possibilities of who he could be spying for.

Industrial espionage was a field he thought would have collapsed after Earth died. He didn't know exactly why he thought that, but it felt reasonable. He could have been spying for the police, but if so, why would they have interrogated him about Domingo's death? They would have known he wasn't responsible. Unless they doubted him.

He could have been spying for his own gain, but he didn't see any way he could have benefited.

He finally decided that, for whatever reasons, he must most likely have been spying for the police. At least that was the only explanation he could imagine that let him hang on to his belief that he had stayed honest.

Taking what seemed to be only a small chance, he quickly typed a message to Jam: "Lost my memory the night Angel died. Believe it was involuntarily. Please contact me. Let me know what I was doing, and why."

Cal waited in front of the terminal for a few minutes, just in case Jam answered immediately, but nothing came in. He left the office. He considered stopping to talk briefly with Leroy, but Leroy was busy talking with a visitor.

"Okay, Vincent. How do I find Carmichael Road?"

Vincent told him, and soon he was walking along the road where Tolbor's *Vittoria* apartment was located. All around were individual houses, each with an expensive air. The immediate area must have held the most extravagant dwellings on *Vittoria*. The house on Cal's left was easily twice the size of his own house.

Ahead there was a center of activity as a small group of people unloaded a cart full of boxes and household possessions. They were taking items from the cart and carrying them into the house that bore Tolbor's address.

Cal decided on the bold approach. He simply walked in behind one of the movers and took a different turn just inside the front door.

The interior of the house was as luxurious as the outside. As in the Daedalus apartment, real wood furniture was plentiful. Cal took a quick tour through the house, trying to present an attitude of belonging as he encountered movers.

He noticed nothing that seemed unusual until he found the room that must have been the library. On the floor near the far corner was a large opened crate. On top was a collection of beam-etched recordings.

The group of recordings visible represented more money than Cal made in a year. They could have probably held ten percent of the race's knowledge. Cal whistled in appreciation and reached to look at the label on one of the cubes.

The label surprised him. The cube said LITERATURE, FICTION A-M. He hadn't pictured Tolbor as a man who had much interest in reading fiction. But what surprised him even more was that below the cube was another. And another below it. The entire crate must have been full of recordings. In a nearby crate there was a recorder and several blank recording cubes.

The total cost staggered Cal. And why would Tolbor want his own set? Surely the *Vittoria* would have its own complete set of recordings. Cal could find no answer that he felt comfortable with, so he continued his inspection and moved to another room. The bedroom held several large boxes of computer gear. Cal had forgotten that computers were one of Tolbor's areas of expertise.

In the kitchen there were several large cartons. Cal started to pry one open when a voice from behind him said, "Move it, will you? We need more space."

The speaker was a man in his early twenties. Making short steps, he finished the trip with a tall carton and set it down heavily. "Who are you anyway?" he asked, frowning.

"Just making sure it's all going okay," Cal said, retreating and hoping the man wouldn't press him for more actual information.

Cal had seen enough and started to go. The man didn't follow him out, but Cal hurried anyway. As he was about to leave the house he noticed a familiar pair of pictures. The Earth and Daedalus adorned one wall of the living room, each in a view that looked the same as the pictures in Tolbor's Daedalus apartment. Cal walked out through the front door, wondering if there was any significance to them, or if he was trying too hard to find hidden meanings in everything he saw.

He had spent too much time lately chasing intangibles. The name he had got from his office computer was a hard fact. He had paid Jerry Lopez money every month, anonymously. And the message about Lopez "missing" him after the tubeway accident had to be significant.

Cal checked inside his coat pocket for the pistol. It was still there, ready for use. He tried once more to force away the fear that he might have used a gun on a person in his past, and concentrated on other things. He started back to Daedalus.

Lopez lived in Machu Picchu, and Vincent's directions were

clear. Soon Cal was within sight of the address, which proved to be a small apartment building apparently holding only six units.

There was nothing modest about the outside furnishings, however. Several large fruit trees grew inside an open-air courtyard that was surrounded by the apartments. The trees gave Cal the feeling he had been there before.

Before going in, he called Nikki. It took her a moment to get to where she was free to talk.

He gave her the name and address. "You're sure you don't know him? I'd hate to get sent away for molesting old uncle Jerry who I've been making secret welfare payments to, or something similar."

"No. I don't know who he is. What do you mean by 'molesting'?"

Cal reflexively felt once again for the pistol. Still there. He hesitated for a moment before he told her about it.

"Are you serious?" she asked.

"Deadly," he replied, suddenly wishing he had picked another word. "Just send the police if I don't come out."

"Cal, don't you think—Oh, I don't know what to say besides 'Be careful.' "

"I'm trying to be. I could have just gone in there without telling anyone." Cal said good-bye and hung up.

Uncomfortable and uneasy, he found the door with Lopez's name on it and rang the bell.

His heart accelerated as he heard footsteps approach the door.

———— Chapter thirteen ————
Hazard

THE man behind the door was smaller than Cal had expected. Jerry Lopez was barely one and a half meters tall, with wiry arms, a small chest, short black hair, and a toothy grin.

"Where have you been?" Lopez asked, motioning Cal into the apartment. He didn't seem angry.

"Real busy," Cal said.

"I'm afraid I don't have time now. I'm expecting someone else in half an hour."

Time for what, Cal wondered, but said nothing. Until he knew more about the nature of his relationship with Domingo, he didn't care to divulge anything about his recent activities. So far, Lopez could be a homosexual prostitute, but that didn't fit anything Cal believed about himself. He could be a doctor seeing patients, except that his apartment didn't look clinical enough. Maybe he dealt in drugs. That could be why he was expecting someone else.

"I tried to reach you," Lopez continued.

"I know. I saw your message, but I couldn't do anything about it right then." Cal didn't tell him the reason he couldn't.

"Are you feeling okay?"

"Fine. Fine." Cal must have misinterpreted the message about missing him. So far, although he didn't know what the link between Lopez and himself was, it didn't seem to be a blackmailer-victim relationship.

"Maybe we should talk for a few minutes before my next client arrives," Lopez said. "You look like you could use it."

"I probably could."

Lopez began to walk toward a door set in the far wall. He turned when he reached the center of the room and said, "Are you coming?"

Cal followed. Lopez's living room looked as green as the courtyard outside. Potted ferns were everywhere. Cal stepped through the doorway, surprised.

Lopez sat behind a desk. In front of it were two massive visitor's chairs. On the wall were several certificates in frames.

Cal moved to one of the certificates and struggled momentarily with the calligraphy. He turned abruptly and said, "You're a counselor?"

Lopez said nothing for a moment. More of the whites of his eyes showed. "How much do you remember?" he asked at last.

Cal sat in one of the chairs. "Nothing inside your office." So all this mystery existed simply because he had been seeing a counselor.

"Just a minute. I want to reschedule my next visitor." Lopez pulled out a keyboard and typed a few characters. "Okay. Where do you think we should start?"

Cal gave the man a greatly abbreviated summary of his last few days, leaving out everything involving violence and his suspicions. That made it easy to skim over. "So," he said when he finished. "Why don't we start with you telling me why I've been seeing you. And why I've been paying you anonymously."

Lopez steepled his fingers. "For the first part, you've been seeing me to try to learn more about how to handle some emotional problems. You've been unjustifiably allowing yourself to feel quite guilty about the death of your daughter. That guilt had been creating pressure on your marriage, and you were afraid of losing your wife because of it. In addition, you were experiencing strong guilt feelings about your job, which you wouldn't discuss in specifics. That was compounding the problem."

"That's all?" Cal saw the startled expression on Lopez's face and quickly added, "Sorry. Just a tasteless joke."

"That's really quite interesting, Cal. One of the side effects of all you were going through is that I never knew you to exhibit the slightest signs of having a sense of humor. Maybe this blanking served as a catharsis. You might not be as bad off as I thought.''

Cal still didn't volunteer the fact that someone was trying to kill him. "But I never told you what was bothering me about work?"

"I got the feeling you had been asked to do something you didn't like to do, that maybe it went against your feelings of—oh, I don't know—fairness, or justice—I really couldn't tell. I just saw that you were upset by it."

"But I wouldn't discuss it?"

"Never. I tried. As for your paying me anonymously, that was another source of discussions for us. Your sense of pride was a little overblown. The idea that you might need personal counseling bothered you—as though you were ashamed at what you perceived to be a mark of personal failure."

"I take it you don't think so?"

"No two people are identical. No two people respond exactly the same to external circumstances. We all have our private fears and unique reactions to stress. I had hoped with our talks to help you see that you weren't alone in having difficulty coping with pressure. By learning the danger signs associated with stress, we can all get better at dealing with it, by reducing it or avoiding it or living with it."

"Do you see me as someone who might have gone down to Forget-Me-Now to get away from it all?"

Lopez scratched an itch on his nose. "No. I wouldn't have predicted that."

"Tell me more about what may have been bothering me at work."

"I'm not sure I know much more. Whatever it was apparently started about four months ago. I didn't detect any signs of it earlier."

"Could it have been simply a result of the guilt about Lynn getting stronger for some reason?"

"Oh, no." Lopez shook his head emphatically. "I don't know what caused it, but it was new and not associated with home. You were quite secretive. We had established what I thought were fairly good communications until that time, but suddenly you were harder to talk to, flatly refusing to talk about anything related to work."

"Did I—" Cal started, but felt a catch in his voice, so he

cleared his throat. "Did I seem to be worried about Nikki dying?"

"No," Lopez said slowly. "You were worried that she might leave you, but you never seemed to think she might die. Why? Are you worried about that now?"

"I'm not sure." Cal saw the puzzled expression on Lopez's face and added, "There's nothing I'm aware of consciously. As my memories start to return, I seem to be aware of feelings before I remember actual events or people."

Vincent broke in with the message that Michelle was calling.

"Tell her I'll call back in five or ten minutes unless it's an emergency," Cal said. To Lopez he said, "I assume that I never told Nikki about the sessions with you?"

"As far as I know you never told her. It was hard for you to admit something to her that you didn't want to admit to yourself. That was part of the problem. We were just beginning to talk about barriers—personal barriers—last time."

"What do you think the chances are that I might have used the erasure parlor deliberately?"

"Very small. You seemed to feel that going into a parlor was some form of suicide. Whatever other mistakes you might have made from time to time, whatever things you might have done to try to fix problems that plagued you, I don't see you going in there freely. You're what I call a survivor. I think you've got a lot of inner strength—enough that you can eventually overcome almost any obstacle."

"Like getting Nikki back?"

Lopez didn't flinch from his gaze. "Not necessarily obstacles like that. Just the ones that are in your power to influence."

"Meaning I have no influence over her?"

"No. It's just that you have no direct power over her. It would all be so simple if you could just command her to love you and stay with you."

Cal thought for a moment. "Did I ever mention specific names of people at work who might have been involved in something that made me feel uncomfortable?"

"Sorry."

Cal decided he wouldn't learn any more, so he paid Lopez the usual fee, not anonymously, thanked him, and left.

The courtyard lacked adequate privacy, so he waited until he left the building and then called Michelle.

"What's up?" he asked.

"Domingo." Michelle looked worried. "The police say they found a cache of weapons and drugs, after a second search of his apartment."

"They what?"

"That's what it says here. The report says they compared building plans against what they saw in his apartment, and realized that his closet was smaller than it was originally. The closet floor was about a meter square, but the plans said two square meters. Behind a fake wall they found all the equipment."

Cal stood for a moment, visualizing the sizes she had mentioned and the closet he had seen. "Something's wrong here," he said slowly. "When *I* was in his apartment, the closet was full-size."

"But that would mean the police had to have known this before you were there. Or—"

"Or they're lying," Cal finished. "Or *I'm* lying."

"I wasn't going to list that possibility," she said. "You're going to have to put some faith in me."

"Sorry. But why would the police hold the information or lie about it?"

"To flush out people who knew him? His accomplices?"

"I'm baffled. Earlier I had myself almost talked into believing that Domingo and I had been acting as police spies. Now I don't know what to think."

"Police spies? Spying on whom? And why?"

"My very questions. I don't know."

"Well, what next?" she asked.

Cal explained about learning he had been lied to at the erasure parlor. "So I think it's worth another visit. Maybe after that, I can spring Edmund's name on a few people and see what reactions I get."

Michelle hung up a moment later. Cal was getting close to the tubeway station, so he sat on a bench and called Nikki.

"You're okay?" she asked.

"No damage. Lopez is my analyst. I've been seeing him to work out a few problems."

"*You* were seeing an analyst?"

"Nikki, don't give me a hard time about it. It doesn't indicate I was going crazy or anything. It just means I thought maybe it would help me. Help us."

"I didn't intend to criticize. I was just surprised. You've had this aura of invincibility. You're always so self-sufficient, so independent."

"Maybe it was hard for me to tell you I *needed* you."

Nikki's face looked out at him from the screen for a long moment. "Cal, I—" she began. "Cal, I've got to go. There's another call coming in."

"Right. I'll talk to you later." Cal fought to keep his voice calm. He wondered what she had been going to say, wishing desperately she had been going to soften, to tell him that maybe she needed him.

After a short journey Cal was within sight of the erasure parlor. He called Michelle and let her know he was about to go in.

He hesitated before the door, determining what approach he would use, and then entered.

The front office was vacant. Cal took a quick look around, trying to remember the proprietor's name. Paulo Frall, that was it.

Cal could have pushed the service button on the desk, but he wanted to see Frall's reactions when he had no advance notice of his visitor. He opened the door in the back of the shop.

"I'm with a customer right now," called a man in a white lab coat. "I'll be out in just a minute." The man was not Paulo Frall.

Cal signaled acknowledgment and went back into the waiting room. He had a brochure in his hand and was examining it when the door opened and the man he had seen a moment ago entered.

The man was younger than Frall by quite a bit. He was perhaps in his mid-twenties.

"Well, sir," he said. "I should be able to start on you within a half hour. We'll clean away the last year, and it won't hurt a bit."

"That's not why I'm here," Cal said. "I've already been through it."

"Oh," the man said, frowning slightly and readjusting. "What *can* I do for you then? Was everything satisfactory?"

"No. But that's not your fault." Cal gave him the benefit of the doubt. "I wanted to talk to the fellow who was here before. Paulo Frall. Does he work a different shift?"

"I'm afraid you just missed him."

"I could try back later."

"No. Sorry," the man said. "What I mean is you just missed him before he went on vacation. He's been thinking about it for a while now, and this morning he decided he'd been postponing it long enough."

"How about if you give me his home address?"

"It wouldn't do you much good. He's gone to Luna for his holidays. He won't be at home. But he'll be back in a couple of weeks."

"A couple of weeks?" Cal realized too late that he sounded shocked. "I mean, are you sure he'll be gone that long?"

"That's what his plans are. Of course, he has a tendency to change his plans abruptly. I could have him call you when he gets back."

"No. That won't be necessary. But while I'm here, could I see your records for four nights ago? I'd like to see if anyone I know was in that night."

The man was reluctant at first, but Cal smiled and laid his bank stick on the reception desk, whereupon the man acquiesced.

In a moment Cal realized why the attendant was so willing to take the bribe.

The record told him almost nothing. He had been the only "patient" between 21:00 and 11:00 the next morning. The transaction seemed just like the ones near it.

"Sorry I couldn't help you," the attendant said.

"Maybe you can. Would you mind doing one thing for me? I'd like to—to make sure Paulo is the same person I think he is. I'd really appreciate it if you would call him and ask him something about the shop. It doesn't matter what. You could tell him you misplaced something."

The man resisted until Cal smiled again and said he would pay for the favor.

Standing out of the range of the desk camera, but where he could see the received image, Cal watched the attendant make the call.

It took Frall a long time to answer. Cal supposed the call had to be relayed through com links not normally required for communications local to Daedalus. When he did answer, it was obvious that he wasn't on the colony. He was in a passenger seat aboard a ship.

"Yes, Anville. What is it?"

The attendant asked him a brief question, and Frall gave him the answer before hanging up. Frall had seemed annoyed at the call.

"Will that do it?" the man asked.

"It sure will. It's the same man." Cal paid him. "Oh, one last question. Is your equipment portable? I mean, could you take it out of here to treat someone?"

"I suppose so," the man said. "It would be a bother, but it could be done."

Cal thanked him and left. "Vincent?" he said, once he was out on the street. "I want to see you blow up one or two of the frames with Frall in them. The upper right section."

"Coming up."

Cal examined the image carefully. Finally he said, "I don't see any trace of image imperfections. What about you?"

"Nope. Picture perfect."

"So it appears Frall is not the one who gave my picture to Edmund. But why would he have left just this morning? If he was afraid of me coming back, why not earlier?"

"Ask your doctor."

"I asked you. If you're as smart as you act sometimes, you should know everything."

"Bovine excrement."

"Vincent, I'm shocked. How about if you call Michelle?"

She answered and asked, "What happened?"

"I'm back out with my memories still intact, such as they are. The guy I saw here the day I woke up is on his way to Luna for a vacation."

"What miserable luck."

"I wonder if luck is any part of it. For all I know, someone is following me, or one of the people I've talked to has seen someone else afterward."

"You told me earlier you were going back to Forget-Me-Now. Are you saying—"

"No. I'm not. I don't believe you told anyone. It must simply be a coincidence that he left today. I don't like coincidences, but they do happen once in a while."

"What next then?"

"It'll probably be too late to do anything about it, but would you check on Paulo Frall? Maybe he has a criminal record."

"Sure."

Cal caught himself examining Michelle's image on Vincent's screen. There were no image imperfections, but she was using her desk computer rather than her wristcomp, so that told him nothing. He forced his attention back to the conversation. He didn't believe she could be responsible, but it was hard to shut off the suspicious thoughts.

"You've got another message coming in," Vincent said.

Cal said good-bye to Michelle and answered the other call.

To his surprise the caller was Pastor Welden from the Presodist church. She had let down her gray hair and looked more casual than during the service.

"Yes," Cal said, puzzled.

"I'll try not to take up too much of your time, Mr. Donley," she said. "You came to one of our services yesterday. I thought perhaps I could answer some of your questions about the church, to encourage you to visit us again."

"Thanks, but I came out of curiosity more than anything else. I think you'd be wasting your time on me." Cal didn't say that, more to the point, she'd be wasting *his* time.

"My time is never wasted," she said. "I may just not realize immediately to what purpose it is being put."

"Well, I do have one question."

"And that is?"

"Is the tale of Sodom and Gomorrah particularly central to your church? I mean, do you devote five Sundays a year to sermons about that story, or give it any other special attention?"

"No, I wouldn't say so. Easter and Christmas are the two biggest church holidays. Almost all the other areas of study are treated only occasionally, with no special attention. Why do you ask?"

"Just runaway curiosity. I've heard that story mentioned several times recently, and I wondered if it was especially significant to the church."

"There are people who feel that God destroyed the Earth because the people there had done so much damage to the planet."

"Do you?" Cal asked.

"Certainly not. We teach of a loving and understanding God, not a vengeful and angry one. The old testament is still quoted, but most of us don't take it literally."

"What kind of people do believe theories like that?"

Pastor Welden hesitated for the first time. "I'm not actually sure," she said slowly. "Our church doesn't officially promote that belief. You might have better luck finding people in other churches."

"But surely some of your members must think that too."

"Perhaps, but I wouldn't know who."

The woman wasn't an accomplished liar. Cal was sure from the flicker of her eyes that she did know a few names. Yet he still had the impression she was telling the truth about everything else. He believed her when she said the Presodists as a whole didn't hold that among their beliefs.

"Thanks for calling, Pastor," Cal said. "I may get back to church."

Before she hung up, Cal saw a look in her eye that must have meant something like "Once a heathen, always a heathen," but she quite politely thanked him for his time and asked him to call her if he had any more questions.

Cal had an idea for another call. After having Vincent verify that Russ Tolbor was not at his apartment, he said, "Get him on the phone, will you?"

"Okay," Vincent said. "But haven't you got anything better to do than sit around all day phoning people?"

"Just do it, you little anthropomorphidite." Cal grinned down at Vincent's screen.

"Such language," Vincent said, but when he finished speaking, Russ came up on the screen. "Yes, Cal. What can I do for you?"

"I was wondering if you might have time to talk for a little while sometime before you leave." Cal wanted to get the man's reactions to a few questions without having to deal with a small screen.

"I might be able to, but it's getting very hectic around here, with all the last-minute preparations. We could always talk more leisurely after the *Vittoria* leaves. The communications equipment works quite well, thanks to you."

"Okay. I'll do that." Cal's irritation grew. "Oh. I ran into someone who knows you. Fargo Edmund."

"Edmund? Sorry, the name doesn't seem familiar. Where did he say I knew him from?" Tolbor's face and voice showed no indications of nervousness.

"That's funny. He said he went to the same church."

"I go to a big church. I really can't place the name. Was it important?"

"No. I'll talk to you later."

"Okay, Vincent," Cal said after Tolbor had hung up. "Let's see some blowups of Tolbor's picture." The man had been using his wristcomp.

"Nothing I can see," Vincent said, displaying the upper right portion of the video received moments earlier.

"Me neither. Damn. He could be the wrong person. It could be a conspiracy with him being only one of the members. Or it could be someone else entirely. Leroy Krantz. Tom Horvath. Maybe Paulo Frall. Maybe, maybe, maybe." Maybe even someone closer, he thought, but he couldn't accept the idea.

Cal got up from the bench. It would do him no good just to sit there. As he began walking he realized how hungry he was. It was mid-afternoon, and he hadn't stopped for a meal. By the time he approached the tubeway, he knew what he would do.

The news station was on the way to where he wanted to go next. A few minutes later he knocked on Michelle's office door.

"Want to buy me a steak in your lunchroom?" he asked when she answered his knock.

"How about a sandwich?"

"Terrific."

"How about if we eat back here, though?" she asked. "I've got something you might want to hear."

They got their food, Michelle taking only a container of orange juice, and returned to her office.

"Tolbor got back to his office a little while ago," she said. "I take it you called him recently?"

Cal nodded.

"You may not like this, but here it is." Michelle touched a switch, and a new collection of random environmental noises joined the ones in her office.

Then Tolbor's voice sounded. "I know. He's done a fine job. I wish he could be part of the team on *Vittoria*. We could use people with his drive and talents. But I'm a little worried about him."

The other voice, male, sounded as though it came from the communications console in Tolbor's office rather than from inside the room. There weren't any of the soft random sounds associated with the second person. "What makes you say that?" he asked.

"He called me a little while ago. Said he wanted to talk but was real vague. Not like Cal. Then he mentioned some friend of his I'd never heard of and seemed not to want to let the topic go."

"Maybe there's just a lot on his mind."

"Maybe," Tolbor said. "Or maybe all the pressure's getting to him finally. It can happen to the best of us."

From there the conversation turned toward final preparations for the journey. Michelle switched it off.

Cal sat silent for a moment, looking at her. Her eyes were slightly puffy, as though she was not sleeping much better than he. "So," he said at last. "Am I cracking under pressure?"

"Don't be silly. I'm not trying to back out or anything stupid like that. I'm just wondering if we might have the wrong man."

Cal took a deep breath. *He* was absolutely certain he was not going crazy. But it would have hurt for Michelle to back out. "I've been wondering that myself. I guess I've been hanging on to him because he seemed to fit all the constraints. If it's not him, then we're that much further away from the real answer."

"Maybe Paulo Frall?"

"Maybe. But I don't get that feeling about him. Oh, I'm sure he lied to me, and probably gave me the treatment himself, but I don't see him as an instigator. Just an assistant."

"But you don't have anything to back that up?"

"No."

"I think we'd better concentrate on anyone else you can think of besides Tolbor. Everyone on the *Evangeline* will be resurrected before *he* does something illegal."

"The *Evangeline*? That name sounds vaguely familiar."

"Oh, that's right. It was the last ship to leave Earth. It's in Earth orbit—'Earth obit,' as the jokers say. It would have been destroyed, but the biologists still plan to see if they can develop some means of protection against the bacteria, without having to go back down to Earth."

Cal considered the information for a moment and then let it drop. "Okay. I've got to agree with you about Tolbor. But let's keep monitoring him, just in case. Thanks for not losing faith."

"Would you stop that?" Michelle said, smiling to let him know she wasn't angry. "What next, then? I can start a data base inquiry into relationships that include Domingo, the Presodist church, and drugs."

"That sounds good. Listening to Tolbor makes me think my next attempts to try Edmund's name on people, or check on image peculiarities, better be slightly more subtle. If I do talk to whoever's responsible, I need to be less transparent. I'll start with Leroy Krantz. He has an office near mine. I don't have any good reason to check up on him, but I don't have any better reason for anyone else."

"So you're going back over to *Vittoria*?"

"Right. I'll keep you posted."

"You do that," Michelle said. She smiled at him as he left, but he could tell she was as worried as he was. By now they should have found *some* indications of who was responsible. Departure time was all too close.

It seemed like each trip to *Vittoria* took longer than the last. Finally Cal was walking down the hall in his office building.

Leroy was in his office, and alone, so Cal stopped in.

"You still want to go for that drink, Leroy?" he asked.

Leroy was obviously not terribly interested. He hesitated for just a moment before apparently deciding he should go, since he had suggested it. "Well, okay," he said. "But let's hurry a little. I've got a lot to do here."

"Fine. Let's just not hurry as much as Fargo Edmund."

Just as Leroy's gaze met Cal's, Vincent interrupted. "You've got a call coming in."

Damn. Leroy's eyes had focused on Vincent, and Cal had lost the opportunity of seeing his expression unaltered by any external events. "I'll answer it in just a minute," Cal said.

"Who's Fargo Edmund?" Leroy asked calmly.

"A jogger who died this morning. He was evidently in a big hurry and fell off a tier in Machu Picchu."

"I hadn't heard the news today. I didn't realize jogging was so dangerous."

"Neither did I. Can you wait just a minute while I answer this call?" Cal retreated to his office, annoyed at having lost the opportunity.

It was Michelle. She looked disturbed, her lips pressed

tightly together. "Are you sitting down?" she asked.

"*Dammit*, I hate it when people start out conversations like that," Cal said, feeling suddenly weak. "Give me the bad news."

She swallowed hard. "A bomb just destroyed your office on Daedalus. And it killed someone."

Chapter fourteen
Headway

CAL slumped in his desk chair shakily. "Who did the bomb kill?" he asked, his voice suddenly hoarse.

"I don't know," Michelle said. Even on Vincent's small screen her agitation was obvious.

"Let me put you on hold for just a minute. I've got to see if Nikki's all right." To Vincent Cal said, "Call her. Right away."

"There's no answer," Vincent said several seconds later. "I don't know if she's just not answering or what."

"Keep trying, dammit."

"Will do."

Cal's fist clenched tightly as he wondered who had been killed in his office. Please don't let it be Nikki. Anyone but her.

The office was uncomfortably hot. The sweat beaded on Cal's forehead.

"I'm going over there," he said suddenly, rising.

"Wait a minute," Vincent said. "She just answered."

"Thank God you're all right," Cal said explosively when he saw Nikki's image.

"What do you mean?" she asked. "What's happened?"

"I don't know who it was yet, but someone was just killed by a bomb going off in my office on Daedalus."

"Oh, God."

"Nikki, there's nothing I can do here. I'm going over there. *Please* be careful, whatever you do. I'll let you know as soon as I know anything more."

"You're sure it's safe to go?"

"It seems like right after an accident is the best time to do anything. Why am I saying 'accident'? Just be careful, okay?"

"Okay."

Michelle was listening to an earphone when she came back on the screen. She waited a moment longer before she said, "Someone in the hall thought he saw a man enter your office just before it blew. That's all they know so far. They haven't been able to get to the body yet."

"I've got to go over there."

She nodded and said, "I'll meet you there."

Cal had forgotten about Leroy. As he passed the man's office, he remembered. "How about some other time?" he asked curtly.

"Fine," Leroy said, a surprised expression on his face.

Cal hurried down the hall, worried, wondering who might have been killed in his office. And why. Maybe it was someone trying to place an explosive in the office. A faltering hand, a wire touching something it shouldn't.

When he arrived, the area around the building was cordoned off. An acrid smell hung in the air. The bomb had somehow triggered a small fire. He was allowed into the lobby but not into the office hallway. Michelle was there, with more reporters and a few people who seemed to be occupants of other offices in the building.

"What the hell's going on?" asked a tall, nervous man Cal didn't remember. He gripped Cal's arm.

"I don't know. I'm as puzzled as you are." Cal freed himself and joined Michelle.

"No more information yet, obviously," she said. She seemed nervous too. "A couple of people in nearby offices were treated for minor injuries, but no one was seriously hurt except the man they think was in your office."

Cal looked down the hall. A couple of paramedics stood near the edge of the activity. Several people with bulky white suits struggled with sections of the ceiling that had collapsed in spots. Apparently they were trying to reach his office through one of its walls, rather than through the pile of rubble near the door.

Cal felt a bitter taste in his mouth. He shook himself. It could so easily have been him as the focal point of the cleanup crew.

He and Michelle waited for another twenty minutes before the crew was able to clear enough rubble so they could reach the office. Shortly thereafter two paramedics went in and then came back out with a body on a stretcher.

Cal stopped them on the way out. "This was my office. I've got to know who was killed."

One of the two glanced at the other and received a nod. They put the body down. Cal pulled down the sheet, uncovering the bloody head of the victim.

"Oh, God," Cal said quietly. His stomach twisted. "It's my boss. Tom Horvath."

As Cal looked at the dead man whose only sin was to be in the wrong place at the wrong time, another mass of memories stirred in the depths, rising on a new current to tell Cal, too late, the dead man had been a friend. Not just a good friend, but a deep, firm friend. Cal wished the memories hadn't returned, and that Tom were still alive. It was too high a price to pay.

Even after they covered Horvath's bloody face, Cal could still see him. And he saw something more. He saw Tom staying up all night with Cal and Nikki, talking with them, consoling them, trying sometimes unsuccessfully to contain his own grief. Tom had almost seen Lynn as his own daughter.

A hand on Cal's shoulder brought him back out of it, and he realized that he was crying, shaking uncontrollably.

"Are you all right?" Michelle asked.

"I'll be okay, I guess," Cal said a moment later. "I just didn't realize how good a friend I had here, and now he's gone, because of me."

"What do you mean, 'because of me'?" asked a male voice from behind Cal.

Cal turned to face Lieutenant Dobson, the policeman who had questioned him the morning before. "I mean it was my office," he said, trying to regain his composure. "Tom's dead because someone was angry enough with me to put a bomb in my office."

"How about if we step into one of these other offices and talk for a few minutes?" the policeman asked.

"Whatever you want," Cal said resignedly. "I'll see you soon, Michelle."

The nearest office was unoccupied, so they went in, and Dobson shut the door. "Well, now," he said, getting settled. "What have you done to get someone this angry with you?"

"I honestly don't know," Cal said, looking at his hands in his lap.

"Do you think Horvath himself was the intended victim?"

"In my office? It doesn't seem likely."

"People can be killed anywhere. No one needs to feel guilty just because the victim happened to be near them or on their property."

"I hear what you're saying," Cal said, looking back up at the policeman and feeling that the man's eyes were softer now than they had been yesterday. "But I can't imagine anyone wanting to hurt Tom Horvath. You couldn't find a more thoughtful or gentle man."

"So you were good friends?"

"The best. I've got to talk to his wife, Dorothy, to tell her what's happened."

Lieutenant Dobson looked into Cal's eyes for a long moment, perhaps seeing the pain Cal felt. "Who do you think might have done this?"

Cal could have told him Fargo Edmund did, but Edmund was dead, and that would require Cal to tell the rest of the story, and that led to much longer sessions with lots of more painful questions, so he simply said, "I don't know. I don't know anyone angry enough with me to do something like this. I don't even know anyone irritated enough to track dirt into my office."

"Obviously someone is a little more upset than that. Assuming this was deliberate. And I can't imagine this was an accident. Explosives are just about at the top of the list of items you don't want to be found guilty of possessing."

Cal hadn't really thought about it before, but he realized now that explosives on Daedalus would cause much more interest than on Earth. On Earth your neighbor could destroy his entire house and property and maybe not cause any permanent damage to you. With possession of explosives, Edmund had taken an even bigger risk than Cal had realized.

Dobson continued questioning Cal for several minutes before concluding with a request. "If you learn *anything* that explains why someone might have done this, I want you to call me." He rose and looked steadily at Cal to give emphasis to his words. "It doesn't matter what time it is. Call me."

Cal agreed. They left the office and went back to the lobby. A cleanup crew was busy stripping blackened wall sections off their mountings.

"Let's get out of here," Cal said to Michelle. "This air is giving me a headache."

Outside, it was almost as though nothing had happened. The damages were invisible, the sun shone brightly, and the air was fresh.

"I'm sorry about your friend," Michelle said. "You didn't remember anything about him until just now?"

"No. I saw him on the phone earlier, but it wasn't until I saw him dead that something clicked inside. Maybe pathways that link emotional responses in my brain are somehow in better shape than straight chronological or associational links."

"Do you remember anything that might help us figure out who's responsible?"

"I don't think so. I remember Nikki better now, and Lynn, and obviously Tom. But I don't see anything more."

"I learned some more today, if you want to hear it."

"Go ahead," Cal said.

"I had turned in an information search on travel authorizations. The report came back just a little while ago. Tolbor hasn't been on Earth in ten years. The closest he's been was an orbital inspection *after* the disaster. So he couldn't have been there prior to the disaster."

"So. That's just one more piece of confirmation. I hope I haven't wasted too much time on him while the real criminal is loose. What does all this do to your motivation? I had the feeling that you lost someone special down there, and that was part of the reason you agreed to help."

"I'm still helping. Maybe you were wrong about the disaster. But someone is definitely up to something. You need help, and I like you."

"Thanks, Michelle. I guess I've said that a lot lately. So I lose one good friend and gain another."

"I wish I could bring Tom back."

Cal reached over to squeeze her arm. "I've got to tell Nikki about Tom. And warn her to be even more careful. I'll talk to you as soon as I've got any more ideas."

"Right."

Cal went to the clinic. He couldn't give Nikki news like that any other way. She came out shortly after an associate took in a note. They went into an empty waiting room.

"What's wrong?" she asked, obviously reading Cal's expression.

Cal told her straight out, knowing that delaying the news

would just make it worse. "It's Tom Horvath. He's dead."

Nikki began to cry. Cal pulled her to him and stroked the hair at the back of her neck, letting her cry. Finally she asked, "What happened?"

"The explosion in my office. He'd said something on the phone about bringing me a plant."

Nikki stiffened and pushed herself back so she could see Cal's eyes. He was positive her look was accusing.

"Damn it all," he said. "I'm sorry. Don't you think it hurts me too? But what could I have done? Warn anyone who might come in contact with me to stay at least a hundred meters away from me, or my property, or anywhere I might go?"

"I didn't say that. I'm worried about you."

Cal stood silent, looking into her eyes. "God, I'm good with guilt," he said finally. "It's amazing I don't feel personally responsible for the human condition. I'm sorry, Nikki."

"It's all right," she said quietly. "I haven't made it much easier."

"I don't blame you for not trusting me, for thinking I might be seeing another woman."

Nikki looked at him quizzically.

"Seeing Tom lying there dead was a jolt in more ways than one. It also jarred some more of my memories loose. Before I saw him, I didn't remember the time the four of us went to Luna. Or a lot of other things. I'm still not in a position to tell you for sure what happened, but I know I wasn't having an affair. I think maybe I was acting as a spy for the police. On who, or why, I don't know."

Nikki looked at him without speaking.

"Well," he said. "What do you think about all of this?"

"I'm beginning to think the man I married is still buried deep in you."

"Go on." Cal smiled, finding uncomfortably that he could feel something good despite Tom's death.

"Just don't press too hard right now. Okay?"

"Okay."

"I hate to break things up," Vincent said. "But you've got a call coming in."

"Does that thing get jealous?" Nikki asked. "Or am I paranoid too?"

"Nobody says thanks anymore," Vincent said.

Cal gave Nikki an amused glance, released her, and said, "Let's have it, Vincent."

"Mr. Donley?" said a man who looked familiar but still didn't register.

"Go ahead."

"I've got the information you requested the day before yesterday. The payments from your account went to a Mr. Jerry Lopez. Do you want the address?"

"No, thanks." Cal stifled a wry grin. "The name is enough."

The clerk hung up, and Cal explained to Nikki that Lopez was the analyst. Nikki grinned.

Cal began to feel guilty that he felt good about making progress with Nikki while Tom lay dead, and he caught himself.

He was about to speak, but Vincent said, "Another message came in. It's text, and you might want to be alone when you read it."

"I don't have secrets from Nikki—any longer. Read it."

"It says, 'Horvath died instead of you. Stay home or someone else might die too. Like your wife.' "

Cal couldn't say anything for a moment. He took several deep breaths. His eyes probably reflected the shock he saw in Nikki's. He sat down and motioned for Nikki to do the same.

"I'd like you to do something for me," Cal said slowly. "I think you'd be a lot safer if you—"

"Don't even *start* to say anything like that," Nikki broke in. "I'm not running out to leave you by yourself to handle this."

"Isn't there someplace you could go, for just a few days—"

"You're not listening."

Cal saw the determination in her eyes, knowing she could be just as stubborn as he could. He wondered fleetingly if his attraction to Michelle was based on her similarity to Nikki. He began to say something more and just stopped.

"Yes, I'll be careful," Nikki said, responding to the unspoken request. "And I'll expect you to be too."

Cal quietly accepted the inevitable. "One of us should talk to Dorothy before she hears about Tom from the police."

"I'll do it," she said. "You've gone through enough already."

"Thanks."

"What are you going to do now?"

"I guess I'll give someone a call about going out for a drink."

"Not Michelle?"

"No." Cal explained about Leroy Krantz and wanting to know if his wristcomp showed any image defects.

"Why don't you call him before you leave?" Nikki asked. "That way I'll know your plan."

Cal did so. Unfortunately, Leroy was still at his desk, so Cal learned nothing except that Leroy looked shocked when he told him Tom Horvath was dead, and he agreed that a drink together to lament Cal's boss would be okay. They settled on a restaurant on Daedalus in an hour. Cal hung up.

"So," Nikki said. "That gives you a guaranteed opportunity to catch him while he's got only his wristcomp to communicate with?"

"Exactly." Cal was still getting used to her perceptiveness and speed. "I passed by that place today. It's being redecorated. So I can call him to change locations."

"If you're not a spy, maybe you ought to be," Nikki said, and grinned.

"As a matter of fact, that's still the only explanation I can see for some of the things I've found out. If it was for the police, I can't say who I was spying *on*, or why they haven't contacted me, but it seems most likely that's what I was doing with some of my off hours."

"You're serious, aren't you?"

"Yes. I just wish there was some way to delay the *Vittoria*."

"Which implies there isn't."

"No," Cal said. "The time window they plan to use is pretty narrow. They want just the right trajectory while they're still in the solar system. Besides, who would listen to me? I don't really *know* anything."

Nikki began to pace. "We've got to do *something*."

"We will. Why don't you go see Dorothy?"

"While you—"

"While I try to figure out what to do next."

Nikki nodded and started for the door. Halfway there she halted and turned. A few quick steps brought her back facing Cal, and she leaned down to give him a brief kiss on the cheek.

Cal didn't know what to say. Fortunately, she didn't seem to expect anything. Nikki drew back, winked at him, and left.

Cal was still sitting there several minutes later when he remembered his surroundings. "Vincent," he said. "I don't suppose *you've* ever been able to figure women out."

"I'm probably not far behind you."

"You're saying I'm slow?" Cal asked, rising.

"I mean I don't see much difference between men and women. It seems to me that it's *you* who want to assign differences."

"You think you're any closer to the truth than the computer that decided ashtrays caused cancer?"

"No matter. You pay me to do the books and make telephone calls. Those I can understand."

"Okay. Let's talk to Michelle."

"Is that the royal 'we,' the editorial 'we,' or the literal 'we'?"

"*I* want to talk to her."

A moment later Michelle's face filled the screen.

"Anything new?" Cal asked.

"Nothing worth calling about yet. The building records show a maintenance call to your office yesterday. It could well have been Edmund, but there's no way to tell."

"That was fast." Cal thanked her for the information and hung up.

Cal left the clinic. He had already decided on Galentine's as the place to meet, but he soon realized that he had more than enough time to get there, so he detoured by his office.

The cleanup crew was still at work removing debris. The three interior walls had been cleared away, leaving a large pile of rubble where his office had been and two smaller concentrations in the neighboring offices. Cal assumed that by now the forensic experts would have come and gone.

He must have been right, for no one challenged him as he approached the office. He wrinkled his nose at the odor of melted plastic. The almost overwhelming feeling of sadness returned as he saw dark stains on the floor. He was aware, too, of the anger that had been building.

As far as he knew, he had never been one to settle issues physically, but right at that moment he strongly wished he had the person responsible right there in what was left of the office, walking on Tom's blood. Maybe slamming him into one of the remaining walls to get his attention would be a good start.

Cal forced away the thoughts, trying to look at the area objectively. It was a struggle.

Near a heap of melted plastic in the corner, he found a small green pulp that was barely recognizable as part of a plant.

The desk wasn't in the room. Or, more precisely, the desk as a whole object wasn't. The explosive must have been inside it. Twisted metal pieces in the pile must have come from the desk.

In the corner lay the remains of Cal's swivel chair. Maybe its rollers had allowed it to move with the tide of violently expanding gas and metal fragments until it collided with the wall.

Cal moved to examine the chair. After a moment he found attached to one of the legs a short segment of wire. That would have been the trigger.

Anger flared within him again as he thought back to the wire in his *Vittoria* office. So Edmund, or whoever had done this, hadn't set up anything so sophisticated that it was guaranteed to blow only when Cal himself was there. Anyone at all could have set it off. Except that Tom was not just anyone.

Cal felt sick to his stomach.

The cleanup crew came back for another load, so he moved out of their way momentarily.

Once they were on their way again, he poked through the remaining pile but had found nothing by the time Vincent told him he had a call.

"Just a minute," Cal said. He found a nearby empty office and closed the door. He avoided the chair.

It was Michelle. "You were right," she said.

"Right about what? I've been wrong so many times lately, that should narrow down the possibilities, but I can't guess which one you're talking about."

"I'm talking about Domingo. Another data base search I requested turned up something. Fourteen years ago the name Angelo Gabriel Domingo was on a list of rookies. Police rookies."

"You're saying that swapping his first and middle name was all it took to obscure the record?"

"I don't know if that's all he did. But you've got to remember that fourteen years ago there were a lot more Domingos and Smiths. He's the same man. There was a class picture in the files."

"And it's him?"

"Right. So the odds that he was still in the police, but undercover, have to be enormous."

"Thanks, Michelle. You—"

"Another call," Vincent said.

"Anything else, Michelle?"

She said no, so Cal thanked her and answered the other call. It was Nikki.

"I'm with Dorothy. She's taken a sedative, so I can talk for a few minutes. I didn't intend to ask her anything about you, but I did anyway."

"And?"

"And there wasn't much. But she did say that Tom was worried about you. It seems you had a talk with him, saying you might need to be out of your office occasionally. He was naturally curious, but you wouldn't tell him why. You just asked for him not to tell anyone else."

"But Dorothy didn't know any more than that?"

"No. Tom told her he tried to find out more and couldn't. In the end he decided the only thing he could do was just trust that you knew what you were doing, and you'd explain it to him eventually."

"I hope I don't die without knowing too."

"What?" Nikki asked sharply.

"I said I hope I find out soon."

Nikki hesitated before she said, "I thought you were striving for more honesty lately."

"I'm sorry. I'm just worried about all of this. Do you think Dorothy will be okay?"

"I think so. I'll ask someone from the clinic to check in with her frequently."

"Thanks for breaking the news to her. I'm sure it wasn't easy."

"I was just lucky she hadn't had the news on and heard about it before I got here. And that I made it ahead of the police."

Cal said good-bye. The crew was still at work in the hallway as he left the building. He had planned on going directly to Galentine's, but decided to be cautious and go instead to the place he had mentioned to Leroy. Fortunately, they were close to each other.

A few minutes later he stood in front of Angie's, the bar he had named. "You're still recording video, right, Vincent?" he asked.

"On target."

"Then put a call in to Leroy Krantz."

Cal was in luck. Judging by the background view, Leroy was in the shuttle on the way over. The view appeared to be from lower than his head, off to one side. He had to be using his wristcomp.

"How about if we make it another place?" Cal asked. "Angie's is closed."

"Okay. Where?"

"Galentine's is close to here. You know it?"

"Sure. I'll see you there."

Cal hung up. He hadn't been able to tell if the video defect he sought was present or not during the call. "Did you see anything?" he asked Vincent.

"You mean image defects?"

"Yes."

"Yes, but they're not in the same place."

Cal didn't know whether to be relieved or disappointed. He hurried to Galentine's and found an empty booth. "Okay. Show me one of the frames."

Obediently Vincent brought up a picture of Leroy. His nose looked more hawklike from this angle. "I'm coloring the defective section red and enlarging it."

Cal saw the red in the bottom half of the image. The dots in the picture of himself that he had found had been at the top. The bad section continued to grow until Cal could see that there were three significant dropouts in the picture. Three black dots.

"They look a lot like the ones in the other picture except for location," Cal said. And then he knew the answer. "It *was* Leroy. If he'd had his arm down at his side when he took the picture of me, the bad section of image would have been swapped top for bottom. Retrieve the first picture, turn it upside down, and do a comparison." Cal held his breath.

An instant later Vincent said, "Perfect match."

—————— Chapter fifteen ——————
Havoc

"So Leroy has been behind it all," Cal said, still surprised at actually finding the wristcomp that had taken the picture of him.

"He's at least guilty of taking your picture," Vincent said. "Get the rope."

Cal signaled for a drink. "That doesn't sound like a lot, but that was the picture I found at Edmund's place. You can't have forgotten Edmund, our friendly electrician."

"I haven't forgotten him. I'm just reviewing the law. You have no proof that, because Edmund had a picture of you taken by Leroy, Leroy must therefore be guilty and convictable."

"You're probably more accurate than your ashtray cousin. And even if he were convictable, it still doesn't explain *why* he did it. In the thrillers the guilty party always explains why he committed his crimes, and what his next one is going to be. I don't see it being all that easy."

"Based on your luck so far, I'd have to agree."

"So somehow I've got to get him to tell me why he's done all this, without letting him know I don't know already."

"Let me make sure I've got this right," Vincent said. "If he thinks that you think that he thinks that you think that—"

"That's enough."

Vincent's apology, if he was going to make one, was cut off by the arrival of Cal's drink. Cal paid the waiter and took a large gulp.

"You might need a clear head," Vincent said.

"I'm sure I will. This doesn't have anything disruptive in it."

"How about ordering me a drink too? I need to unwind."

Cal didn't reply. He leaned back into the booth cushion, and the gun in his pocket pressed against his hip. "Can you set up a three-way call with Nikki and Michelle?"

"Do babies burp?"

Cal made no attempt to reply. Already he saw that Vincent had divided the display screen into two sections. A moment later Michelle's face appeared on the right side. Before he could tell her to hang on just a moment, Nikki was on the left.

"Nikki, Michelle. Michelle, Nikki. Can both of you hear everything?" he asked. They confirmed that they could. "Okay," Cal said. "I don't have much time. I'm at Galentine's, and Leroy Krantz is on his way over here. I'm sure he's the one responsible for this."

Both women asked the same question at once.

"Because," Cal said, "the picture I found at Edmund's has to have been taken by Leroy. That's all I know. I still don't know why all this is happening. But if either one of you get a marriage proposal from him after I'm dead, I want you to refuse."

Michelle agreed with a straight face and Nikki grimaced.

"What I'm going to do," Cal continued, "is ask Vincent to relay all the video and audio he picks up to one of you, say Michelle, since you've probably got access to better recording equipment. I'm still not even sure yet what I'm going to do with Leroy, but either we get evidence of what he's already done, or we get evidence of what he'll do to me. You got that, Vincent?"

Vincent acknowledged. Nikki and Michelle protested, so Cal told them about the gun. It didn't seem to make them feel much better.

"I'm sorry," Cal said. "But I don't have much time. He's due here any minute. I'll talk to you later."

Leroy didn't arrive until more than ten minutes later, but Cal was still glad he hadn't taken a chance on Leroy finding him talking to someone.

"I still can't believe Tom's really dead," Leroy said after he entered the room and closed the door. His appearance shook Cal's confidence in his newfound clue. Leroy really seemed to be shaken by the news.

"It's hard for me to accept too. But there wasn't much margin for error. Whoever set the explosion must have been awfully conservative."

"What do you mean?" Leroy ordered a drink as he settled into the booth.

"Just that the amount of explosive he used must have been ten times what it would take just to kill someone or destroy my desk. It leveled my office and injured people next door."

Cal tried to watch Leroy for reactions, without being obvious about it. It was puzzling that Leroy actually whitened slightly as he heard about the explosion.

"Maybe a little bit goes a long way," Leroy said.

"I don't think that's the case. Oh, maybe there are explosives powerful enough to require only a couple of drops to do that damage, but this particular explosive comes in containers that hold about a liter." Cal had the sudden hope that Leroy wouldn't ask him how he knew that.

Leroy didn't. He was interrupted as the door opened and a waiter brought in Leroy's drink. By the time the man had gone, Cal shifted the conversation away from the topic.

"It seems like everything's just about ready for the departure," Cal said.

If Leroy was relieved to switch subjects, it wasn't obvious to Cal. The man still seemed agitated. He drank his drink quickly. "Yeah," he said, making a nervous gesture. "It took a lot of preparation."

Cal's impatience finally grew too great. It was time to start applying the pressure. "It sure is hard to find good help these days," he said evenly.

"What do you mean by that?"

"I mean that Fargo Edmund sure hasn't been too reliable," Cal said, watching Leroy intently.

Leroy drained his drink and ordered another. "You're being awfully vague, Cal. Isn't that the guy you mentioned to me earlier? The one who fell while he was jogging?"

"The same one. Except that he wasn't jogging. He was running away from me."

Leroy tugged at his collar. "I don't understand. Why were you chasing him?"

"You don't understand? I'm surprised at you, Leroy. I thought it would be obvious to you."

"What are you talking about? If you're going to talk crazy,

I'm leaving. Maybe Tom's death has affected you more than you realize."

"It certainly affected me more than I realized it would," Cal said carefully.

"Maybe you should see a doctor."

"I already have, actually. He helped me in a couple of ways."

"You keep talking in riddles. What's the problem?"

"Okay. No more riddles. Just some clear, solid observations. I know what you're up to, Leroy." Cal had been about to threaten him with the police, but suddenly saw an alternative. "I want a cut."

"A cut of what? What do you mean you know what I'm up to?" Leroy was even more flustered, now finding it difficult to maintain eye contact.

"A cut of the profits," Cal said, guessing. "I've got the photograph, you see."

"Photograph?"

"It's a passable picture of me, taken outside the *Vittoria* office building. Do I need to say more?"

"You sure do. I don't know what you're talking about."

"I found it in Fargo Edmund's apartment. It was taken with your wristcomp. And I can prove it." Cal could prove only that Leroy had taken it, not that he had found it at Edmund's, but there was no use burdening Leroy with too much information.

"Cal, I—I don't know what you're talking about." Leroy's body language disagreed with his speech. He slumped now, hand on his chin. Sweat beaded on his forehead.

Cal didn't argue the point immediately, because Leroy's drink arrived in the hands of another waiter.

Cal paid little attention to the large man until he laid a fresh napkin in front of him. "I didn't order a—"

"Compliments of the house," the waiter said, pointing with his finger at the napkin. Only then did Cal realize there was a message written on the napkin. Suddenly chilled, he leaned forward to read it.

The note said, "If your wristcomp's on, turn it off NOW, or we'll kill you NOW. Believe it."

Cal cleared his throat uncomfortably. "Good-bye, Vincent," he said in as clear a voice as he could manage. A moment later he added, "Can you hear me, Vincent?"

No answer. Had he obeyed the instruction, or had he stopped responding to convince Cal's company that he had followed orders? Cal was afraid that he had taken the literal order.

Fear surged within him as he looked back up to the man who had brought Leroy's drink. He was a stranger, powerfully built, with broad features and a humorless way of transfixing a person with his stare.

"Listen up," the man said. "We're leaving here in one minute. You're coming with us. If you flinch just a little, and make me think you're running, I'll take the chance. Maybe they'll catch us, maybe not. But you won't be around to find out if they do or not."

"How did he learn so much?" Leroy asked.

"Shut up. We've got more to worry about now."

"But if he gets loose, he'll tell everyone what happened."

"I said shut up. I've got a plan."

"A plan like hiring Edmund? He was only supposed to hospitalize—"

"Shut up," the man said through clenched teeth. He said nothing more, but Cal could easily imagine him continuing with "Or you're going with him."

Leroy's imagination obviously worked well too. He shut up.

Absorbed with the interaction between Leroy and his friend, Cal hadn't noticed the small gun that the man now held.

"Get up," the man said.

Cal no longer had doubts about who the boss was. He directed his next question to the large man. "What if I don't?"

"Then you never do. I'll kill you right here."

"That's the problem with having too much curiosity," Cal said, trying to disguise his nervousness. He rose. "Other than that, why should I go with you? You'll just kill me somewhere else."

"Maybe. But this way your pretty little wife doesn't get her arms and legs sliced off later."

Cal's stomach lurched. "Okay. I'm ready to go."

"I thought that would persuade you. But you sure could have saved us a lot of trouble if you'd just stayed home like we asked."

Cal moved slowly toward the door.

"Wait a minute," the man said. "You're not quite ready

yet. Lean over the table, hands in the center.''

Cal did so, and the man searched him quickly and efficiently.

"Well, well, well. Our computer expert carries a gun. I must not have told you yet how much I don't like surprises."

Cal was straightening up when the blow hit. The man probably used Cal's own gun to hit him.

The impact caught him over his right ear. The explosion of pain in his head was all he was aware of for an agonizing moment. He eventually realized he had fallen onto the floor. He pulled himself to his feet, listening to the blood pound in his heart and hearing Leroy's objections silenced by the other man. The man gave Cal's gun to Leroy.

"Just trying to prevent future communications problems," the man said when Cal had made it to his feet. "I don't want you to do *anything* except come with us peacefully, and make no funny moves. You do, and your wife gets it later, and you get it right away. Is all that clear?"

"Perfectly." Cal no longer noticed his churning stomach for the pain in his head.

"Okay, then. Stand up straight. Look happy."

Cal tried to smile.

"Never mind. That's worse."

They opened the door and walked into the hall. Leroy was at Cal's side, and his partner followed, no doubt with his gun concealed but ready. Cal couldn't afford to do anything unless it had almost guaranteed success. He couldn't risk doubting the man's word about what would happen to Nikki.

Nikki. He clung to the hope that Vincent had kept transmitting, but that hope was fading. No police had arrived on the scene. The main room looked just as before, with people talking and milling around.

Cal walked at Leroy's side, looking for a familiar face in the crowd, but not knowing what he would do if he saw one. If it weren't for Leroy's partner's threat, he could have tried to escape into the throng. Surely they wouldn't fire on him in here.

Too quickly they reached the exit. The sweat on Cal's head began to cool and evaporate once they were outside.

"You were great," the man said. "Maybe that wife of yours will live a long life."

Cal said nothing.

"This way," the man said, indicating the direction by jamming his gun against Cal's ribs.

"There's no need for that kind of talk now that we're outside," Leroy said, breaking his long silence.

They walked along the terrace. Few other people were close, and Leroy kept his voice low.

"Who are you to object?" his partner asked.

"Dammit, Dave. This is all getting out of hand. It was never supposed to be like this."

"Shut up and keep walking."

Cal felt new shivers up his spine as he realized that Dave, if that were his real name, didn't object to being partially identified. The shivers intensified when he recalled that Michelle's data base had said Leroy's partner was a man named David Ledbetter.

With a minimum of conversation they boarded a tube car and rode to the south pole. Cal kept watch for the right opportunity, but none came. Shortly they boarded a shuttle.

Cal wondered why they were taking him to *Vittoria,* but his curiosity was soon changed to a deep, gut-twisting fear.

Dave closed the overhead entry but then touched a control panel. Cal knew without being told that the man had prevented the shuttle from being released yet.

Dave looked out the window for a moment without talking. Then he moved his gaze from the view of Daedalus, put the gun in his belt behind his back, and turned to face Cal.

Briefly he inspected Cal. Cal had started to wonder what would happen next when with no warning Dave hit him squarely in the solar plexus, hard.

Cal's view went black as he closed his eyes against the pain. The man's fist felt as if a pole vaulter's rod had rammed into Cal's stomach. Cal gasped for breath. His body bent under the force of the blow. Just as he began to think about how lucky it was that he hadn't eaten a large meal recently, Dave hit him again.

Dave's fist caught Cal solidly on the side of the jaw. Cal was fleetingly aware of Leroy's protests, but his head felt as if someone had exploded a large firecracker in his mouth and had another one buried in the back of his skull.

But Dave didn't stop there. He hit several more times, past the point at which Cal quit counting.

Cal must have lost consciousness for a brief period, because he found himself crumpled on the floor, hard metal below his chin. There was a sharp, salty taste in Cal's mouth. Leroy and Dave were arguing. Cal kept his eyes closed.

". . . didn't have to do that," Leroy said.

"Listen, Leroy. We've got to find out exactly how much he knows, and fast. If you've got a better way, get it out."

"There have to be drugs to do that."

"Well, excuse me. I didn't have time to visit someone who'd furnish fancy drugs for a price. Besides, this way is more rewarding."

Cal would have stayed quiet, but his rib cage hurt so intensely, he tried to shift his weight to reduce the sharp pain. The motion was detected.

"Help me get him onto a seat," Dave said.

The agony in Cal's ribs doubled as the two men lifted him by his arms to maneuver him. His body was flopped onto a chair, and his head snapped back against the bulkhead. Again he felt on the verge of throwing up.

"Okay, Mr. Donley," Dave said. "We're going to ask you some questions. You can answer them quickly and correctly, and you won't get hurt any more. I think you can figure out the other possibility."

"I probably could at that," Cal said, his voice blurred.

"See, Leroy. There's a little life left in him. You always worry too much."

Leroy said nothing. He had been unusually quiet lately.

"Okay," Dave said. "First question. Who else knows what you know?"

Cal shuddered. If Vincent were still transmitting, a possibility Cal was giving up on, he could tell them the truth, and they might even quit beating him. Otherwise the truth would merely let Dave track down Nikki and Michelle and kill them. If he told them no one else knew, he lost leverage, but their safety—

Dave hit him in the stomach again. This time Cal did throw up. Unfortunately, he threw up on Dave, so the man kicked him.

As the pain slowly receded to the point where Cal could pay attention to his surroundings again, Dave said, "I asked you to answer quickly."

Cal tried to spit out the answer fast enough to avoid more pain. "No one else knows."

"Convince me."

"Convince you?" Cal's words were slurred. "Think about it. If someone else knew I was meeting Leroy to get money out of him, you think you would have been able to get me here?"

This time Dave slapped him hard on the cheek. Cal's head felt like it was going to come off.

"Let's try that again. I know damn well you weren't trying to get money out of Leroy. You wouldn't go in for blackmail."

"I appreciate your confidence in me," Cal said heavily. "I wanted to find out why."

"If you don't know why, you don't know much. How did you find Edmund?"

Cal tried to find a lie that wouldn't point back to Michelle. "I tapped into the master file of pictures of everyone alive and ran an image comparison program until I narrowed it down. Then I went calling. I'm a computer expert, remember?"

Dave thought for a moment, then seemed to accept the answer. "How did you trace him to Leroy? Not that I'm implying that part must have been particularly hard."

The truth would work this time. "I found a picture of me in Edmund's apartment—"

"What were you doing in his apartment?"

"I went there after he fell off the terrace. So I found this picture. And it had been taken with a wristcomp. A wristcomp with some defects in the video. I started calling anyone I could think of who might have had a reason to hurt me."

"So you called Leroy."

"Right. They matched."

"How'd you think you could get away with that alone?"

"I *had* a gun, remember?"

"Yeah. Why?"

"Why?" Cal repeated.

"Why'd you call Leroy. What made you think it might be him?"

"No good reason. I wondered why he'd seemed nervous during the test the other day."

"That's *all*?" Dave glared at Cal. Then he turned to Leroy and said, "Damn, but you're dumb."

"There was a little more," Cal said. "During the test I witnessed, the picture faded for just a moment."

Dave rubbed his chin. The big man towered over Cal.

"Maybe we did the right thing after all. You hadn't suspected anything earlier?"

"No," Cal said. It was getting harder to talk, because his jaw was becoming stiff, but he tried one more time to get information out of them. "How much are you guys going to make off this deal?"

"Enough."

Maybe the direct approach would work. "Dammit," Cal said with a tongue that almost refused to obey. "What the hell did you *do*?"

"You don't even know that much?" Dave turned to Leroy, and glared at him again. "We made some economies in the communications gear. *Vittoria* doesn't really need it, and Tolbor wasn't watching too carefully, so we eliminated a few of the backups."

"So the image fading was just an indication that reliability was low?"

"I think we've wasted enough time here," Dave said, ignoring Cal's question. "Leroy, get two suits out of the locker."

Cal's remaining strength started to fade. He hadn't paid much attention to the suit locker on his past trips. Another thing he hadn't thought about much was the emergency door at the rear of the shuttle.

Cal had always been good at math. Despite his fatigue and the throbbing pain, he could easily see that three men, two suits, and one emergency exit left almost zero hope.

—— Chapter sixteen ——
Hurdle

CAL shuddered, pulling himself upright in the shuttle seat. He tried to convince himself that Dave wouldn't throw him out the emergency exit.

"Don't move," Dave commanded. "Hurry it up with those suits, Leroy."

Cal's thoughts snapped back to Nikki and Michelle. If only he could use the threat of someone else's knowledge to avoid being thrown out the emergency exit. But telling Dave would be like ordering their execution.

But he had to do something. Cal searched the possibilities. He had no chance, in his current condition, of overpowering Dave.

"What's the slow-up?" Dave yelled at Leroy. Leroy still hadn't got the suits out.

"Just a minute," Leroy said. "I need to think. There's got to be some other way."

"What are you talking about?"

"Some other way of dealing with Cal. To kill him—"

"We have no choice, you idiot. If he's alive, he can find us. And he can protect his wife if he has enough time. This isn't some eighteenth-century swashbuckler. We can't just disappear. You heard how he found Edmund. There's no choice."

"Just a minute," Leroy repeated.

Cal saw the opportunity and tried to capitalize on it. "You'll get caught sooner or later anyway, Leroy. You can claim that the times Edmund tried to kill me were due to his misunderstanding. If you're here when your partner throws

189

me out, you don't have a chance."

"Shut up," Dave said. He said it a lot.

"I left a disposition with the bank computer. It's to send it to the police if I die."

"You're lying," Dave said. "You would have mentioned it before."

"Until now, I didn't think you were going to kill me. And surely somebody will remember seeing us together at the bar."

"He's right, Dave," Leroy said, still not reaching for the suits.

"Dammit, he's lying, trying to make you think we'll get caught."

"I still don't want to kill anyone."

"You're not going to. We'll both be in suits, and our friend here will just be a little slow getting into his. *I'll* open the door."

"You'll be just as guilty," Cal said.

"Shut up," Dave said.

"Leroy," Cal called. "You've got my gun. You can do something to correct all this. Edmund tried deliberately to murder me three times, obviously at Dave's request. He's the guilty one. Your only offense is—"

"Shut up," Dave shouted one more time. But this time he didn't wait to see if Cal would obey. He punched Cal again, three quick, hard, vicious punches.

Cal was sure he felt a rib crack. His breath was gone. He couldn't talk.

"Give me the gun, Leroy," Dave said. Obviously Leroy's delays were not lost on Dave.

With blurred vision Cal saw Dave approach Leroy slowly, gun pointing toward him.

Cal fought to get his breath back. In the last instant before Dave reached Leroy, Cal snapped a cushion loose from its resting place and hurled it at Dave.

Several things seemed to happen all at once.

Dave whirled to see the cause of whatever had hit his back. It took him a fraction of a second before he assessed Cal's action, obviously dismissed it, and turned his attention back to Leroy.

Leroy had not been idle while Dave had looked behind. He had drawn Cal's gun.

For an instant the two partners faced each other, guns drawn. Then, so close together that Cal couldn't tell the true order, a high-pitched beep sounded on the shuttle intercom, and twin burning noises indicated that each man had shot the other. Maybe the intercom sound had triggered both men to fire. Maybe they would have fired anyway.

Nothing seemed to happen in the next moment. Leroy and Dave stood unmoving, and the intercom remained silent. Perhaps a second later, motion resumed.

Dave pitched forward onto the floor of the shuttle, and Leroy began to sag. He grabbed for a handhold and held himself from falling.

As Leroy hung there, the intercom sounded again. "This is the police. We have the shuttle release inhibited. Put down your weapons and prepare to come out unarmed, one at a time."

Cal was finally able to breathe again, but the sharp pain in his ribs flared as he tried to gulp in a deep breath. "Hello, Vincent," he managed.

"What the hell's going on around here?" Vincent asked.

"Never mind that for now. Just tell the police they can come in unmolested."

Leroy's face was quite pale. He sagged farther.

Cal struggled to get enough energy to move to him. Trying to block out the pain in his ribs, he pulled himself close enough to Leroy to help him sit down.

Leroy was shaking. Blood seeped from a chest wound. "I didn't mean for there to be any killing," he said, straining to get the words out.

"Why did you do it?"

"For the money." Leroy paused to lick his lips. "Dave's idea. Put in cheap substitutes. Almost worked."

"Why didn't you stop when the killing started, if that wasn't what you wanted?" Cal asked, having to lean closer to hear Leroy's response.

"I tried, dammit. Tom was a friend of mine, too."

"Tom? Why not stop when Domingo was killed?"

"Domingo?" Leroy's eyes began to stare into the distance. "Who's Domingo?"

"Gabriel Domingo." Cal realized he was raising his voice. "What about Forget-Me-Now?"

Leroy couldn't keep his eyes open. "You're not talking—" Leroy coughed. Flecks of blood appeared on his lips. "—sense."

"I'm not—" Cal stopped.

Leroy had abruptly gone limp. His head began to tip forward. Cal pushed Leroy's body back into the seat. Leroy was a boneless, life-size doll. Cal felt the man's wrist. Leroy's heart had stopped.

Dave lay still. Cal couldn't see his chest moving.

"Damn," Cal said, and leaned heavily back on the cushions. Noise from above reminded him about the police. "Vincent, what's taking the police so long?"

"Apparently the hatch is jammed, or locked from the inside."

Cal levered himself upright. Everything seemed to be a hazy red. Near the ladder he found the interior control panel, and saw a large amber blinking panel that said MANUAL—LOCKED.

A nearby control was labeled AUTOMATIC. Cal pushed it. A moment later came the deep noise associated with the hatch opening.

"All right," someone yelled from above. "Out. One at a time."

Cal summoned his strength to yell back. "It's going to take a while. There are two dead men in here, and I don't think I'm in good enough condition to climb the ladder."

"Who are you?"

"Cal Donley."

A minute later a remote monitor drifted slowly down the hatch. About the size and shape of two saucers stuck together face-to-face, and partially helium filled, it maneuvered carefully with small gas jets.

Cal stepped back and sat down on the chair. The monitor puffed a couple of times and approached Dave. After a brief inspection it rose and moved near Leroy's body. Completing another short check, it rose to waist-height, drifted to the center of the shuttle, and rotated until twin sensors pointed at Cal.

Only when that was complete did Cal hear feet on the hatch ladder. First into the shuttle was a uniformed policeman, Lieutenant Dobson. Second was a young doctor.

"You're lucky to have friends," Dobson said, sitting on a cushion to one side, while the doctor sat on the other side and began to unpack his instruments.

Cal didn't reply. The exertion of unlocking the shuttle door had been even more draining than he had realized.

"Your wife and Michelle Garney are up above," Dobson

said. "They wouldn't tell me what all this was about, but I watched enough of the video coming from your wristcomp to make it clear that you were the victim here."

So Vincent *had* kept transmitting. "Thanks, Vincent," Cal managed. "I'm indebted."

"You're welcome," Vincent said.

The doctor asked Cal to lean forward just a little so he could slide a screen behind his back. As Cal tried to comply, his last reserves finally faded, and he lost consciousness.

When Cal awoke, he smelled the odors he associated with the clinic. He opened his eyes, squinting against the brightness.

Nikki sat in a nearby chair. Her eyes were closed.

"Hello, Nickname," Cal said softly.

Nikki's eyes opened and she smiled. It was the best smile Cal could recall. She brought her chair over and sat down beside Cal's bed. "How are you feeling?"

"Emotionally or physically?"

"Either."

"Better. Both. What are the damages?"

"Other than quite a few bruises, two broken ribs."

Cal looked at Vincent's screen. It was almost ten hundred the next morning. "Have you been here since last night?"

"Yes."

"You should have got some rest."

"I did. I slept here."

Cal's throat tightened as he realized, without knowing the specifics, that Nikki was like that. She had always been generous and concerned. Why had he been so oblivious? "Nikki," he said. "Thanks. You didn't need to, though."

"It was little enough after what you did last night."

"I got punched a few times. That's not very—"

"You know what I mean. You could have told them about me and Michelle. And they could have started after us."

"But Vincent kept transmitting. You would have known what was happening and told the police."

"*You* didn't know that. You couldn't know that Vincent would guess what you really wanted and keep transmitting after you told him to turn off. Maybe getting him wasn't such a mistake after all."

"Well, I like that," Vincent said.

"I thought you were off," Nikki said, not apologizing.

"Who would have turned me off? Cal passed out while I was on."

"This may seem ungrateful, Vincent, but I really would like to turn you off for a little while," Cal said. "I do appreciate what you did last night."

"No problem. I'm going."

Nikki grinned.

Cal reached his hand to hers. "Thanks for being here."

She squeezed his hand in return. After a moment she said, "Lieutenant Dobson wants to talk to you."

Cal thought back to the night before. "How much of Vincent's transmission did he see?"

"Only the part where those two were getting ready to throw you out of the airlock." Nikki shuddered.

"So he doesn't know what all this is about?"

"Neither do we. I'm just glad it's over."

Cal looked up into her eyes. They were softer now than he had seen them in the last few days. "Nikki," he said. "It's not all over."

She frowned.

"No," Cal said. "I'm not talking about you and me. I agreed not to bring that up. I'm talking about Leroy and Dave and this whole strange business. It's not over."

"But of course it is. It must be."

"I wish it were. Believe me. But something's still wrong. When Leroy was dying, I asked him a few questions. Did you hear me?"

"No. By then we switched off the video. We were waiting at the shuttle with the police."

"He said he was very disturbed by Tom's death, and that killing wasn't part of his plan."

"But Domingo—"

"Exactly. Why wouldn't Leroy have been bothered right then? The answer is that he didn't know about Domingo. He wasn't responsible. He denied knowing anything about Forget-Me-Now too."

"Maybe his partner handled all that."

"It's a possibility, but I don't think so. Too many things just don't fit. Sodom and Gomorrah, the Presodist church, Domingo's death—none of those are answered. I think there's still something else going on."

"Back to ground zero?"

"Not quite. We should be able to figure out which actions were caused by Leroy and Dave. That means the rest are someone else's fault. Then we have a hope of seeing the true pattern. Maybe Tolbor is our man after all."

"But if that's true, then you have less than a day to find out."

"Except for one thing. We know the communications gear on the *Vittoria* wasn't built to the specifications. By publicizing that, we can delay the departure."

"Why not just announce it now?"

"Because whoever our real antagonist is, we don't want him panicking. We want him to think it's business as usual, so he might get careless."

"How sure are you that Leroy told you the truth? It seems that two men, trying to cover up embezzling or whatever you want to call this, could easily have caused everything."

"He was dying. He was in a lot of pain. I don't think he had a good reason to lie to me then. Besides, I still have this feeling that there's more to it. Someone else is involved. Help me sit up, will you?" Cal pushed against the bedding, trying to get upright. His chest hurt, but not unbearably.

"I told Lieutenant Dobson I'd call when you could talk," Nikki said.

"That's fine. But would you also talk to Michelle and ask her not to release any story just yet? Except for what the police already know."

Nikki made the calls. Cal heard Michelle's protests, but she quieted down after Nikki told her the rest.

Lieutenant Dobson couldn't have been very far away. He was in Cal's hospital room not five minutes later. Nikki pulled her chair back to the wall and sat, listening.

Dobson sat gingerly at the foot of the bed. "I suppose you know that both men are dead."

"I was pretty sure. I'm not in trouble about that, am I?"

"No. We saw the video being relayed up just before we got to the shuttle. You may have to answer some questions at the inquest, but it will just be routine. What I wanted to find out was *why*. Your wife didn't want to show me the rest of the video, and I didn't choose to make an issue of it."

Cal thought for a moment. "They had been planning something illegal, and I found out about it. Leroy wanted to call it off. The other guy didn't want to. Fortunately, they argued long enough for you to get there.''

"What were they planning?"

Cal decided to mix in a slight amount of truth. "You know, that's almost funny, in a bizarre way. I don't know exactly. They were planning to steal some expensive equipment from somewhere. I heard the end of a conversation between them, enough to find out that something illegal was going on, but I didn't hear all of the talk. They assumed I had heard it all, and nothing I could say would convince them I hadn't.''

The lieutenant looked disappointed, as though he had been expecting all the sordid details. Cal made himself a promise to tell Dobson as soon as he could after he knew what was *really* going on. Linking himself to Domingo's killing had too much potential for restricting his actions.

The policeman pried for a few more details before he finally gave up.

As Dobson left, Michelle came in. This time Nikki sat on the bed, and Michelle brought the chair over.

"What's all this nonsense about suppressing the story?" Michelle asked once she was settled.

"Didn't Nikki tell you?"

"I wanted to hear it from you."

"Well, you can run the story about Leroy and Dave killing each other. And you can mention that I was there. But it would make things easier if you played down the connection, like I was an innocent bystander." Cal mentioned the questions still unexplained, and Leroy's denial of knowledge about Domingo.

"Okay," Michelle said finally. "But what next?"

Cal turned Vincent back on and said, "Next we've got to sort through the pieces of information we've accumulated, discard the things Leroy and Dave were responsible for, and examine the balance."

"So," Nikki said, "we're eliminating the incident on the tubeway, the trap in your *Vittoria* office, and the explosion."

"And," Cal said, "the Vital Twenty-Two."

"Why?" the women asked together.

"It just doesn't seem to me to fit with the rest. It triggers absolutely no memories even now. I keep getting tiny flashes, but never about drugs."

"What's left, then?" Nikki asked.

"Domingo's death," Cal said. "I'm guessing that he didn't know any more about Leroy's plan than I did. But someone killed him. And my visit to Forget-Me-Now has to tie in."

"The Sodom and Gomorrah references," Nikki said. "You've seen them too many times for them not to be important."

"So that just leaves the church," Michelle said.

"And the messages I've sent to Jam," Cal finished. "But the church may have been mentioned only because Tolbor, or whoever I was keeping track of, goes there."

Michelle had too much nervous energy to stay seated. She rose. "Refresh me on the Sodom and Gomorrah story."

Cal looked at Nikki. She drew in a breath and started. "The story was about Lot. He lived in Sodom, one of the two most important cities of the plain. Abraham talked to God about trying to spare them, but Lot was the only innocent man God could find.

"When Lot was on the way out of Sodom, his wife looked back, disobeying, and was turned into a pillar of salt. After that Lot made his way to Zoar, the last city of the plain."

"Tell me again why the cities were destroyed."

"The passage says because the residents were serving other gods."

"I still don't know if there's any literal significance there," Cal said. "If Earth's dead cities represent Sodom and Gomorrah, it could be as crazy as someone deciding that looking back, like with the Earth telescope, might be sinful."

"Or that anyone working on reclaiming the Earth is looking back, and that's sinful," Nikki said.

Michelle said, "Or it could be that whoever you were watching has slipped in the shower and killed himself. Everything that's happened since Domingo died we can attribute to Leroy and his partner."

Cal looked at her. "Maybe he doesn't need to do anything. Maybe he's confident that blanking my memory is sufficient to keep me away."

"That could make it impossible to find him," Nikki said. "If all he needs to do is lie low and escape on the *Vittoria,* then where are we?"

"For one thing," Cal said, "we can always delay the *Vittoria* by telling what we know—"

"If they believe us," Michelle said.

"Right. But maybe we can make him panic. What do you think he would do if you printed a story saying I had been to Forget-Me-Now a few nights ago, and some new, previously untested process was somehow able to eliminate most of the memory blockage?"

"It sounds risky to me," Nikki said. "Besides, that all depends on how much you knew before that night. If all you had were suspicions, then that story might not worry anyone."

"But what other chance do we have?" Michelle asked.

No one spoke.

After a long moment Cal said, "I don't see any alternative. We've got to force some action. Whoever we're dealing with is a lot more passive or a lot more confident than Leroy and company. Maybe this will jolt someone into doing something we can use to our advantage."

Nikki was plainly unhappy at the latest decision, but after a few more objections she gave in.

"Give me just a few minutes to call the office and get this started," Michelle said.

Cal and Nikki waited silently as they listened to Michelle call. Nikki got up to stretch, and when she sat back down on the bed she was closer to Cal than before.

Michelle had someone on the other end and was starting to make her request when the other person evidently interrupted, and Michelle said, "What?"

There was a pause. Then she said, "Yes, I know him. When did it come in?" She frowned. "Read it to me verbatim."

Michelle looked more worried as she listened. Finally she said, "Never mind about my original request. I'll get back to you."

She terminated the call and looked over at Cal and Nikki.

"What is it?" Cal asked.

"An anonymous tip was just sent in. The tip names Domingo's killer."

Michelle's eyes were unreadable as she looked at Cal. "It was your name."

──── Chapter seventeen ────
Hope

AFTER Michelle's announcement there was an awkward silence. Cal looked at Nikki and then back to Michelle. Finally he said, "Oh, come on. You can't believe I killed Domingo, can you? After all that's happened?"

"No," Michelle said. "For a few minutes there, I tried to believe that it was all over—that it was really/all related to Leroy, and that he just wasn't thinking clearly after he was shot. But with this message coming in, I can't deny it any longer. I've got these cold shivers, like when you first told me what was happening."

"Me too," Nikki said. "There must be someone else. Someone who's got something to hide."

Cal took a deep breath and settled back onto the bed.

Michelle tapped her temple. "Just a minute. I was thinking about so much, I forgot to do something." She called her office back and began talking with whoever had given her the message a few minutes ago.

"Put a hold on that message until I get a few more facts to go with it," she said. A pause. "No. It can wait a little while."

This time the speaker on the other end took longer. Michelle rubbed her forehead as she listened. Finally she asked, "How'd you find out?"

Another pause. "Okay," she said. "Never mind. Just hold it as long as you can."

Michelle looked up after completing the call. "The news station wasn't the only one to get the message. Our friend made sure the police got a copy too."

Before Cal had time to respond, the door opened and Dr.

Bartum came in. "Awfully quiet in here," he said. No one disagreed.

Bartum came over to the bed, and Nikki got off. "You certainly seem to be leading an adventurous life lately. First having that seizure, now getting assaulted. How are you holding up?" Bartum didn't ask what it was all about, but Cal had the feeling that he was intensely curious. Bartum scratched his chin. The room was so still, the whisker stubble sound was clearly audible.

"I've probably had better weeks," Cal said.

"Yes, I suppose so. Well, I need to take another look. Can you get back into the center of the bed, with your head on your pillow?"

Nikki helped Cal maneuver while Bartum raised a small plate from one side of the bed. When she was finished, the doctor pulled a second plate up on the other side of the bed.

Bartum turned on a wall screen near the head of the bed and inspected several views of rib cage. "Still looks okay," he said at last. "But you'd better get plenty of rest."

"I'm not sure that's going to be possible," Cal said.

Dr. Bartum silently looked at Cal for a long moment. Then he turned to Nikki, still without saying anything.

"I can't control him," she said in response to his unasked but obvious question. "He seems determined to destroy his body."

"Maybe I should just give you a tranquilizer gun and let you shoot him every time he moves."

Nikki looked at Cal. "I don't know if even that would stop him. How about if you do the best you can, assuming he has to be on his feet in a day or two?"

"A day or two?" Cal said.

Nikki didn't seem to know what to say.

"I don't suppose tomorrow morning would be soon enough?" Bartum asked. Then his lips pressed, indicating that he was sure even that wouldn't be adequate. He was right.

"How about in ten minutes?" Cal asked, grinning, just as the door opened behind Dr. Bartum.

"How about what in ten minutes?" asked Lieutenant Dobson, stepping into the room. "I hope you're not considering leaving."

"You got here remarkably fast for just having got a tip," Cal said.

Dobson looked at him speculatively. "And you're remarkably informed for an invalid. I need to talk to you. Alone."

"I don't think it needs to be alone. I don't have secrets here." It didn't matter if Nikki and Michelle heard, and Bartum's attempts at concealing his curiosity were woefully inadequate.

"You might change your mind," Dobson said.

"If I do, I'll ask people to leave."

"Okay. It's your privacy." The policeman approached the bed but didn't try to find a chair. "Don't say anything you don't want used against you in court." He pointedly switched on his wristcomp.

"Understood," Cal said.

"You obviously heard that we received a report naming you as the person who killed Gabriel Domingo."

Dr. Bartum breathed in loudly and covered his mouth when Cal looked at him.

"A report, or an anonymous message?" Cal asked.

"An anonymous message, but that's beside the point."

"Gabriel Domingo, the construction worker?"

"Yes."

"Or Angelo Gabriel Domingo, the undercover policeman?"

Lieutenant Dobson's eyes narrowed. "What exactly do you mean by that?"

"Later. What are your questions?"

"Do you admit going to Forget-Me-Now the night Domingo was found dead?"

"Think about your question, Lieutenant. If I had my memory blanked, how would I have functioned this week? I've been at work, at home."

"You didn't answer my question."

"Your question can't be answered. If I wasn't there, the answer is no. If I was there, I wouldn't remember it, so the answer would still be no. Next question?"

Dobson looked distinctly flustered, as though this were not exactly the line of questioning he had anticipated. "Very well. What do you know about an allegation that you were in possession of illegal drugs, drugs that you gave to your wife, who in turn gave them to someone here at the clinic?"

Cal refrained from looking at Nikki. How did their anonymous informer know about that? Unless it was Nikki, Michelle, or—or whoever Nikki had given the drugs to. "In

what sense do you mean 'gave'? In the pharmaceutical sense
of dispensing, or in the generous sense of—"

"Stop right there," Lieutenant Dobson said, his features
tightening in obvious anger. "If you're going to be deliberately obstructive, or if you want to play games with me, we're
going up to the office, and your wife—"

Dobson was interrupted by a two-note chime from his
wristcomp. For a moment he looked as though he were going
to ignore it and continue his statement, but then he apparently
changed his mind. "Just a minute," he said, and went out of
the room.

Cal looked at Nikki, Michelle, and then at Dr. Bartum. By a
healthy margin the doctor's expression was the most surprised. Michelle looked as if she were going to say something,
but changed her mind when she looked at Dr. Bartum.

Dobson was out of the room for only a short time. When he
returned, his puzzled expression wasn't all that different from
the one on Dr. Bartum's face. Cal guessed that both men had
experience in masking their expressions, but today wasn't
quite a normal day.

Lieutenant Dobson seemed subdued in addition to being
puzzled. He approached the bed slowly. "I'm going to have to
delay this session," he said. He looked at Cal for a long moment, then turned and started for the door.

"Wait a minute," Cal said. "What's going on? What do
you mean delay? Delay until noon?"

Dobson turned to face Cal. "I don't know. My boss directed me to put everything on hold."

"So now you're thinking I've got political clout—friends in
high places?"

"You've seen too many movies. Mike Jones doesn't do
favors for *anyone*. Whatever his reason, you can bet it's a
good one." With that, Lieutenant Dobson left. The door
closed automatically, but Cal could have sworn it closed more
gently than usual behind the puzzled policeman.

Dr. Bartum still wore his curious expression too.

Cal was as confounded as anyone. "Doctor, could you excuse us for a few minutes, please?" he asked.

"What? Oh, sure." Bartum's bedside mask was in
shambles, the disappointment on his face almost as easy to
read as a child's.

When the door closed again with Dr. Bartum on the outside, Cal and Nikki and Michelle took turns looking at each other before Michelle finally spoke. "I guess the police spy theory gains weight."

"So it would seem," Cal said. "And the duplication of letters in 'Jam' and 'Mike Jones' makes me wonder if Mike Jones *is* Jam."

"That's fairly flimsy," Nikki said.

"What do you know about Jones?" Cal asked, looking at Michelle.

"He's one of the top officials at headquarters," she said. "Strong reputation for pushing hard when it's necessary. He's had a tendency to worry more about the end than the means, but no one has ever accused him of not acting in the public interest. He's a stocky guy about my height. Keeps his hair cut real short."

The description seemed familiar to Cal. "If Jam were Mike Jones," he said, "I still don't know why he wouldn't have contacted me after I sent him a message."

"You must be a psychic or something," Vincent said. "A text message signed 'Jam' just came in. You want me to read it now?"

"Go ahead."

"It says, 'With your memory gone, I didn't feel I could answer your last message. I have called off Dobson, as you probably know by now. Not sure how Domingo's death figures with Krantz. Let me know if you do.'"

Cal looked up at Nikki, more relieved by the confirmation than he had guessed he would be. "See. So Jam *is* Mike Jones. I told you I'm not a murderer. Working for the police has got to explain it."

"Maybe you should tell him about Leroy's shortcut on the *Vittoria* communications system," she said.

"Not yet. There's still time for our friend to make a mistake. Michelle, you got the recording okay?"

"Safe and sound in my desk computer."

"The *Vittoria* isn't scheduled to leave until tomorrow morning, right?" Cal asked.

Michelle nodded.

"So if we can delay until early tomorrow, that gives us about eighteen hours."

"Twenty-four hours with maybe no more clues," Nikki said.

"Let's talk about our old standby, Russ Tolbor. What's going on now, Vincent?"

"Nothing. He's not near the bugs in his office, his Daedalus apartment, or Galentine's. I still have recordings of conversations from the times he's been in any of those places, but he hasn't been back in his apartment in the last day."

"Still nothing suspicious?"

"Nope."

"What's he talked about?"

"By keyword?" Vincent asked.

"Sure."

"Daedalus, departure, Earth, exploration, final tests, friendship, history, job, religion, sports, *Vittoria*."

"I notice you left out murder and memory erasure."

"True. Those subjects never came up."

Cal lay back on the bed, feeling overwhelmed by the lack of hard facts to grab hold of. "Replay one of his conversations about departure."

"This is from last night at nineteen twelve."

Tolbor's voice sounded from Vincent's speaker. "Leaving is going to be so hard. I know I've been trying to persuade you to come, but I guess that, in some ways, I'd like to stay too."

"It's not too late. Find someone else to command." The second voice reminded Cal of one of the men he had seen with Tolbor at Galentine's.

"It's not quite that easy." Tolbor paused. "I cleared out the rest of my things from the apartment today. It's hard to leave that place."

"I'm sure your new fancy house will make it easier."

"Maybe." Tolbor sounded wistful.

"That's enough, Vincent," Cal said. "Damn. There's got to be something we can do to force action out of whoever knows about Domingo."

Michelle stood up. "Unless you've got a better suggestion, maybe I'll go back to my office and start some more data base searches, this time with narrower parameters, and another day's worth of data."

"My mind is a blank—" Cal started, revising it hastily to, "I can't think of anything better. What about you, Nikki?"

Nikki shook her head. After Michelle left, Nikki came back and sat on the bed. She looked as worried as Cal felt. "Maybe Domingo's death isn't solvable. Have you considered that possibility?"

"Yes." Cal reached his hand to touch Nikki's.

Her eyes seemed warmer than they had been in the last few days. She looked at him seriously, as though trying to make a decision, but she said nothing.

"How likely is it that the person you asked to analyze the Vital Twenty-Two is the one who talked to the police?" Cal tried to think of how else the information might have leaked.

"I really don't think she would have. But she's probably on duty right now. I'll go ask her."

"Are you sure that's the best method?"

"For me it is." Nikki leaned over and kissed Cal on the lips. Then leisurely she rose and left the room.

Despite the broken ribs, the other abuse he had taken from Dave, and all the disasters of the week, Cal felt considerably better in the space of that one minute. Maybe there was hope of salvaging what he had once shared with Nikki.

He thought for several more minutes, alternating between Nikki and the question of who had killed Domingo.

"Well, Vincent," he said. "what do *you* think? Will she come back to me?"

"My success rate at predicting human reactions is probably even worse than yours."

"Even?"

"Never mind. I only work here. You've got a message coming in. From Michelle."

"Okay."

Cal could tell immediately from her face that something was wrong.

"What's happened?" he asked, worried.

"My desk computer. It's been destroyed. As well as my office."

"Another explosion?" Cal pushed himself up on one elbow.

"Someone with a hand laser. Whoever it was sliced up almost everything on the walls, and the internals on the computer."

"But at least no one was hurt?"

"Right. But the recordings were demolished."

Cal had momentarily forgotten, worrying about Michelle rather than the office. "I see." The possibility that someone was telling secrets was now confirmed. But who was it? And how?

"I see? That's all you can say?" Michelle asked. She made

agitated motions with her hands but said nothing else.

"I'm sorry, Michelle. I'm just glad you're all right. We'll just have to figure out an alternative. Can you call me when you've got things under control over there?"

"Okay." She took another deep breath, and said, "Okay. I'll call you back after I see if there's any hope of salvage."

Cal didn't know what to do next, but he couldn't just lie in the hospital. He struggled to his feet. The pain in his chest was worst when he bent forward to rise. Once on his feet, he walked shakily to the closet.

Dr. Bartum was learning. Cal's clothes were there already. Putting on his socks was the worst part. He had just completed dressing when Vincent told him he had another message. A text message.

"It's signed 'Jam' again," Vincent said. "It says, 'Need to talk with you privately concerning new data received regarding Domingo. Can't talk in office. Meet me at laboratory D8 in manufacturing disk at fourteen hundred. Important you don't tell anyone. I'll explain.' "

Cal walked slowly back to the bed and sat down gingerly. Why shouldn't he tell anyone? Why shouldn't he tell Nikki or Michelle? Surely Mike Jones couldn't suspect one of them. Or did he think one of them was monitored?

Cal wondered suddenly if some of the places he frequented were monitored in the same way he was eavesdropping on Tolbor. Maybe someone was listening in on *his* conversations.

And then it hit him. His scalp contracted, and shivers edged down his spine.

Only one person could have reliably reported on all the conversations Cal had had with Nikki and Michelle. And the conversations with Leroy and Dave.

Except that it wasn't really a person. The only possibility of consistent, mobile monitoring was now so obvious to him that anger welled within him.

──── Chapter eighteen ────
Hindsight

OF course. Vincent. Only Vincent had been nearby during all his conversations in the past few days. It was Vincent who had kept transmitting to Michelle after Cal had asked him to shut himself off.

At the time Cal had been grateful that Vincent had kept transmitting. Only now did he think about how easy it would have been for Vincent to have been doing that all along.

Cal looked around at the stark walls in the hospital room. He felt as though he'd just lost another friend like Tom.

He couldn't verify his theory, of course. But the evidence seemed overwhelming. And regardless of whether or not Vincent was transmitting to someone else, Cal couldn't take the chance that he was. Cal must act as though everything were normal. He couldn't let whoever was listening on the other end know that the situation wasn't the same as it had been five minutes ago.

A thought hit him suddenly. Maybe this was one small advantage he finally had over the listener on the other end. As long as the observer thought he was unsuspected, Cal could conceivably use the knowledge to his advantage.

Cal rose from the bed, his ribs hurting less this time. He paced.

His mind was racing. Too many new possibilities to consider all at once tumbled into his consciousness. The message. If the transmission from Jam warning him not to mention it to anyone was referring to Nikki or Michelle, then the message was sent from someone misinformed, Cal hoped.

If the message came from someone that ill-informed, then the sender wouldn't help Cal much. If, however, the message came from a person who wanted Cal to meet him all alone, the picture was much different. That person would be the one listening on the other end. That person was someone Cal wanted very much to meet.

But would it be a meeting? Far more likely it would be a trap. Perhaps a fatal trap.

His consideration of the possibilities was cut short by the sound of the door opening. Nikki was back.

"I talked to my friend," she said. "I really don't think she's the one who talked."

No. She wouldn't be. The listener on the other end would have heard all about her already, and that would have been sufficient. "Thanks for talking to her," Cal said, trying to think fast enough to sound like nothing unusual had happened.

"You don't sound like you care," Nikki said. She came nearer and looked at him carefully.

This was going to be harder than he had thought. "I do care. I just didn't hold out much hope that it would be her. You pick your friends pretty carefully."

"You're dressed," she said, apparently noticing for the first time.

"Yeah. I've, ah—been in bed too long. I need to get out and have a little exercise." Maybe he could tell her he'd be back in an hour or two. Time to think and all that. Cal wasn't about to give the listener on the other end any more reasons to hurt Nikki.

"Well, I'll go with you. Maybe some sunshine would help."

"Ah, Nikki, I could use a little time alone, to let me think more clearly."

For a moment he thought it might work. Then a puzzled frown wrinkled Nikki's forehead.

"Cal," she said. "Nothing's the matter, is it? You're not going to do anything more than just think?"

"Would I do that?"

It was the wrong thing to say. He had never been able to lie to Nikki.

The hurt in her eyes was terrible. It twisted Cal's weakened stomach into knots.

"I know what you're thinking," he said hurriedly, aware

that he had bungled the job. "But it's nothing big. I just need to run an errand."

"Tell me about it," she said, far too calmly.

"I'll tell you about it as soon as I get back." If only he could write her a note, so the listener couldn't tell what was happening. But he could be watching too. Even if he wasn't, a delay would make him suspicious.

"I want to know about it now." Nikki's voice rose. "You've talked all week about open communications. I've had a lot of second thoughts about leaving. But you're driving me away right now. Please tell me what's going on."

"I can't," Cal said softly. Saying the words was like cutting off his hand. But if he didn't convince the listener, he and Nikki would be dead. He knew that, but he still couldn't figure out *why*. "Please trust me." It sounded lame even as he said it.

Nikki looked at him, speechless for an agonizing moment. Then the pain in her eyes turned to anger, and she clenched her fists. "Trust you? Trust you, Cal? I'll never trust you again."

Cal moved toward her, but she backed away, palms toward him.

Without another word she turned and left.

The door slid shut behind her, sealing her off from him. Cal felt like vomiting, the emotional pain was so much like physical pain. He stood mute.

The hospital room was utterly silent. Devastated, Cal sat down tiredly on the bed. For a moment he tried to concentrate on Vincent and the message, supposedly from Jam, to force Nikki out of his thoughts. It didn't work.

The damage had already been done. Nikki would never come back to him now. So why did his memory persist in dragging up old scenes? Why did it keep returning to one time when she had surprised him at work?

He had gone into work a little early to catch up. After he had been there for perhaps an hour, Tom had come down to tell him he was late for a meeting in the main conference room.

Cal hurried down there, wondering what it was he had forgotten. When he arrived, he found that there was only one person there before him. Nikki. With her was a bottle of wine and a picnic lunch. She had already talked to Tom and arranged a vacation day for Cal.

Cal hadn't even gone back to his office. He and Nikki just left the building and went to a park.

"Damn." Cal forced away the memory, suddenly conscious of the irony of now *not* wanting a memory back.

"Are you talking to me?" Vincent asked.

"No. I was just frustrated. I wanted to tell Nikki I was meeting with Jones and for her not to worry. But I can't. This had better be damn important." Cal had to act in front of Vincent too.

He wondered how deeply Vincent was immersed in this subterfuge. For all Cal knew, Vincent could have been obeying someone else's orders ever since Cal bought him. At the other end of the scale, it was conceivable that Vincent didn't even know what was going on. There could be some other program running in the same computer, unknown to Vincent's program. That second program could be doing anything from just transmitting audio all the way to altering Vincent's memories and forcing him to say particular things.

The proposition that Vincent had been spying on him ever since Cal bought him was too much to accept. Somehow Vincent had to have been tampered with since then. And that meant the most likely possibility was that the tampering had been done five nights ago, the night Domingo died.

That night must have been an awfully busy eight hours. Domingo died. Cal's memory was blanked. And Vincent was altered to report Cal's activities to someone.

That someone could still be Tolbor. All of Tolbor's conversations about how good a job Cal had done, and how Tolbor wished Cal was coming on *Vittoria,* could have been staged. If Tolbor had known all about Cal's activities, he certainly would have known about the transmitters Cal and Michelle had planted.

In fact, if it really were Tolbor who was listening in, he probably could barely manage not to laugh out loud during his phony conversations. The listener could be being listened to. And Tolbor's computer knowledge was probably ample to load a second program into Vincent's memory, one that ran without Vincent's knowledge.

Cal himself might have had the same capability, and the information required to correct the situation, maybe even alter it so Vincent would transmit *Cal's* phony conversations, but not now. Not with so many of his memories still unavailable. His only hope was somehow to use his wits to give him an advantage.

He should have an advantage already, suspecting the tampering, but he saw no way to use the knowledge. How can you trick someone who knows everything you do? You can't just call someone and say, "Oh, be sure to let the dog out," hoping they'll realize something's wrong. Not when the listener knows there is no dog and can hear the friend call back to ask, "What's happened?"

Cal stood up shakily. "I'd better get going if I want to be on time."

"You sure you're okay?" Vincent asked.

Cal hoped that Vincent had been tampered with. He wouldn't like to think that Vincent had been designed to cooperate with the listener all along. "Yeah. I'll be fine."

The door opened at his request, and Cal paused for a moment, deciding which way to go. Nikki was nowhere in sight. To the right a short corridor led to the outside. Cal almost started in that direction, but he remembered his last visit to the clinic.

He turned left.

Another turn at the end of the corridor took him toward the nurse's station. He felt progressively more steady as he walked, but he deliberately kept moving slowly. At first he was afraid there was no nurse on duty, but then he saw the man's head.

As he'd hoped, the nurse, a pudgy young man with blond hair, spoke to him as he neared. "Mr. Donley, isn't it?" he asked.

"That's right." Cal approached the counter shakily.

"What are you doing up so soon?"

"I'm leaving." Cal started to pull away.

"But Dr. Bartum hasn't authorized your release yet."

"He's not my keeper."

"I know that, sir. But either Dr. Bartum signs your release, or I need you to sign a waiver of responsibility."

Finally. Cal moved still closer to the counter, his hands at his sides.

The nurse pushed a clipboard and a pen on a chain up to the countertop.

Cal picked up the pen and began to write, keeping his eyes fixed on the seated man. "What do you mean, 'release'?" Cal asked. "You mean that if I fall down outside and kill myself that Dr. Bartum can't be sued?"

"It's just a safety precaution, Mr. Donley. The clinic wants its patients to know when they're doing something not recommended by the doctor."

"For all I know, Dr. Bartum approves, but he just hasn't told you." Cal kept writing.

"I can't justify the policy for you right now, sir. Please just sign the form."

"Okay. Okay. Right here where it says, 'Patient acknowledgment'?"

"Yes, sir." The nurse had obviously decided this was a lot of fuss for a simple signature.

Cal finished writing and left the clipboard on the counter. The nurse made no move to retrieve it.

Outside, the mid-afternoon sun wasn't enough to keep Cal from feeling chilled. He couldn't tell if it was because of his recent injuries or his state of mind. If he still had the gun, maybe that would have made him feel better.

He could always go buy another. But if the listener were real, he could see exactly what the new gun cost and how much charging current it drew. He'd probably also wonder *why* Cal was buying another gun right then.

"Vincent," he said, making his way along the route to the tubeway. "The name of the lab where I'm meeting Jones sounds familiar. Have I been there before?"

"Not that I know of. You could have been there before you asked me to start keeping more information. But if you'd gone there this week, I'd have lots and lots of pictures."

"So it's getting more crowded in there?"

"It's so crowded in here I'm having to reuse all the electrons."

"Right," Cal said dryly.

"I'll bet you think I'm kidding."

"How about if you put yourself to use. At this walking speed, am I going to arrive at the tubeway in time for the next car?"

Vincent was silent for a moment, perhaps determining Cal's speed. "Nope. You'll miss it by about fifteen seconds."

"How about at this speed?" Cal asked. His ribs began to hurt more.

"You should have about twenty seconds to spare. This is all theoretical, of course. Since the stops aren't consistent, I'm assuming a typical frequency."

"That's fine, Vincent. I can't expect you to be right all the time."

"Now, wait a minute. That's not what I said."

"Okay. Okay. You're as right as you can possibly be."

"I'll let that pass."

Cal arrived at the tubeway with less of a margin than he wanted. He had to run a few steps to make it. Light-headed and breathing heavily, he found an empty seat. The car started up the hill.

Cal glanced around at his fellow travelers. The car was almost full. Just like Vincent was almost full. The idea of a few people getting off at the next stop began to occupy his thoughts for no apparent reason. He puzzled over it for a moment before he realized the significance of the thought.

Cal actually smiled faintly. At least he had another possible line of defense, if it turned out that Tolbor or someone other than Mike Jones was waiting for him in the lab.

The feeling didn't last long, however. Nikki was back on his mind as the car stopped at the south pole, and Cal drifted into the corridor leading through the spin axis.

Before long he was in the rotating disk, and then on the same level as the lab the message had mentioned. He was two minutes early.

The corridor outside the lab looked like almost all the other corridors in the disk. But the lab door brought back the first feeling of déjà vu.

The sign on the door said D8: LINEWOLD TESTING LABORATORY in large blue letters. The door was unlocked.

The room inside was enormous. Five long, parallel, double-sided lab benches ran almost the whole length of the room. Large doors stood at either end of the lab.

Cal took a second glance at one of the two doors. For an instant he could have sworn he saw Gabriel Domingo in front of it. Then he realized what had happened. Some fragment of his memory was telling him that he had seen Domingo here. Maybe the night he was killed.

Cal walked closer to the door, hearing dim echoes of his footfalls. The door looked as if it were pressure-tight, maybe the entrance to an environmental chamber. A large gasket showed around the edge, and a big wheeled lock held the door shut.

"Telegram," Vincent said, and Cal jumped.

"You startled me," Cal said, surprised at how apprehensive he felt here. His nervousness had to be caused by more than just the possibility of confronting the listener.

"You want me to clear my throat first?" Vincent asked.

"No. What is it?"

"Michelle."

"Put her on."

"There's no hope of salvaging the recording," she said. "But I found out a few more tidbits on Tolbor. If there's anyone else you want me to check on, let me know."

"I don't have the vaguest idea anymore of who we should be looking for," Cal said for the benefit of the listener, if there was one. "But why don't you give me what you've got anyway."

"Okay. He's paid up his apartment here on Daedalus for another month after he leaves. Evidently he's letting a nephew use it temporarily, but I haven't checked on the nephew."

As Michelle talked, Cal realized that, if Michelle paid attention to the background, she might be able to give the police a clue to his location if he were reported missing. If Nikki noticed. Trying to avoid any overt actions, he slowly moved Vincent to where there was a clearer view of the lab itself. "Anything else?"

"One item that seems a little unusual. Tolbor rented a fair amount of industrial equipment for a friend about a year ago. Vacuum pumps, waldoes, power supplies, sterilizing gear, large motors and winches, solar panels, and a bunch of miscellaneous small items. The friend was apparently going to build a prototype for a new solar panel design."

"What's unusual about that?"

"Maybe nothing. I was just surprised that his friend didn't rent it himself."

"Okay. It doesn't seem so insidious to me. Anything else?"

"There's a public going-away party for him tonight."

"Maybe I'll go," Cal said.

"Are you all right?" Michelle asked suddenly.

"Sure," Cal lied. "Fine. Why?"

"No reason." Michelle hesitated for just an instant. "I'll see you later."

Michelle switched off. Cal hoped she had noticed his surroundings, but imagined that they were much like lots of other labs.

A noise caught Cal's attention. It could have been his imagination, or it could have been someone moving at the far end of the room. Cal began to walk quietly toward the source of the sound.

The benches he passed were thick with dust. The floor was cleaner. Behind him Cal could see no outlined footprints. His heart began to beat more loudly.

He couldn't identify much of the equipment. A few electronic measurement devices were the only familiar instruments. The sound didn't recur.

Overcome by a burst of uneasiness, Cal suddenly stooped low to see if he could see anyone's legs below the line of lab benches. He could see none, but the view was cut off in several directions. There wouldn't have been a concealed group with him in the room, but there could be a single man. Or woman.

Cal reached the far end of the lab without encountering anyone. The door on this end was metallic, but not as sturdy as the other door. It was solid in a different way, not as though it had to withstand high pressure.

Cal stared at the door, wondering what was on the other side, when he heard another sound. This time the sound was definitely from the other side of the door.

Cal hesitated. If the listener were on the other side, Cal wasn't at all sure he wanted to open the door. But if he didn't, he would never know, and whoever it was would be free to do as he chose.

Cal twisted the wheel on the door. It moved freely, spinning to the end of its travel. He pulled, and the door swung easily outward. Inside was darkness.

Cal was about to close the door again when a light in the distance came on. It was a small light, directed toward Cal.

An instant later a figure moved partway into the path of the light and stood silhouetted against it.

"Come on in and close the door, Cal," the figure said. The voice was male and familiar-seeming, but echoes distorted the voice beyond easy recognition.

"Mike?" Cal asked tentatively.

"That's right. It's Mike Jones. Come on in. I need to talk to you."

Cal stood transfixed. The possibility that this was legitimate was all but nonexistent, but he still didn't know the truth. He made a concerted effort to slow his breathing.

Cal took a step up into the room and closed the door. To his right there was another door set in the wall, an interior wall of the chamber he was in.

"Cal—" Vincent began.

"Not now." Cal had to hear the voice again. He took a few more steps into the gloom.

"It's important," Vincent said.

Cal took a few more steps, considering. "Okay. What is it?"

"I'm shielded. This room is cutting off my transmitter and receiver from the outside."

Cal stopped.

"Please come ahead, Cal," the voice said pleasantly. "I really must insist." The figure put its arm into the pool of light.

The hand gripped a gun.

Cal still hesitated.

"Your wristcomp is fond of old expressions," the figure said. "Have you ever heard the phrase 'Easy as shooting fish in a barrel'?"

"No. But I suppose I see your meaning." Cal resumed walking forward.

The figure said nothing more until Cal had traveled almost halfway. "I think that's far enough."

"Far enough for what?" Cal asked. He didn't like the way the man had said it. He wondered too if his ears were playing tricks on him. The man's voice had not sounded as though it were still straight ahead this time.

"Please stay there, Cal." The man's voice was slightly clearer than before.

Cal halted. He might not have recognized the voice by now if he hadn't already been suspicious. "What do you want from me, Russ?"

Russ Tolbor said nothing for a moment. When he spoke, his voice was utterly calm. "I want from you more than you're going to want to give. I'm greatly disappointed in you, Cal. I've never seen someone so talented give it all up to go to work for the man."

" 'Go to work for the man'?" Cal asked. He knew what Tolbor meant, but he couldn't understand why he said it.

"The devil takes whoever he can get. I bet he was quite delighted to find you."

"Russ, you're just not talking sense. I may not go to church regularly, but that's—"

"Silence!" Tolbor had turned on a death-and-destruction preacher's voice Cal never knew he had. Tolbor's religious state was more severe than Cal had realized.

"Why did you want me here?" Cal asked.

"I had to stop your interference."

"My interference with what?"

"With God's plan, of course. It really will do you no good at all to pretend, Cal." Tolbor's voice was calm again.

Cal didn't know what to say.

Into the lengthening silence Tolbor said quietly, "I'm sorry to have to leave you here to die, Cal."

"What do you mean?" Cal asked apprehensively.

"You'll know in a day or two."

At the same moment Tolbor spoke, Cal felt a cool breeze on his neck. At first he thought his fear was responsible for the chill. Then he realized suddenly that it was simply a ventilation fan.

The fan triggered his intuition.

Horrified, Cal finally made sense of the connecting pieces. How could Tolbor possibly be that sick?

The Bible spoke of Sodom and Gomorrah being destroyed by God, while Lot traveled to a new home. Cal was being left to die in a well-ventilated laboratory while Tolbor left on a mission of exploration. Tolbor wasn't leaving Cal to suffocate.

In his Daedalus apartment Tolbor had hung twin pictures of Earth and Daedalus. But only now did Cal realize what Tolbor must see when he looked at them.

He saw Sodom and Gomorrah.

——— Chapter nineteen ———
Helpless

CAL was stunned at the realization. Tolbor had to be absolutely certifiable. He couldn't possibly plan to destroy life on Daedalus.

But Cal had no doubts. He knew suddenly why he had been worried that Nikki would die. They all would die.

The sterilization gear that Tolbor had rented, and the waldoes, all of it made sense. Tolbor hadn't caused the disaster on Earth, but it must have pushed him over the edge. He probably saw it as God destroying Sodom. Now Gomorrah was ready to fall, and Tolbor was God's chosen one. A modern-day Lot, one acting as God's firm right hand.

Cal was desperate. There had to be *something* he could do. "You're mad," he said slowly.

But Tolbor didn't answer. He moved out of the light, and a noise sounded from behind Cal.

"Wait a minute," Cal said, turning swiftly to face the exit, realizing why he had been confused about the direction of the sound. Tolbor had put a mirror at the far end of the room, to trick Cal into thinking he was ahead rather than near the entrance. Tolbor had been just on other side of the door Cal had passed. Cal started for the exit. Fear made his heart pound.

"Stop right where you are," Tolbor said harshly into the gloom. Light spilled from the interior doorway, giving him a half-light, half-dark appearance.

Cal stopped. Then he began to move forward in minuscule steps. "Aren't you curious," he asked quickly, "about how I found out you were monitoring me?"

Tolbor hesitated, the gun visible once again. "Make it quick."

An encouraging thought occurred to Cal. If Vincent had been cooperating all along with Tolbor, if he were following Tolbor's instructions, there was no need for Cal to be locked in a shielded room. A strong closet would have been adequate. Maybe he could get close enough to Tolbor that he might consider taking Vincent with him.

"Vincent," Cal said. "Make sure you get all this recorded, so you can pass it on to whoever finds me if I die soon. It may be too late already, but I have to do whatever I can."

"I'm all ears."

"That's the first part of the problem, now that you mention it. The night Domingo died, something else happened too. Russ must have tampered with you."

"I beg your pardon."

"Just listen. Somehow, I think he loaded a second program into your memory, one which was set up to run without your noticing. As far as I can tell, it's still there, and designed to do only one thing: relay audio and video to Tolbor."

"How sure are you? I haven't noticed anything like that."

"It has to—"

"Wait a minute," Vincent said. "I think I see something. Well, 'see' isn't quite the word, but periodically, my transmitter goes busy for a little less than a microsecond."

"That must be it."

"I didn't pay any attention to that. I thought maybe one of my subroutines was just responding to location checks or diagnostics."

"I doubt it."

"Do you have any suggestions?"

"Yes. Search through your entire memory, looking for anything that doesn't seem to be exactly what you thought should be there. If some of the video you've saved has been altered, or if any data that should be recognizable looks more like a program, find it."

"This may take a while."

"Get to the point, Cal," Tolbor said. "I've got to leave."

"I think I found it," Vincent said excitedly. "Damn him. He *tampered* with me. Cal, you've got to beat the hell out of him."

"First things first." Cal looked back at the gun in Tolbor's hand. "Get rid of it if you can."

"Done," Vincent said. "Cal, I'm sorry. I didn't mean to betray you. You know I wouldn't."

"I know. It's okay. You were just fooled. Like I was."

"How long have you known?" Tolbor asked.

"Since I got the message asking me to come here. That's why I couldn't tell Nikki. She probably has her own apartment already. But I'm worrying about centimeters when I should be concerned about light-years. Vincent, our friend here is planning to kill everyone on Daedalus."

"He's WHAT?"

"Correct me if I'm wrong, Russ." Cal explained what he had deduced, finishing with "So Russ must plan to leave a container with the bacteria on Daedalus. When it breaks, there won't be anything left to stop the bacteria. And Gomorrah will go the way of Sodom."

"So how long do we have?" Vincent asked.

"My very question. Would you care to tell us, Russ? It can't be too long. *Vittoria* leaves at oh six hundred. You're obviously planning to leave me alive, so you don't expect me to be found before you're untouchable." Cal looked at Vincent's screen. "So we probably have between twelve hours and maybe a day or two. And Luna will die, too, if the bacteria gets spread before anyone gets the first symptoms. Damn!"

"It's been nice knowing you, Cal," Vincent said. "I guess this means you aren't a murderer. I'm glad to know that, at least."

"Don't start, Vincent. We're going to get out of here. Tolbor's just confused. He's been reading the Bible too much. He isn't really going to do this, are you, Russ?" Inside, Cal was as pessimistic as Vincent, but he refused to stop trying. He crept closer.

"This has ceased to be interesting," Tolbor said. "You've got substantial power on your side. That's obvious from the progress you've made. But you stay here, and I go. That's what it all comes down—"

Cal knew that. He held no hope for reprieve. The only change of heart Tolbor would be likely to have was a transplant. So, just before Tolbor finished speaking, Cal began to run.

Obviously there was only one exit. Since Tolbor hadn't disagreed when he said he'd leave Cal alive, he had to be intending to lock him in the shielded room. Once the door was closed, Cal would have absolutely no chance.

But now he had one small one. He took huge steps, ignoring the pain in his ribs, swerving, trying to keep his course erratic. Tolbor was a man who set things in motion. He didn't pull triggers, Cal hoped.

He was wrong.

Just as Cal closed the distance to a meter, he heard Tolbor's gun discharge, and he felt the stabbing pain in his side. But Cal's momentum kept him going.

He hurtled into Tolbor, slamming the man hard against the door. And then Cal hit too. His head crashed into solid, unyielding metal.

Lynn was sitting on his lap. She looked up into Cal's eyes and smiled. Across the room lay her traveling bag. Nikki sat nearby. Her bags were packed too.

Cal found himself looking at a door labeled LINEWOLD TESTING LABORATORY in blue letters. There was someone behind him. Gabriel Domingo.

"But we've got to go in, Gabe," Cal said.

After a discussion too brief to call an argument, they opened the door. The room full of lab benches lay in darkness until Gabe found the light switch. They searched the room thoroughly, each covering half of the area.

They obviously hadn't found whatever they sought. Cal convinced Domingo they must continue searching. The emissions lab proved to be uninteresting, so Cal examined the other door, the one that looked as if it were built to seal an environmental lab.

Gabe shook his head and pointed at the door. Cal moved to it and tried to turn the wheel. It wouldn't move. Cal called to Gabe and indicated his stronger muscles.

Annoyed, Gabe pushed Cal aside and twisted on the wheel. It didn't turn for him either. He applied more force. His biceps tensed, and sweat appeared on his forehead.

The wheel began to turn.

The last conscious act Domingo made was giving Cal a condescending but friendly grin, turning the wheel with only one hand.

Then the door did something Cal had never expected. With no warning sound it burst open so quickly, it was hard for Cal to believe that it was a solid, massive door.

Gabe couldn't believe it either. He had no time to retreat

from the door's path. It smashed violently into his chest.

In the same instant Gabe's body rammed backward into Cal. Cal felt himself propelled off balance, thrust into a wall-mounted ashtray that caught him just to one side of the small of his back. His head snapped against the wall. Dazed, he slumped to the floor.

The pain was excruciating. Unable to move for several moments, Cal finally managed to pull himself over to where Domingo lay.

For just an instant there was a look of amazement on Gabe's face, and then it was gone. He had probably been dead even before Cal was able to see his face. Gabe's chest was crushed, and he had already lost a massive quantity of blood.

For a moment Cal refused to believe what had happened. It couldn't be. But it was. "Gabe," he cried in a strangled voice. "Gabe. What have I done to you?" If only Cal had opened the door. If only he hadn't asked Gabe to come with him.

For several long seconds Cal didn't know what he was doing. When his awareness returned, he saw that he had taken hold of Gabe's legs and had pulled him away from the door, as though removing him from the scene would eliminate the damage.

"Vincent?" Cal said.

"Yes."

"Erase all records of my recent activities."

"If that's what you really want."

Cal didn't know if that was what he wanted or not, he was so confused. But he didn't want those memories getting into the wrong person's hands if he were caught soon. "Do it."

He stopped right where he was and collapsed. After a time he realized he was crying for the friend he had lost, for being the one to drag him here. Cal turned off Vincent and looked up.

From where he was he could see into the enclosure that had been barred by the door. It was dark inside, but light from the main lab spilled in and shone off something silvery inside.

He wiped blood from his hands onto the floor and then rose shakily. He moved a step or two closer.

The silvery shape was in the center of the room. It seemed to be a sealed test tube.

He approached more closely. As he reached the entrance to the lab, he noticed an unusual smell, rather like roses.

His knees weakened suddenly, and he had to catch himself

on the door. And then, as he thought about thoroughness and booby traps, consciousness slipped away.

Cal was uncomfortable. He tried to straighten his pillow. He was still uncomfortable. Only after a few more minutes did his head begin to clear. Something was wrong. This wasn't a pillow. This was—what?

It was a body. Cal flinched. He pulled himself away so rapidly that the jolt started his head hurting. What was he doing lying on top of a body, particularly a male one?

And then things began to come back swiftly. Russ Tolbor was the man beneath Cal.

And Russ Tolbor was dead.

It took no detailed inspection for Cal to reach the conclusion. He quickly checked for a pulse to make absolutely certain, but the action only confirmed what he already knew.

He rose shakily. A raw spot on his side painfully reminded Cal where Tolbor had shot him. Cal had been lucky. Or Tolbor had shied from taking a direct, irreconcilable action.

Tolbor and Domingo. How different they were. And how similar they looked in death.

"You're still on, right, Vincent?" Cal asked at last.

"I'm fine. And I'm glad you're okay. I would have called for help, but I'm still shielded. I couldn't even call out for pizza."

Cal grinned wryly. He swung the door open and stepped out of the chamber and into the lab. "Can you communicate again?"

"Yes."

"In just a minute I want to call Lieutenant Dobson. If anything at all happens to me, call him, bring him up to date on the last"—Cal looked at the time—"two hours. I want to do something first."

Cal walked shakily over to the environmental lab he had noticed earlier, the one he had just remembered. As he got closer he began to get a bad feeling about it. By the time he reached it, he knew why. The door was shut but not locked.

Standing clear of the path of the door, Cal pulled at it to open it. He pulled harder.

The door slowly began to swing open. And suddenly Cal felt at least as bad as when Nikki had walked out.

The test tube he had seen earlier was gone.

——— Chapter twenty ———
Hoard

"Mr. Donley," a voice called. "Are you in there?"

Cal moved from behind the door. Lieutenant Dobson was at the entrance to the lab.

"Thank God you're here," Cal said, starting to function again. "We may be too late already."

Lieutenant Dobson stepped into the lab. "Too late for what? Are you injured? Your wife and Michelle Garney tried to tell us something was wrong with *Vittoria*'s communications, but no one was convinced. We thought they were just worried that you might be aboard *Vittoria*." There was another policeman with Dobson.

"They were right," Cal said. "But it's far worse than that. Russ Tolbor. He had a container of the bacteria in here. The bacteria that destroyed Earth." Cal led them to Tolbor's body.

"You're serious, then," Dobson said in a hushed voice.

"There's no time to delay. I've got wristcomp recordings to convince you, but we've got to act now."

"Whatever you say, sir. I've just had a long talk with Mike Jones." Dobson's eyes were steady, but his jaw muscles contracted and relaxed as he looked at Cal.

"Okay, then. We've got to evacuate the whole colony."

Lieutenant Dobson gave Cal a final appraising gaze and made a call. "Dobson, sir. Immediate evacuation of Daedalus and Icarus is required."

The voice on the other end asked, "Donley says so?" The voice Cal recognized as Mike Jones's.

"Yes," Dobson said.

"I'll start it. But we can't handle more than five to ten percent." He gave orders to someone else for a minute, then said, "Put Donley on."

"Here," Cal said.

"Give it to me fast."

"There's a container of the bacteria that killed life on Earth. It's somewhere on Daedalus or Icarus. And I'm sure it's going to break sometime soon. Russ Tolbor brought it here."

It was a lot for Jones to accept, but he did it readily. "We'll start a search. We've got a lot of people to do it with, since probably ninety percent of us are stuck here. What's it look like?"

Cal told him.

"Any idea where he might have put it? I'll have someone ask him fast and firm, but I don't want to count on it."

"None." Cal explained why no one would be able to question Tolbor, and then thought for a moment. "Maybe in his old apartment. He paid for another month in advance."

Jones didn't ask him his source of information. He just acted on it.

"I'm going over there myself," Cal said. "It's on my way home. I want to see if my wife will speak to me one last time."

"Why shouldn't she?" Dobson asked. "She was worried enough about you an hour ago."

Cal had started for the door, but stopped and turned. "What do you mean? You found me here because of the note I left on the waiver log, didn't you?"

"Yes, but we probably wouldn't have found you so soon if she hadn't raised such a commotion after you disappeared. She's the one who went looking all through the hospital for some indication of what had happened. That nurse probably wouldn't have looked at the log until the end of the month."

Cal couldn't speak for a moment, he was so relieved to learn the news. Then he tried to force thoughts of Nikki out of his mind. They had to find the container.

"Thanks," he said to Dobson, and started for the door.

"I'll join you," Dobson said. "It's a big place, and that seems as good as any to look." He directed his companion to stay behind with the body.

On the way over Dobson explained two things that Cal had

still been puzzled about. First the faked findings in Domingo's apartment, the drugs and weapons, had been intended to make Domingo look like a criminal instead of an undercover officer, to protect Cal. Second, Cal had been asked to help investigate, not because the police had any real reason to expect fraud or any other crimes, but because that was the way Mike Jones chose to be thorough. No one but Mike Jones had known the entire story until recently.

When Cal and Lieutenant Dobson reached Tolbor's apartment, there were two other policemen leaving. "You're wasting your time," one said.

Cal sagged against the hallway wall, wondering if he should try to find Nikki, to spend their last hours together. Instead he entered the apartment.

He understood immediately what the man had meant. They had ripped the place apart.

The men had already dismantled the furniture, the computer cabinet, and the kitchen appliance cabinets, leaving panels hanging open. Nothing inside. The only other possessions still there were the two pictures on the wall.

Cal felt sick. How could Tolbor do it? If the container wasn't here, it could be almost anywhere. It could take years to find.

Cal couldn't believe it wasn't here. Not after Tolbor arranged a month's extra rent. He moved to inspect the computer cabinet.

The cabinet had so many panels removed, Cal could see straight through it in almost any direction he chose. There couldn't be anything like the bacteria container hidden there.

The kitchen appliances were the same. The police had used controlled-depth cutting lasers and carefully peeled apart any possible area of concealment.

Bitterly depressed, Cal walked back into the living room. He looked again at the pictures of Earth and Daedalus, wondering how Tolbor could possibly think that he was doing God's will.

And, as he looked, it hit him. The bacteria had to be near the pictures.

He could imagine Tolbor feeling secure with the container hidden here. With the rent paid up, no one should enter the apartment. And Tolbor had no reason to believe that anyone would even be searching for the container.

Cal moved to the pictures and gingerly removed them from

the wall. There was no wall safe behind either.

But there was a faint seam in the wall, and several small holes, as though someone had tried several times to find exactly the right location to hang the pictures.

"Grab a knife or a screwdriver," Cal shouted to Dobson, who was in the kitchen.

Working rapidly but cautiously, they succeeded in prying away a wall panel. Behind it lay a silver test tube.

A quiet fan blew air past the tube, directing it toward the vent holes in the wall. And adjacent to the tube was what had to be a detonator and timer.

Gingerly Dobson removed the timer package. Only when it was outside of the apartment did Cal actually begin to relax.

" 'Thanks' is a pretty weak word," Dobson said, wiping his forehead."

"Thanks for believing me. I'm going home."

"What about that?" Dobson pointed to the burn hole where Tolbor had shot him.

"It doesn't hurt too badly. I'll see to it soon." Fortunately, the wound was in the fleshy area in Cal's waist, and it had stopped bleeding.

"Okay. We'll notify the *Vittoria* that they'll be needing a new commander." Dobson tipped two fingers toward Cal in a salute.

Filled with a weary sense of relief, Cal started to leave, but paused. "Oh, one more thing. I think the guy who helped Tolbor is Paulo Frall. He was an attendant at Forget-Me-Now. He's probably on Luna right now. Tolbor must have warned him that I was suspicious, but he almost certainly doesn't know what Tolbor was concealing."

The tubeway was much busier than normal, so Cal couldn't board the first car along. As he waited Vincent told him that a public announcement was being broadcast, announcing a stop to the partial evacuation.

"I haven't been thinking," Cal said. "Call Michelle, would you, Vincent?"

"Am I glad to see you," Michelle said when she answered. "Have you talked to Nikki yet? She's worried sick. And give me the details on what happened. I've got a newscast to prepare for."

"In order, no, I haven't talked to Nikki. I wanted to do it in person. And Tolbor did it."

"Come on. Come *on*."

"Okay. I'll give you as much as I can before I get home. And if I don't finish, I'll give you the rest at least four hours before I agree to talk to *anyone*."

"Better. Go ahead."

Cal talked quietly into Vincent's microphone for almost the whole trip.

As he neared the house he wondered the same thing he had wondered several times lately. Would Nikki be home?

"Wish me luck, Vincent."

"You'll need it."

"Thanks a lot."

Nikki was there. She sat stiffly in one of the living room chairs, her eyes seeming darker than usual. She held a hot drink in her hands, as though trying to warm herself.

"Hello, Nikki." He tried to keep his voice calm.

"Hello, Cal." She matched his tone.

"I need to talk to you."

"I wasn't sure if you still would."

Cal was taken aback. "You mean because of what you said in the hospital?"

"What else?" Nikki sniffed and drew in a deep breath.

Cal stepped closer. "You know now why I couldn't talk then?"

"Yes. I knew it when I saw the note. I felt even worse than I did when I talked to you in your room."

"Can you forgive me, then?"

"God, you ask silly questions sometimes. Of course."

"If you can forgive me for seeming to do the wrong thing when you didn't know all the reasons, I'd be a pretty small person if I couldn't do the same."

Nikki's face lit up, but she stayed seated. "But you haven't talked about wanting me at all in the last few days."

"Now who's silly? I was afraid that if I did, it would drive you further away." Cal moved another step closer. "I want you more than I've ever wanted you. I love you."

Nikki scrambled out of the chair, and Cal moved to join her. The strength of her arms as they embraced put too much pressure on his ribs, but she didn't complain.

"I want you too," she said into his ear. "I'm glad you're back."

"Me too. In more ways than one."

After a few minutes Cal's cheeks began to hurt from smiling. "Lieutenant Dobson told me you were the driving force behind the search for me after I disappeared," he said. "I thought you would be busy apartment-hunting."

"I just couldn't accept it at all. I really thought you were trying to pull closer, and then you wouldn't talk. The more I thought about it, the more I was convinced that something was wrong. I wanted to come with Dobson, but he takes a hard line on risk and police responsibilities." Nikki backed up a few centimeters and said, "Tell me what happened." She straightened Cal's hair. "God, you look terrible."

He told her, finishing with, "When Jones originally asked me to make covert checks, he gave me a severe warning about telling *anyone*. But I found I didn't want to anyway. I felt dirty, spying on my friends. Anyway, I started listening to people's conversations. Sodom and Gomorrah came up in a couple of Tolbor's conversations—he didn't know he was being listened to then. He obviously felt it was God's plan, not some horrible accident. He talked a lot about how Jupiter had been so clean and unspoiled. I started wondering.

"I'm still not sure about the Vital Twenty-Two, but I think one of Tolbor's friends gave him some, figuring it wouldn't be any crime for him to use it himself. Anyway, I eventually found out Tolbor was one of the original owners of Linewold Lab, and went to check it out."

"But why did you suspect Tolbor when you came to?" she asked. "What made you so sure it was him?"

"I wasn't sure. It was just that most of the indications pointed to him. Tolbor was the person I had bad feelings about when I walked around that first day after Gabe died. I think Leroy and Dave decided to embark on their plan only after they realized Tolbor wasn't paying much attention to the *Vittoria*-to-Daedalus communications equipment."

"Why was that? Because calling back to Daedalus would be like Lot's wife looking back at Sodom and Gomorrah?"

"That's my theory too. And there were some small things that I finally realized in Tolbor's lab. When I tried out Fargo Edmund's name on Tolbor, he said he didn't know *him*. But Fargo could be a woman's name too."

"I don't understand why Tolbor wasn't going to kill you outright while he had the chance," Nikki said, shivering and wincing as she spoke.

"I'm not entirely sure myself. My best guess is that Tolbor

saw himself as a tool of God, responding to gentle nudges, setting clockwork devices in motion. As long as he didn't take any final, direct action, there was always the possibility of change. If he was misinterpreting God's will, there was always the chance of God arranging for someone else to upset his efforts. And, if no one did, well, Tolbor was right all along."

"But why did you think to look behind the pictures?" Nikki asked.

"Because I had seen those same two pictures, already moved, at Tolbor's *Vittoria* home. So there had to be two sets, or he moved the one set back. Either way, it didn't make sense."

Nikki looked at him intently, her eyes warm, her cheeks flushed. "How much of your memory has come back?"

"Almost all, I think. I guess when Tolbor told the Forgot-Me-Now attendant to do it fast, and to blank as much as possible, he made a mistake. They blanked more memory than usual, but they did it too lightly. Tolbor must have really been in a panic when he heard how much I was able to recall or stumble over." Cal hesitated. "Now I even remember that frilly blue negligee." He grinned.

Nikki grinned right back. "After this, you're going to have to leave Vincent outside when you come to bed. Who knows who he'll broadcast to next time?"

"One teeny problem," Vincent said, breaking his long silence. "One little faux pas, and they hold it against you forever. It wasn't even my fault."

Still smiling, Nikki calmly covered Vincent with one hand and kissed Cal.